Stay for a spell

"Better knock first." Hal was in no hurry to enter the wizard's castle, which was understandable, considering what happened the last time he'd entered a sorcerer's castle unannounced.

Emily laughed. "Don't worry about it. It's a test."

Hal said, "Mmm?"

"You know the sort of thing. The door looks impossible to open, so no one even tries. I'll bet we just have to give it a push and it will come right open." She leaned on it with the palm of her hand, and sure enough, it swung back silently on massive but perfectly balanced hinges.

Emily stepped inside and turned around. "You see, magicians love tests like these. They want to know if you're the type who can be fooled by appearances, or if you're persistent enough to seek out the truth. Or something like that. Kind of silly, I think. If they—"

The door slammed shut, instantly cutting off her words. No matter how hard Hal pushed, it stubbornly remained closed.

Ace titles by John Moore

HEROICS FOR BEGINNERS
THE UNHANDSOME PRINCE

THE
Unhandsome Prince

JOHN MOORE

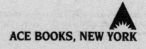

ACE BOOKS, NEW YORK

THE BERKLEY PUBLISHING GROUP
Published by the Penguin Group
Penguin Group (USA) Inc.
375 Hudson Street, New York, New York 10014, USA
Penguin Group (Canada), 10 Alcorn Avenue, Toronto, Ontario M4V 3B2, Canada
(a division of Pearson Penguin Canada Inc.)
Penguin Books Ltd., 80 Strand, London WC2R 0RL, England
Penguin Group Ireland, 25 St. Stephen's Green, Dublin 2, Ireland (a division of Penguin Books Ltd.)
Penguin Group (Australia), 250 Camberwell Road, Camberwell, Victoria 3124, Australia
(a division of Pearson Australia Group Pty. Ltd.)
Penguin Books India Pvt. Ltd., 11 Community Centre, Panchsheel Park, New Delhi—110 017, India
Penguin Group (NZ), Cnr. Airborne and Rosedale Roads, Albany, Auckland 1310, New Zealand
(a division of Pearson New Zealand Ltd.)
Penguin Books (South Africa) (Pty.) Ltd., 24 Sturdee Avenue, Rosebank, Johannesburg 2196,
South Africa

Penguin Books Ltd., Registered Offices: 80 Strand, London WC2R 0RL, England

This is a work of fiction. Names, characters, places, and incidents either are the product of the author's imagination or are used fictitiously, and any resemblance to actual persons, living or dead, business establishments, events, or locales is entirely coincidental.

THE UNHANDSOME PRINCE

An Ace Book / published by arrangement with the author

PRINTING HISTORY
Ace mass market edition / May 2005

Copyright © 2005 by John Moore.
Cover art by Walter Velez.
Cover design by Annette Fiore.
Interior text design by Kristin del Rosario.

ISBN: 0-441-01287-6

ACE
Ace Books are published by The Berkley Publishing Group,
a division of Penguin Group (USA) Inc.,
375 Hudson Street, New York, New York 10014.
ACE and the "A" design are trademarks belonging to Penguin Group (USA) Inc.

PRINTED IN THE UNITED STATES OF AMERICA

10 9 8 7 6 5 4 3 2 1

To my fellow Drone Rangers

On a hot day in late summer, when puffy white clouds were floating in a hazy blue sky, when birds were twittering in the trees and bees were buzzing around the flowers, when a gentle breeze was puffing the dandelions and great black clouds of gnats were making themselves really, really annoying, the most beautiful girl in the Kingdom of Melinower was standing in a swamp.

The swamp was fed by a clear and cheerful brook that ran slightly to the west of a cluster of houses and shops. Hence the village name of Ripplebrook. The brook originated in the highlands to the north of the village and vanished into the Sturgeon river some ways to the south, and for the most part flowed quickly and merrily, but slightly below the village was a shallow bowl in the surrounding countryside, a lowlands covering some several square miles. Here the brook spread out and became a swamp.

Many centuries later it would be called a wetlands. Great and ultimately futile attempts would be made to preserve it. Its protectors would talk of the beauty of nature, of the birds that made their homes in the wetlands, of the snakes and salamanders that lived in its waters, and of the importance of pond scum to the ecosystem. But these were earlier times and this was a fairy-tale kingdom, and to the villagers of Ripplebrook, the swamp was merely a swamp.

And it was an ordinary swamp at that. It was not one of those swamps where rare newts and butterflies are found, where exotic lichens and strangely perfumed orchids grow. It was not even one of those scary swamps, with craggy trees and twisting vines that grab at you and make you jump and send a tremor of fear down your spine. The will-o'-the-wisp did not glow at night, luring unwary travelers to their doom. It did not—and this is really pathetic—it did not even have quicksand. The Ripplebrook swamp was nothing more than a completely boring and utterly dismal bog.

Caroline certainly did not think highly of the place. Nonetheless, there she was, barefoot and ankle deep in black mud. Murky green water rose to her knees. Her plain white dress was soaked to the waist. Her arms were muddy up to the elbows, and there were crusts of dried mud on her ears where she had swatted at mosquitoes and great splotches of mud in her hair where she had pushed it out of her face. All in all she was one tired, wet, muddy, angry, and mosquito-bitten girl, and now she glared at Prince Hal as though this were his fault.

Not that the Prince was in any better shape. He had

transformed with his old clothes back on, so at least he wasn't naked, and that was something to be grateful for. But there was mud *under* his clothes, so they'd have to come off anyway. And he was soaked to the skin. He was dazed and disoriented, as only one who has spent the last seven weeks as a frog can be. He had no idea where he was or how long he had been there, or who this girl with the blue eyes, and the blond hair, and the mosquito bites could be. So he spoke the first words that came into his head.

"Are there leeches in here?"

"Yes," said Caroline. "So let's go." She grabbed him by the wrist and started leading him out of the swamp. Hal followed along readily enough, having no better idea where to go. With his free hand he batted at the cloud of insects. Caroline led him through a patch of cattail reeds and into shallower water. Emerging from the water, incongruously, was a stack of wooden frames with netting. "What are these?"

Caroline stopped and looked at them. "Frog traps. I'd set them up, then beat the water with a broom and herd the frogs into the nets. Sometimes I would get a dozen or more in one go. I bought the lumber in town and wove the netting myself."

"Very clever."

"The traps saved time."

She let go of his arm and just let him follow her. They came to a small island in the swamp, where a grove of mossy trees gave some shade. Under one tree were two bushel baskets with woven tops. Caroline lifted one of the lids. From inside the Prince could hear croaking.

"A lot of frogs," he said.

"You don't know the half of it," said the girl. She lugged the basket to the water's edge and tipped it over. The frogs spilled out across the water and disappeared gratefully into its murky depths. "After I kissed the frogs I'd put them in these baskets, then take them to the outlet of the swamp and let the stream carry them away. That way I didn't waste effort catching the same frog twice."

"Clever," said the Prince again. He helped her carry the second basket to the water's edge and empty it. Back at the tree he saw her staring at a sheet of paper. It had been tacked to the bark with tuppenny nails. She tore it off and crumpled it. "What was that? May I see it?"

She tossed it to him, and he unfolded it. It seemed to be a strange design with small squares and check marks. He looked at her questioningly.

"It's a map of the swamp," Caroline said. "When I started this, I drew a map of the swamp and marked it with a grid. As I cleared out the frogs in one sector, I'd mark it on the map and move over to the next square in the grid. Of course, some frogs migrated back into the empty areas, but not so many as you'd think. I also netted the tadpoles and dumped them in the stream, to keep them from filling a sector with new frogs."

This was clever enough that the Prince didn't even bother to say so. "How long have I been here?"

"Seven weeks." Caroline took the map from his hand, tore it in half, and let the wind carry the pieces away. "Water under the bridge, now."

"Seven weeks," murmured the Prince. Aloud, he said, "And you are . . . ?"

"Caroline," said Caroline. She lifted the hem of her muddy dress and made a solemn curtsey. This was so unexpected, given the context, that Prince Hal could think of no other response than to give an equally solemn bow.

"Hal," he said. "I'm afraid we haven't been properly introduced . . ."

"But we've already kissed," said Caroline. "So let's get on with it." And she trudged back into the swamp.

By this time Hal's head was starting to clear. He had tumbled to the fact that she was angry with him for some reason, and that conversation was not going to be cheerful. So he remained largely silent. And it was only a short, but buggy, walk to the edge of the swamp from the island. "I cleared this area of frogs last month," said Caroline. "That's why the mosquitoes are so bad."

"Of course," said Hal.

She pointed to some shallow ditches. "I dug those to drain that section. The frogs just moved to deeper water, but the higher concentration made them easier to net."

"Good Lord! You did all this yourself? It must have been an enormous amount of work."

"It was." She led him up a rise to a small cottage. The mists that rose from the swamp were considered unhealthy by the villagers, and the rents for cottages that lay on the swampy side of the village were correspondingly low. Caroline's was the lowest rent of the lot. The thatch on the roof was wearing thin, and the door sagged on worn hinges. The cottage was nothing more than a single room, with a dirt floor and a small fireplace. There were no windows, nor a bed, merely a bundle of ticking on the floor, with a blanket. There was a single stool for sitting. And just inside the door were two oaken buckets of water.

Early on Caroline had realized that each day, as she returned from the swamp, she would be too tired to fetch fresh water to clean up. And so each day she would set aside a bucket of water before leaving for the swamp. And each day she would set aside a second bucket of water for the Prince.

It became a ritual. Optimistic at first, she was certain each day that she would be returning before evening with a handsome prince, and so every morning she set aside water, soap, and a towel for him. As the days went by, and each successive frog turned out merely to be a frog, she clung to the ritual with grim determination. Not setting out the second bucket would be conceding that she wasn't going to find her prince today. And if she wasn't going to find her prince in that swamp, then what was she doing out there?

Now she set one of the buckets outside the door and handed Prince Hal a robe, a bar of soap, and a towel. "I'm sorry, Your Highness, but a girl needs her privacy. You'll have to wash outside. Then we'll go to the village, and I'll call for a meeting of the town council."

"What's this?" said Hal. He was looking at the towel—soft, fluffy, cotton, and new—and the bar of fancy, milled soap. Caroline had a threadbare piece of linen and a small chunk of brown tallow soap.

Caroline suddenly realized how tired she was. She sat

down on the stool, pulled her dress up slightly, and inspected her feet and ankles for leeches. Not finding any, she let the hem fall back down. "Well, Your Highness, there were a lot of girls looking for you at first. I think every girl in the village came down at least once to try her hand at catching and kissing a frog. Amanda told us that a maiden's kiss would break the spell and whoever kissed the right frog would marry a handsome prince."

"I know how the spell works," said Hal, a little tightly.

"We were all in it together, Lisa and Tiffany and Christine and, well, everyone. We'd have parties here in the evening, because my place was closest to the swamp. Two of my girlfriends—Ashley and Brenna—brought the towels and stuff, so you'd be able to clean up after we found you."

The Prince looked around. "Where are they all?"

"They all dropped out a month ago. After Amanda died, there was no one to keep goading them on."

"The sorceress is dead? That was her name, Amanda?"

Caroline nodded. "Took a fever and died a couple weeks after your unfortunate encounter with her. Oh, she teased us all with stories of how we could marry a handsome prince and help rule over the kingdom. But after she died, most of the girls stopped believing the story. Or decided that even if it was true, it was impossible to find one frog in all that swamp. I kept at it, so they left the towel, soap, and robe with me. And here you are."

"Well," said Hal. "Thank you." He put the fluffy towel

and perfumed soap in her hand and took the old towel and homemade soap. "These will be fine for me." Caroline accepted the exchange wordlessly and shut the door behind Hal.

The Prince banged on the door, and she immediately opened it. "I have just one more question for now. It seems to me that you're angry for some reason. What is it?"

"You're not handsome," said Caroline, and shut the door.

Ripplebrook was not a very large, nor a very rich village by any means, but it was big enough and prosperous enough to have a Town Hall with two stories. A very nice one, too, all done in local stone, with a slate roof and blue-painted trim. Upstairs housed the tax records, the birth and death records, the surveyors' records, and the deeds and titles to the surrounding farms. Downstairs was where the town council had its meetings, when it was deemed necessary to have meetings, which was not all that often. On Thursday nights it had bingo.

But today the council had called a special session. Old Twigham was leading the proceedings. He was thin and white-haired and kept bees. He was always elected to the council, and the other members deferred to him, by virtue of the fact that he was the oldest resident of the village. The remaining councillors were from the village's more successful merchants, for few others had the spare time to serve on committees. The council members were all seated on one side of a long, narrow table. Twigham sat at the center of the other side. To his left was Caroline, now freshly scrubbed, in a clean dress (her only other dress), with her long hair tied back. She looked very pretty, except for the welts caused by mosquito bites. And she looked very determined.

At Twigham's right arm was Emily. She was the daughter of Amanda, the recently deceased sorceress. She was pretty, petite, and a year younger than Caroline. And she was not happy.

"Handsome," Caroline was saying again.

"What's wrong with Prince Hal?" said Emily. "I think he's sort of cute."

"Cute is not handsome. The deal was to marry a *handsome* prince."

"I think he looks fine."

"He's short. To be handsome you have to be tall. Tall and handsome are synonymous, practically."

Emily looked out the window. The Prince was waiting, out of earshot, in the courtyard of the Town Hall. He was talking with a gaggle of curious girls, and more were arriving by the minute. "He's not that short. He's almost average height."

"Below average is not tall. He's skinny, and he has zits."

"Lots of teenage boys are skinny. And we all have *some* zits!"

"Not that sort of skinny. He has no build at all. His chin recedes. And his ears stick out."

"Oh come now! His chin recedes but a little. Make him grow a beard if it bothers you. And he can grow his hair long to cover his ears. Guys with long hair are sexy anyway."

"And look at his nose."

"His nose is just . . . his nose is . . . lots of teenage boys are skinny!"

Councilman Durley interrupted at this point. "Emily, you're dissembling. If a young man is handsome, he's handsome even without a beard or long hair. Yes, I'm sure we all recognize that handsome is to some degree a matter of personal taste." Durley, in his salad days, had fancied himself something of a ladies man. He now had two rather good-looking boys of his own, and thus felt himself qualified to speak on the subject. "But still, I am equally sure that we'd agree that our honored guest would not be attracting much attention from the girls were he not a prince. If he were but a common lad, well, I expect that the word to describe him would be more along the line of . . . um . . ."

"Dweeb," said Councilwoman Tailor.

"Yes. Quite so. And then there's the question of inheritance."

"What?"

"Prince Hal is not the heir apparent. He is the third son and not in line for the throne."

"What does that have to do with anything?" said Emily. "The deal was to marry a prince. There was nothing about ascending the throne."

"Yes, there was," said Caroline.

"Caroline is correct," said Tailor. "Your mother talked

about this constantly, Emily. She spent considerable time alluding to Hal's handsome appearance and his right to inherit the throne." Councilwoman Tailor was a widow. Her own two daughters had devoted the better part of a week to kissing frogs. The councilwoman herself had slipped down to the swamp one night to kiss a few. She did not admit this.

Emily had been packing to leave town when the council summoned her. She had two years to go on her apprenticeship and was growing more and more impatient at what she felt was an unreasonable delay. She pounced on the councilwoman's words. "Alluded, perhaps yes! But Mummy never actually *said* that the Prince would be the heir. For that matter, I don't think she actually said what he would look like. Maybe Mummy thought he *was* handsome. Maybe she was speaking in a relative sense. You can't hold someone to an agreement like this!"

"We certainly can," said Councilman Dunbury, who was an attorney. "I have given the council my opinion that Amanda's words constituted an oral contract. I'm sure she never expected that a single enchanted frog could be found in all that swamp, that she'd never have to make good on her claims, but there it is. Your mother was a powerful and respected sorceress, but she was not above the law."

"Oh, sure," said Emily. "You can spout off judgments like that all you want, now that my mother is dead. You wouldn't be talking like this if she were here."

"No doubt she'd be turning all of us into frogs. Nonetheless, for a contract to be valid there must be an exchange of consideration—that is, both parties must contribute something of value. Caroline contributed her labor—a great deal of hard, unpleasant labor—and deserves something of value in return."

"But she gets to marry a prince! So what if he's a bit of a dweeb . . . ?"

"All right now," said Twigham. "Let's not be disrespectful to the young man. He is royalty, after all."

"My point exactly," Emily said to Caroline. "How many of us commoners get to marry any sort of a prince at all? You should look upon the glass as being half-full rather than half-empty."

"My glass is full of swamp water," said Caroline. "And I've been wading in it for seven weeks."

Durley stood up. "It is clear that—"

"It is clear that it is time for a break," said Twigham.

"First I want to say that—"

"Break time," said Twigham firmly. He rapped the table three times with his knuckles to signify order. "I'm calling a recess. We will meet back here in half an hour. Emily, you will remain here with me."

Twigham's standing in the village was such that few were willing to flout his authority. Caroline was the first to leave, going out to join Hal in the courtyard, throwing a resentful glance back over her shoulder at Emily. Durley followed, then the rest of the council. As soon as the door closed behind them, Emily turned to Twigham and wailed, "They're all picking on me!"

"You're absolutely right," said Twigham.

Being a teenager, Emily was not used to having adults agree with her. "I am?"

Twigham had produced a pipe from one jacket pocket and a pouch of tobacco from the other. He proceeded to begin that complicated stuffing and tamping thing that pipe-smokers do when they need time to think about what they are going to say. Apparently he was a fast thinker, though, because he stopped with the pipe only partly ready and set it down. "Emily, your mother was a skilled sorceress, greatly respected throughout the kingdom, and in this village. But she was not well liked."

"You liked her."

"People were afraid of your mother, Emily. At my age there is little to fear anymore. You learn to take the long view."

"She did have a bit of a temper," the girl admitted.

"Brigands and highwaymen tended to give our village a wide berth, once they learned a prominent magician had set up shop here. So we got some advantage from it. Often, though, Amanda was able to run roughshod over people's feelings because they were afraid of her. But Emily, that affair of the frog."

Here Twigham stopped talking and started working on his pipe again. Emily sat silently until he got it lit. He took a long pull, let out the smoke, and started again. "Amanda made fools of us all. I don't know whether you've noticed, but every family in Ripplebrook has at least one girl. Every one of those girls would like to marry a handsome prince. Well, your mother led them all a merry chase. The girls were all out there slogging through the mud, kissing frogs, and generally looking ridiculous. And by extension, making their families look ridiculous. You know how it is in small villages. People remember every slight. Some can hold a grudge for generations. Now the town council has an advantage, and they think that it's payback time."

"Okay, fine. I can understand that they didn't like Mummy. I can understand that they'd all be ticked off a bit. But my mother is dead! Any chance they had for retribution is gone. This has nothing to do with me. *I* didn't turn the poor guy into a frog."

Twigham picked up his pipe and started to tamp it again, but immediately put it back down. "Emily, if the villagers decide that Caroline deserves compensation, they will take it out of your mother's estate."

"No! They wouldn't!"

"I think they would. They're talking about it already. Your mother had her craft to protect her. You are still an apprentice and have none. They know your mother had a tremendous store of magical books, worth a pretty penny. They're liable to confiscate the whole lot. Dunbury will collect his fee for making it legal. And if I know Durley and Tailor, they'll take a percentage for themselves before handing the crumbs to Caroline."

"Caroline!" Emily practically spat out the name. "She makes me so mad, the way everyone lets her push them around. It isn't enough for her to be the most beautiful girl in the village. And the most popular also. Now she wants my library."

"Hmmm. Emily, when the Smiths had typhoid fever, and we had to quarantine the house, who went inside to tend their baby?"

"Caroline," Emily said reluctantly.

"At the village faire, who volunteered to organize the charity auction?"

"Caroline, yes, yes, I get the picture. She's beautiful, she's popular, and she's a saint, okay? But Twigham, I can't lose my mother's library." Here the girl stood up and pounded her small fists on the table. "I can't! I can't!"

"Calm down, my dear. I understand."

Emily unclenched her fists but remained standing. "Do you know how Mummy was able to apprentice me to a first-class wizard like Torricelli? It's not easy, you know. The top magicians only take on a few new kids each year, and competition is tough. But every magician in the Twenty Kingdoms would like to get a peek at Mummy's library." Emily finally sat down. "Twigham, without those books, I'll just be another sorceress wanna-be, studying under some third-rate spell hack."

"I understand perfectly," said the old man. "That's why you should bring Caroline to the city with you."

"What!"

"Bring her with you to the City of Melinower. Hal is returning there. The two of you can travel with him. It's not safe for a young woman to travel alone anyway."

"I am *not* taking *that girl* with me. I am going there to study. I'm not a tour guide."

"You are not listening. You have to set that girl up with a handsome young man. Your best chance for doing that is in Melinower."

"With a prince? I have no more chance of marrying her to a prince than I have of marrying one myself."

Twigham's mouth quirked up at the corners, and he

looked like he was about to say something amusing. But he forced himself into a serious expression. "I understand your mother had many friends and clients in the city. You should have no problem getting an introduction to the better families. Once the boys see Caroline, nature will take its course."

"But a prince? Mummy didn't have those kinds of connections."

Twigham shrugged. "A duke, then. An earl, a count, a baron. Even a wealthy merchant's son. I suspect Caroline is not that picky. She just doesn't want to spend the rest of her life in this village, sitting at a spinning wheel. She'll forget about princes if she meets a good-looking boy who can keep her in style. A girl who looks like Caroline will have plenty of opportunity to meet men. Well, once those mosquito bites fade, anyway."

"Hmmm." Emily thought this over. Twigham made it sound easy, but men always thought it was easy for a girl to attract the right boy. Girls knew better.

Still, Emily knew she had to do something, and quickly. If word got out that a lien might be placed on her mother's books, her chances of getting a good apprenticeship would be greatly diminished. It would be better for her to arrive in Melinower with the Prince, rather than get there later and have to face a lot of exaggerated stories.

She looked at Hal in the courtyard. He was freshly scrubbed, and the village merchants, eager to score points with the royal family, had brought him clean clothes. The village girls were gathered around him, offering baskets of homemade jams and jellies, freshly baked rolls, or bundles of flowers. The Prince accepted all the offerings graciously. Emily thought he would be a very nice person to travel with, and she certainly thought he looked presentable enough. Still, she had to admit that Caroline had the facts on her side. Hal was the kind of boy who, if you asked his friends what he looked like, they would tell you he had a great sense of humor.

She also saw that Caroline was standing beside him, acting a trifle possessive, in Emily's humble opinion. She considered the girl. Perhaps Twigham was right. She'd rest easier if Caroline was with her in Melinower, away from the town council, rather than back home in Ripplebrook stirring up trouble.

"All right," she told Twigham. "You're right. I'll do it. Wait! What if she won't go?"

"I'll have a talk with her and the council," said Twigham. "She'll go. And I'll make sure the council doesn't take any action while you are gone."

"Thank you," said Emily. She kissed him on the cheek. "For an old man, you're pretty sharp."

"I like to think so myself."

"But if you think this is going to be one of those situations where two girls start out disliking each other, then have some sort of adventure and end up being best friends, well, forget about it. That isn't going to happen."

"The thought had never crossed my mind," said Twigham.

Caroline was attractive enough to inspire jealous spite in all the other girls of the village, except for one very helpful fact—she never competed with them to win the other boys. Caroline simply didn't want any of the village boys. She had long ago determined that she was not going to stay poor, and she was certainly going to get out of Ripplebrook. In her day and age this meant marrying and marrying well. Not one of the villagers saw any reason to dissuade her. Marrying a prince (or, for the boys, a princess) was a common enough fantasy. Now they rallied around Caroline the way they might rally around a local sports hero who was about to play the big game. And nearly every one of the girls wished that she, too, had spent more hours in the swamp, kissing at least a few extra frogs before giving up.

Emily was in quite a different position than Caroline.

She had inherited from her mother a tiny castle, complete with a narrow tower from which eerie lights gleamed. The castle was right on the edge of the swamp—in fact she was Caroline's closest neighbor—but in the sorcery business a nearby swamp was okay. At night mists rose from it and shrouded the castle, making it look dark and foreboding, exactly the way Amanda thought a sorceress's castle should look. Especially when she did the eerie tower light thing. Emily was petite, and dark-haired, and had deep black eyes. Her appearance was going to work out very well for her, because a sorceress was expected to look a bit mysterious and exotic, and deep dark eyes are always a help there. For the same reason, Emily's mother had always insisted that she dress in formal sorceress attire when visitors came to the castle— silken black robes, with high heels and bloodred lipstick and nail polish. "If you want to succeed in the magic business, you have to look the part," Amanda taught her. "People trust a sorceress who looks like a sorceress. The customers aren't going to give hard money for enchantments to someone who looks like a pauper." Emily had taken her mother's teachings to heart and continued to dress like her even after Amanda's death. Emily was also considered something of an outcast by the other children. They didn't tease her—they were smart enough to know you didn't tease the daughter of a woman who could turn children into vermin—but Amanda taught her daughter at home instead of sending her to the village schoolhouse. Thus she hadn't had the chance to mingle with the other children and make friends, join a clique, gossip with girls, and banter with boys.

The result was that now, as she silently rode her horse alongside Prince Hal, Emily was coming to an important realization.

She had no idea how to talk to a boy.

At least, in her own mind, she didn't. Where the road was narrow they rode mostly one behind the other, with the Prince taking the lead, so that any trouble they might happen to meet would be confronted first by a young man with a sword. Where the road was wider, and this happened more and more frequently as each day brought them closer to Melinower, they would ride three abreast so they could talk, the Prince in the center on a dark gelding, Caroline on a large bay, Emily on a dappled mare. A packhorse with their supplies followed. The village merchants had provided Caroline with a horse, and her girlfriends had forced upon her gifts of clothing. "You can't go to the city without a proper wardrobe," they said, and Caroline, who did not like to ask favors, had reluctantly accepted. Hal was riding the horse that had brought him to Ripplebrook—it had been housed in Amanda's stable since then. Emily was riding her own horse. It was late summer, and the sun was warm, the pace of the horses lulling, and the words flowed easily from all three young people: yet Emily *felt* that her conversation was awkward. She would make a statement about something simple, the beauty of the countryside, for example, then immediately decide that she had said something stupid. Then Hal would give her an easy smile and say something back, and Emily would stammer out a reply. Except that she knew that she wasn't stammering, but it just *seemed* like she was. Sometimes

Hal would address a question to Caroline, and Emily would feel a little pang of disappointment in her stomach and a desire to break into the conversation and turn the Prince's attention back to herself. That would have been rude, of course, and she never actually did it, but it bothered her that she *wanted* to do it.

On the third night away from Ripplebrook, after they had hobbled the horses and set them to graze, set up a camp in a clearing in the woods, built a fire, and were sitting around it, Caroline asked Hal how he came to be turned into a frog.

"I mean, Hal," said Caroline. (Both she and Emily were calling the Prince by his first name now, at Hal's insistence) "Amanda can't just turn anyone into a frog. She can't just say, 'Presto, you're a frog' and you change. You have to have wronged her somehow. Am I right, Emily?"

"Well—right," said Emily. Uncomfortable with this question, she was watching Hal carefully across the fire. "These types of spells are like curses—they're done in revenge. That's a simplification, of course, it's not all cut-and-dried and there are a lot of gray areas." She swallowed nervously, because what she was saying was tantamount to accusing Hal of a crime, and he was royalty after all, and there was no telling how he might take it. "But if you tried to do it to some innocent chap on the street corner, nothing would happen."

"So Hal," Caroline went on brightly, "what was your crime?"

Emily winced, but Hal answered cheerfully, "Tried to steal some philosopher's stone from the sorceress."

"Philosopher's stone? The stuff that turns lead into gold?"

"Brass," said Emily.

"Brass into gold," said Hal, "is the way I heard it also. Anyway, Dad learned that this sorceress in Ripplebrook got some, or made some, and sent me off to get it."

"You tried to steal the philosopher's stone? That doesn't sound very princely. Aren't you supposed to be honest and truthful and virtuous and things like that?"

"Oh no." Hal shook his head, a trifle irritably. "You're thinking of knights. The ruling class just takes what it wants."

"And so she got angry and turned you into a frog."

"That's about the size of it."

"All that trouble for something that doesn't even exist."

The Prince shrugged. "That's the downside of being a prince. Dad sends me on these off-the-wall quests, and there's not really much I can do about it."

"What? What are you saying?" Emily was confused now. "You think the philosopher's stone doesn't exist?"

Now Caroline looked surprised, and so did Hal. "You mean it does?"

"I've got it right here," said Emily. She rose, went to her saddlebags, and rummaged around in them for a while. When she returned she had a small leather bag with a rawhide cord for wearing around the neck. She tossed it to Caroline. "Mum spent years working on this."

Caroline opened the bag and looked inside. "This is a joke. It has to be. Amanda couldn't have had the philosopher's stone."

"I don't know why you'd say that," said Emily. "I didn't follow the formulation myself very carefully, but that is what she came up with."

"Come on, Emily. Figure it out. If your mother had this stuff to change brass into gold, why wasn't she doing it?"

"You need a lot more than just the philosopher's stone. Red mercury, for one thing. And a whole lot of preparation. And it won't work on just any old hunk of brass. It takes a particular alloy called virgin brass. And then you need a girl who can—um—help with the preparation."

"Can you turn brass into gold?"

"Me? I can't do anything until I finish my apprenticeship. As for alchemy, I wouldn't begin to know where to start. Neither did Mummy. Near as I can figure, she was making this on contract for someone else. Who, presumably, had a supply of red mercury and virgin brass lined up."

"I'm pretty sure Dad has neither," said Hal. "He probably just heard about this somewhere and fixed on it as yet another one of his get-rich-quick schemes. And another excuse to get me out of the city."

This last line was spoken casually. A little too casually was Caroline's thinking, and she zeroed in on it. "You and the King are not on good terms?"

Hal hesitated before speaking. "Ah, well." He looked into the fire. "Dad has high expectations." And here he looked directly at Caroline. "He wants his sons to look a bit more princely."

Caroline had the grace to look embarrassed. There was an awkward silence.

Hal broke it by standing up and saying, "Well, I think it's time to gather more wood for the fire."

"Wait," said Emily. She held out the leather bag. "Hal, go ahead and take it."

"The philosopher's stone? No, I couldn't."

Emily continued to hold out the bag. "Please take it, Hal. It's of no use to me, and after living in a swamp all that time, you've earned it."

"That's really generous of you, Emily, but no."

"It will help you get back in your father's good graces. Take it, please. Consider it a gift to the King from his loyal subject, Emily."

Hal sat back down. "Well, if you put it that way." He let Emily put the bag in his hand. "I appreciate this, Emily. I thank you on behalf of His Royal Highness, the King."

"His Majesty is welcome."

Something in the way that Emily looked at Hal, something in the way her eyes held his, triggered just a little bit of tension in Caroline's spine. She broke into the exchange by asking, "How do you make it, anyway?"

"I don't know. It's distilled from virgin's milk, then vitrified."

Both Hal and Caroline stared at her. "Distilled from what?"

"Virgin's milk. Don't ask me. I don't know what it is either. I didn't even know about this until I read Mummy's notes after she died. And she didn't keep notes on the really secret stuff."

Caroline said, "And virgin's milk is from a . . . ?"

"I don't know! Maybe it's just a name for something

innocuous. Don't look at me that way. It didn't come from me, I'll tell you that!"

The conversation was getting a bit too personal for the Prince. He said, by way of changing the subject, "Why is it called the philosopher's stone?"

"That's easy. Hold it in your palm and see."

Hal opened the leather bag and poured the contents into his cupped hand. The contents turned out to be an oblong white stone about the size of his thumb, something like a large pearl but more translucent. He held it to the firelight and gave Emily a questioning look.

"Close your hand around it, then close your eyes. Tell us the first thought that comes into your head."

"*Cogito, ergo sum,*" said Hal, with his eyes closed. He opened them in surprise. "I think, therefore I am?"

"Rationalism," said Emily. "Pretty typical for the first time."

"Let me try," said Caroline. Hal passed her the stone. She shook it in her hand as though she were getting ready to roll dice.

"Just hold it still," said Emily.

Caroline closed her eyes. A few moments later she murmured, "Virtue is to be found in moderation." She paused for a moment, then continued, "Socrates is a man, all men are mortal, therefore . . ."

"Socrates is mortal," Hal and Emily finished with her. "Classic logic," Emily added. "Also pretty common."

"Did you ever do this?"

"Oh sure. A couple of times. The first time Mummy gave it to me she let me ramble on about mind-body dualism for half an hour. Of course I couldn't understand what I was saying." Emily put the stone back in its leather bag and returned it to Hal. "But it was enough to make me understand the power of philosophy and why the secret of preparing a philosopher's stone has to be carefully guarded."

Hal and Caroline exchanged looks. "Why?"

"Philosophy is dangerous. Entire armies have been bored to death with it."

"Ah, of course," said Hal. "I well remember my tutors lecturing on the difference between denotation and connotation. I still consider it a miracle I survived. Students were dropping three classrooms away."

"Hmm," said Caroline. "We're getting into tall tales now?"

"Not at all. I was able to keep awake by holding matches to my toes. Being the only student to finish the lecture, I aced the course."

"I think it's my turn to get the firewood," said Caroline. "And then hit you over the head with it."

Hal excused himself and disappeared into the woods. The two girls could hear twigs crackle beneath his feet as he moved into the darkness of the trees. As soon as she judged he was out of earshot, Caroline hissed, "What are you doing? He's *my* boyfriend. You can't go around giving gifts to another girl's boyfriend."

"What!" said Emily. "What are you talking about? Prince Hal isn't your boyfriend."

"Of course he is. I found him. I freed him from the spell. Now he's obligated to marry me."

"You already rejected him! You said he was a dweeb!"

"Yes, but . . . but . . ."

"I'm here with you two only because I'm supposed to help you find a handsomer husband."

"Um, right. But *until* then, Hal is my boyfriend, so don't get any ideas, okay?"

"I don't have any ideas," snapped Emily. "And Hal is a real person with feelings of his own, you know. You can't just treat him like some sort of pawn to be moved around the board and played games with."

"Oh, look who's talking. At least I didn't turn him into a frog and abandon him in a swamp."

"That wasn't me! That was my mother."

"Yeah, and why did she do it?"

"Hal told you. Because he tried to steal the philosopher's stone."

"Yeah, right. What was she really mad about?"

"What do you mean?"

"Figure it out." Caroline moved around the fire and sat next to Emily. "Teenage boy breaks into castle. Teenage girl lies sleeping alone. Mom comes along, finds teenage boy sneaking about outside her daughter's bedroom, what is she going to think?"

"Hal wouldn't do something like that!"

"How do you know? You heard him say it, that the ruling class takes what it wants."

"Caroline! That's an awful thing to say about Hal! Especially as he has been so nice considering all the nasty stuff that happened to him."

"Well." Caroline looked a bit embarrassed. "No, I didn't mean to say he tried to do something to you. I'm just saying that maybe your mother *thought* he was trying to do something to you. That would have given her a lot more incentive to put a spell on him than just trying to swipe a bit of condensed milk."

"You didn't know my mother well. She was very possessive about her magical stuff. She didn't even let me in on her best stuff, and I was her apprentice. And her daughter."

"Okay, okay. It was just an idea."

The two girls fell silent. Caroline stared into the dying fire. Emily seemed lost in speculative thought. They heard a crunching of twigs. It was Hal, returning with an armful of branches.

Emily leaned forward and whispered to Caroline, "Do you really think he tried to do something with me?"

"Oh, for goodness sake," said Caroline. "Go to bed, Emily."

They rode through an area of thick oak, aspen, and wild pear. It was an area that could only have been sparsely inhabited, for Caroline saw little sign of woodcutters. "Gundar's Forest," Hal told her. "It's an old name, so don't ask me who Gundar was." Although it was a clear day, and the sun was high, the heavy shadows gave her a spooky feeling. So she was not pleased when Hal turned off the road onto a narrow and even more shadowy trail.

"Just a little detour," he called back. "It won't take long. We'll be back on the main road in no time."

"Where are we going?"

"There's a girl I have to check up on."

The trail was narrow enough that the horses had to walk single file. Caroline turned her head back to look at Emily and mouth the words, "A girl?" Emily could only shrug in reply.

They started to climb. The trees got thicker and closed in on the trail. It was still wide enough to ride, but Caroline found herself bending low over the saddle to get under the overhanging branches. The trail went up a steep hill, then disappeared. She was sure the Prince would soon dismount and lead his horse, but no. He continued to pick his way through the trees, leading them back and forth along narrow switchbacks, gradually working their way higher and higher. Finally, as Caroline's horse was starting to foam, they broke out of the trees and crested the hill. The peak was clear of trees, barren and hot in the noonday sun. Below them, thick green forest spread in all directions. In the center of the clearing stood a tower.

The Prince had reined in his horse at the edge of the woods and waved the girls over. He pointed across the hills. "See. There's Melinower. Another day's ride or so should bring us there." Caroline glanced only briefly at the smudge of buildings in the distance, nodded, and turned her head back to the tower.

A stone tower in the middle of a deserted wood is intriguing under any circumstance, but this one fairly dripped with mystery. It was high, some sixty feet at least, and narrow, and perfectly round, but it was the stonework that gave it a foreboding aspect. The tower was made of black stone, dark and smooth and uniformly featureless. It rose straight up to a narrow turret. Caroline could see a small window just beneath the top—there were no other openings. She dismounted and walked up to the base. Peering at it closely, she could see that the black stone was not perfectly smooth. A grid of fine lines had been etched into each block, giving it a dull, matte finish.

Hal came by and looked over her shoulder. He, too, touched the stone. "Pretty clever, eh? This tower was built as a prison. If the walls had been perfectly smooth, I was going to try using suction cups to climb up the side. But because it's textured, that idea didn't work."

"What? Why did you want to climb it?"

"Had to rescue a damsel in distress."

"Rescue who?" This was from Emily. She had also tied up her horse, and joined them.

"Some mad sorcerer kidnapped a girl and locked her away in this tower. Dad assigned me to bring her back. Except that after I broke into the place, she didn't want to leave. Don't ask me why. Anyway, as long as we were going by, I figured I'd better stop in and see how she is getting along. Maybe she's changed her mind and wants to go home now."

As he spoke, he was walking around the base of the tower, with the two girls following. A number of shallow holes had been dug throughout the clearing. At first Caroline thought someone was trying to start a garden, but the holes had been dug haphazardly, in no particular pattern. On the opposite side of the tower, a crude door had been smashed through the stonework. Broken chunks of hard black granite still lay around the open-ing, which was covered with a thick blanket. Hal ap-proached the door and made as if to draw back the blanket, but then hesitated. He studied it for a long mo-ment, while Caroline and Emily watched, perplexed. Then he backed away from the door and drew the two girls aside.

"There's one more thing, before we go in," he said. "Don't say anything about her hair, okay?"

"Why?" said Caroline. "What's wrong with it?"

"Nothing, it's fine. Just don't get her started, okay?"

Caroline exchanged glances with Emily, who gave her usual shrug. "Fine."

"All right, then." The Prince walked up to the door, rapped on the stone with his knuckles, then drew the blanket aside. "Hey, Rapunzel, it's me, Hal. Anyone home?"

"Come on in," said a voice.

Because the walls of the tower were necessarily thick at the base, the room Hal led them into was rather small, although pleasantly furnished, with a polished wood parquet floor and simple, light oak furniture. It was lit by a single torch, plus the light coming through from the opening. A spiral of stone steps ran along the inside of the wall, to a mezzanine about ten feet above the floor. This had stairs to another mezzanine above it, and so on. Caroline could barely make out the wood floor of the upper apartment. Then her gaze ran to the girl sitting on the floor, and her eyes widened in surprise.

The girl was young and pretty, perhaps a year older than Caroline, and she was sitting cross-legged on a thick rug, with a few cushions scattered around her. In one hand she held a silver brush, with bristles of elephant hair, and in the other a silver mirror. A tortoiseshell comb lay on a pillow in front of her. Around her was her hair.

There was such a mass of it that Caroline first assumed that she had collected it—that this girl, located in a strange tower in the middle of the woods, had somehow started a wig-making business. As far-fetched as that idea was, it was no stranger than the truth. For Caroline quickly realized that this incredible length of golden hair all belonged to the girl. And it was still attached to her head.

The torchlight shone on the dark yellow mane, occasionally reflecting a red highlight. The hair lay coiled around the girl in great soft loops, loosely tied at intervals with yellow ribbon. It seemed to fill half the room, piled higher than the backs of the chair, and more coils and loops ran up the stairs. Caroline thought she had pretty good hair herself, but this girl's hair was perfect. In all that length of gold, Caroline could not spot a single split end or frizzle.

"Rapunzel," the Prince was saying, "these are my friends Caroline and Emily. Caroline, Emily, meet Rapunzel."

"Charmed," said the girl, in a low, soft voice. "Please have a seat. I hope you'll excuse me if I don't get up. It takes rather a bit of time to get all this arranged so I can relax."

"Thank you," said Caroline. Then, before she could help herself, continued, "You have beautiful hair."

The Prince glared at her momentarily, but sat down with an air of resignation. He kicked at some of the parquet tiles, which were loose and shifted under his toe.

"Well, thank you," said Rapunzel. She held up the hairbrush. "Today I've been using a brush with a wide pin design. It increases air circulation at the root to add volume for a softer look. I've also been misting it to keep the strands straight. I know you're probably thinking that I shouldn't brush my hair when it is wet, but I've found a little bit of moisture makes the brush glide more smoothly and reduces frizzing. But you know that only works when the humidity level is high. If the air is especially dry, as it gets sometimes in Melinower during cold weather, you know, when we have a cold clear winter day, then that's when I get the flyaway hair effect, which can lead to tangles, especially after it's all been washed, and I'm trying to dry it. So I use a moisturizing detangler, which helps to take out the snags, and also adds texture. Sure, that takes away some of the gloss, but it actually helps bring out the highlights. Of course, that's only true if you use it with the wide pin volumizing brush."

"Of course," said Emily.

"Shush," said Hal. "You're just encouraging her."

"But if you really want volume, well you can't do without a good conditioner." Rapunzel kept talking as though she hadn't heard. "My preference is an oil-based conditioner—the one I'm using now has five essential oils—jojoba oil, almond oil, sesame oil, wheat germ oil, and banana oil, to replace the natural oils that your hair loses through shampooing. It's the shampooing that is really tough on your hair, especially if you use a shampoo that contains alcohol—that will really dry it out. But even if you use an alcohol-free shampoo, you still need to use a conditioner to add back in the essential oils that have been washed away with the dirt. What do you wash your hair with?" she said to Caroline.

"Uh, soap."

"Well, soap is not the optimum thing to wash your hair with, although it can be acceptable if you live in an area where the water is exceptionally soft. Otherwise, it mixes with the minerals in the water to give a dull coating to your hair. It's the same thing that causes soap rings around your bathtub, and you know how difficult those are to remove. Fortunately, there are now what they call swimmers' shampoos that remove mineral buildup without causing damage or dullness. Still, they're pretty harsh shampoos, so you definitely have to use a conditioner after you use a harsh shampoo, with perhaps a color enhancer for brighter highlights. Then again, a lot of girls who wash their hair with soap use rainwater, which avoids the whole hard water issue. But you can't always count on having a bucket of rainwater around when you want it."

Caroline actually found this kind of interesting, but she could see that the Prince was getting that eyes-glazed-over look, so she decided to help him out and change the subject. At the first hint of a pause, she interrupted with, "I hear you were held prisoner here. Did you suffer much?"

Caroline saw Emily leaning forward to catch Rapunzel's answer. "Oh no," said the blond girl. "The wizard who kidnapped me didn't mistreat me, except for casting that spell that made my hair grow long. Of course, I was still pretty happy when Hal showed up to rescue me."

"I'm sure," said Caroline. She looked at the crude doorway. "It must have taken some time to knock those stones out."

"Oh, that wasn't it. Hal made that opening after the wizard was gone, for me to come and go. He first got in by climbing up my hair."

Caroline stared. Behind Rapunzel, she saw Hal shaking his head and putting a finger to his lips. Caroline ignored him. "He climbed up your hair?"

"By the time Hal showed up, my hair had already grown long enough to reach from the top of the tower. So I braided it into a rope ladder, and Hal was able to climb up."

This seemed so patently absurd that Caroline was sure a punch line was going to follow. But the girl seemed perfectly serious, and Hal wasn't smiling, and there was all that mass of golden hair to consider. Rapunzel went on, "At first I thought I'd do a French braid, as it would be tighter and stronger. But it shortens the hair too much, and I didn't have that kind of length yet. An English braid is looser, but of course it's just a French braid in reverse, so there was still the length problem. So I finally just decided to go with an ordinary braid. I was afraid it wouldn't be strong enough, but it held up fine, long enough for Hal to get to the window and subdue the wizard. But whatever style of braid you try, you still have to prepare your hair by dampening it first. This makes the hair slide more easily. You can wet it totally, and it will slide even better, but then you better expect to have wet hair the rest of the day, because it takes a long time to dry after it has been braided. I used a perfume atomizer to spray it with a fine mist of water. Anyway, the plan worked, although it was a very long and tedious braiding job. I certainly don't want to have to do it again. But when you're going to put that sort of stress on your hair, do you know what the most important thing is?"

"Strong roots," Hal muttered under his breath.

"Strong roots," Rapunzel told Caroline. "That's why I like to use a shampoo with a good nutrient base, to feed the hair roots. I'm getting good results with a mixture of lettuce and fern extracts. It also contains lemon peel and citrus extracts, with some rosemary, sage, and nettle. I was also following it up once a week with a hot oil scalp treatment—almond oil and rose hip oil, with oatmeal for a mild abrasive affect. This was supposed to thoroughly cleanse the scalp and remove any dead or flaking skin. But I couldn't see that it made any difference. I guess I already have a pretty healthy scalp."

Rapunzel went on in this vein for quite a while. It was afternoon, in fact, before her monologues ran down, and the three travelers managed to extract themselves from the tower. They rode their horses back down the trail in silence, and it wasn't until they reached the main road that Emily finally spoke.

"Personally, I always use a brush of wombat hair and nautilus shell, to add more body."

"I always condition my hair with oatmeal, honey, almond oil, and raisins, plus half a teaspoon of baking powder," said Caroline. "Then bake in a medium oven for forty minutes. For extra volume, of course."

"Of course."

"Hey," said Hal. "Now don't you two get started."

"I think we should do Hal's hair," said Emily. "Something really needs to be done about it. Don't you think so, Caroline?"

"Oh, absolutely. Perhaps a light, layered, shag cut for that man-about-town look."

"With a bushy mustache."

"Jeez," said the Prince, and rode his horse down the road in front of them.

"Wait," said Emily. She spurred her horse to catch up with him. "Hal, you haven't told us everything. Who is this girl and how did you get to know her and what is she doing there?"

"There's nothing to tell. Some wizard kidnapped Rapunzel and shut her up in that tower. Dad sent me to rescue her. It's one of those things you've got to do when you're a prince. Bandits and highwaymen, well, when they get too thick, you send out the army to run them down and hang them. Kidnappings are different. You can't use that sort of brute force, because the kidnapper might kill the victim. It's the merchant class that has the most trouble. They've got money, but they don't have knights or soldiers of their own. So they expect the King to do something. That's what they're paying their taxes for, they figure."

"Why not just pay the ransom and go after the wizard afterward?" said Caroline, who had also ridden her horse up while Hal was talking.

"He didn't demand a ransom."

"No ransom? Then why did he kidnap . . . oh."

"What?" said Emily. "What 'oh?' "

Caroline lowered her voice. "Figure it out. Old man, pretty girl. He must have seized her so he could . . . you know. To violate her."

"Oh," said Emily. "Oh, that's terrible. That poor girl."

"No," said Hal. "She swears he didn't lay a finger on her. Just cast a spell to make her hair grow long."

"Why?"

"Maybe he just had a thing for long hair. Anyway, she won't leave the tower, now. I knocked a door in the base so she can get in and out, but there she stays."

"Maybe she doesn't want to talk about it," said Emily. "I'll bet he did things to her. Now she doesn't want to go home because she's ashamed."

"I still call it mysterious behavior," said Caroline.

"Well, she's got clothing and enough food to last out the summer. Not to mention plenty of stuff to put on her hair. I'll check back when the leaves turn and see if she's ready to return to the city."

Caroline drew her horse alongside Hal's. "So this is what a Prince does? Rescue girls? Do you slay dragons also?"

"Not so many dragons around Melinower these days. The area is pretty well settled. But yeah, if a dragon showed up, I suppose I'd be the one to take it on. My brothers . . ."

Here the Prince stopped, as if he'd said too much and was looking for a way to back out of the subject. He opened his mouth to start talking again, then shut it without saying anything. He drew his horse a little away from the girls and started inspecting the mane, as though searching for burrs. But Caroline would not let the matter drop.

"What about your brothers? Can't they slay a dragon? Aren't they strong enough?"

"Hmm? Oh sure. No problem. They're both big, muscular guys, good in sports and combat."

"Handsome?" said Caroline. "Are they handsome?"

Emily shot Caroline an irritated look. Caroline affected not to notice.

"Yeah, plenty handsome. The thing is . . ." The Prince stopped again and considered his words. "Ah, the thing is that Dad considers that one of them is the heir to the throne, and he doesn't want to risk his heir. So, he tends to assign me to the more dangerous stuff. Dad figures I'm kind of, um."

"Expendable," said Caroline. Emily slipped her foot out of the stirrup and kicked the blonde girl in the shin. Caroline ignored her.

"No, no. Don't get me wrong. It's not like he wants me to get killed—nothing like that. It's just that he prefers me to be out of the kingdom, out of the public eye. I'm kind of a disappointment to him. I don't fit his image of what a prince should be. Not princely enough, you know. But I'm okay with it. It's good experience and a chance to get away from the castle."

Hal said this lightly, in a relaxed, easygoing tone of voice that Emily thought would not have fooled a child for five seconds. Had she been alone with Hal, she would have tried to say something consoling.

"Sure," said Caroline. "So let me see, you have two brothers, right? And they're both handsome? What are they like?

Someone, thought Emily, *should really strangle that girl.*

She tried bringing it up with Caroline when they stopped for lunch. The hilly road had tired out the horses. Hal, spying a grassy meadow, thought it would be a good place to let them graze for a while. While he was removing the saddles and currying the horses, the girls decided to build a fire. Emily picked up a stick and said, with assumed carelessness, "It's not exactly tactful to keep reminding Hal that you're rejecting him."

Caroline lifted a branch, noted that the wood was slightly rotten, and tossed it aside. She said—and her nonchalance was not a pose—"I doubt he cares. He's a prince, we're commoners. He wouldn't give us a second thought if it wasn't for the spell."

"I'm sure it bothers him that the girls prefer his brothers."

"Yeah, probably." Caroline added another stick to the pile in her arms. "I spent so long thinking of him as a frog that it's hard for me to relate to him as a boy. I think this is enough wood, don't you?"

"Uh-huh." They carried their loads back to the clearing

where their blankets lay and stacked it on the ground. "So, what was it like to kiss him?"

"Who?"

"What do you mean, who? Hal!"

"It was like kissing a frog."

"Well, I mean, after he changed. While he was changing. The end of the kiss when he was changed back."

"It didn't happen while we were kissing. I kissed him, I dropped him in the water, I reached for the next frog—and there he was. Instant prince."

"Oh. So you don't know what it's like to kiss him?"

"Same as any other boy, I would imagine."

"Um, yes. I suppose."

Caroline stopped and looked at the dark-haired girl. "You're telling me you've never kissed a boy?"

"I didn't say that!"

"But you never have."

"It's different being a sorcerer's apprentice," said Emily defensively. "There's a lot of studying to do. You don't have a lot of time to go out and socialize."

"Hey, don't worry about it. It's no big deal."

"Okay." Emily stuffed some dried grass and shredded bark under the stack. She took a small knife and a piece of flint from her bag and started striking sparks. "So you have kissed other boys, then?"

Caroline was amused. "Oh sure, a few. I don't do it very often. I think it's cruel to get a boy's hopes up if you don't intend to do anything with him."

"There's magic in a kiss," said Emily. "Well, I guess you ought to know as well as anyone. But since I'm an apprentice sorceress, I have to be especially careful."

"So you're not going to kiss Hal?"

Emily started. "What? What makes you ask a question like that?"

"You brought it up. You must have been thinking about it."

"Certainly not!"

"Not that it would matter to him. A boy who is a prince, even if he's not good-looking, can get all the girls he wants. You can bet that Hal has been with more girls than you've had hot dinners. You'd just be one more in a long line."

"I would not! I mean, I don't care. Frankly, it doesn't matter to me what he does. I was just making conversation."

"Right. Are you going to light that fire, or what?"

Emily looked down, where she was still striking sparks from the flint. They were falling on bare dirt. She moved her hands and aimed them at the tinder.

Caroline said, "I thought sorceresses were supposed to be able to start fires magically."

"We do. It's one of the first things we learn. But I'm still an apprentice, so all I have is a learner's permit. I can't do anything unless accompanied by a master or journeyman."

"How can they stop you?"

"Magically."

"Oh, right. Well, I guess that makes sense. We all know the stories about sorcerers' apprentices and the trouble they get into."

"What stories?"

"Oh, you know. Like the one about the sorcerer's apprentice who cast a spell to make the broom carry water from the well, then couldn't get it to stop after the castle was flooded."

"Oh that." Emily suddenly became very absorbed in the tinder, striking the flint with great precision. "Ha-ha. Yes, I've also heard that story. Um, you think maybe this tinder is damp, and that's why it's not catching?"

"Wait, you've done magic before. I know you have. Last year, you said that spell over Suzanne to make her breasts get bigger."

"That was a joke."

"No it wasn't. She started pushing out right after that."

Emily gave the other girl a disbelieving look. "Caroline, that's the oldest trick in the book."

"But it worked."

"For any group of teenage girls, someone's got to be the last to develop. She gets worried about it, so she goes out and buys a charm, or a potion, or starts doing chest exercises, and then her breasts get bigger, and she thinks it worked. All that happened was that she was about to start growing anyway." She struck another spark into the tinder, which caught into a gentle flame.

"Um, right. I knew that, of course. I was just testing you." Caroline covered the tinder with dried twigs. They quickly built this up into a crackling fire, but Caroline decided she wasn't done teasing the younger girl. She said, "So a sorceress has to be careful about who she kisses."

"An apprentice does. The kissing isn't the problem, except that it can lead to the other thing."

"And that's a problem?"

"Well, sure."

"Ah," said Caroline. She rocked back on her heels. "It's starting to make sense. A philosopher's stone is made from virgin's milk. Gold is made from virgin brass. A sorcerer's apprentice has to be a virgin. I sense a continuing motif here."

"It's called the Law of Transformation. When something changes state, there's a release or an acceptance of energy. So the transformation of a virgin to a nonvirgin is what powers the transformation from an ordinary person into a magician. Or something like that. Provided it's done right, and the energy isn't just dissipated. At least, that's the way Mummy explained it to me."

"No wonder she was so upset when Hal tried to get into your room," Caroline said wickedly.

"Will you stop saying that! He just wanted to get the philosopher's stone."

"I know. Just kidding. So you're going to be poring over books for years to come while my new husband is keeping me warm. You have my sympathy."

"Yeah, right. Don't feel sorry for me. We can still do the other thing."

This got Caroline's attention. "What other thing?"

Emily wasn't sure if she was still being teased. "You know what I mean."

"No, I don't."

"I have to spell it out for you?"

"Apparently so."

Emily cocked her head and looked at Caroline, then

decided that maybe she really did know something the older girl didn't. "When the boy licks the girl's—"

"Ahhhh!" Caroline clapped her hands over her ears. "Never mind. Don't tell me! I'm not listening! That is gross. That is totally gross."

"Well, you asked."

"I didn't think you were going to get graphic. That's disgusting."

"I didn't say I was going to do it. I just mentioned it as an option. Anyway, how could it be more disgusting than kissing frogs?"

"I wasn't kissing frogs for fun. And yes, it was disgusting. That's why I want everything that I was promised."

Her words reminded them of the uncomfortable situation that had led to the two girls being here, and Emily decided not to continue the conversation. She picked up a jug. "I'll fill our water jug from the stream."

"Fine," said Caroline. Then she giggled.

"What?"

"I was just thinking. A boy who spent several months as a frog ought to be able to do some really cool things with his tongue."

"Now who's being disgusting?" said Emily. But she looked thoughtful.

She headed off to a nearby stream, but once she was hidden by the trees, she changed direction and cut through the woods until she was almost at the clearing where the horses were hobbled. Hal was just finishing up. Emily slowed to a walk that just happened to intercept him as he turned back toward the campfire. "Oh hi."

"Hi."

She held up the jug. "I was just going to get some water."

"The stream is that way," said Hal. He nodded in a direction some 180 degrees from the path Emily was traveling.

She looked over her shoulder. "Oh, is it? Thanks. So, how are the horses?"

"Fine."

"Good," said Emily. She made no move to continue to the stream, or to get out of Hal's way. It seemed to Hal that she was waiting for something, and she was. Emily was by no means certain how a girl got a boy to kiss her. It wasn't the sort of thing she could have asked her mother, nor was it covered in any of the books she had read.

At least, not in those terms. There *was* magic in a kiss, that much her studies had made clear. More than a few spells could only be broken with a kiss. But what to do if you weren't under a spell? Emily had the vague idea that all a girl really had to do was get herself alone with a boy and wait. Apart from exceptions like the frog spell, kissing was really a boy's job. Surely they were trained for these situations.

She waited through some awkward silence. "You look very nice," said Hal.

Good, good. That's a start, Emily thought. "Why, thank you." She moved a little closer to him.

"It's a nice afternoon for walking in the woods."

"Uh-huh," said Emily. She had rather heard that some women had only to look at a man in a certain way, and he would get up and cross the room just to give her a kiss. She did not, unfortunately, know what that look was supposed to look like. She concentrated on trying to look kissable.

"I can help you get water," said Hal. "Let me take that jug for you." She raised the jug toward him, her fingers around the handle, and he put his hand over hers.

Better and better, she thought, not letting go of the jug, just letting his hand stay of top of her hand. She turned her face up to his and tilted it a little, thinking, *Here it comes.*

"What's Caroline up to?" said Hal.

These were not the words Emily had been anticipating. "She's fine," she said, snatching the water jug back out of the Prince's hand. She turned away. "I guess you think you're pretty lucky," she snapped back over her shoulder.

"Huh," said Hal. "What? Lucky about what?" He caught up with her, took the jug out of her hands, and put her arm in his. Walking toward the stream, he continued, "What are you talking about?"

"Oh, you know. All the boys think Caroline is just so, *so* fine. And now you're required to marry her. Oh, tough break. Would you be so casual about it if someone else had kissed that frog? Someone maybe . . . not so pretty . . . someone else. Oh never mind."

"First of all," said Hal, "let's get some perspective here. Caroline is not the prettiest girl I've ever seen. In fact, she is not even the prettiest girl in your village. I can think of someone who is a lot prettier."

"Who?"

"Oh, come on. You know who I'm talking about."

Emily suddenly found it hard to catch her breath. "No, tell me."

The Prince slipped his arm around her waist and lowered his head, so his lips were next to her ear. "Surely you can guess," he murmured.

"No." Emily swallowed hard. "I haven't the slightest idea."

"Mrs. Crossley, the schoolteacher. I think she's lots prettier than—ow!" he finished as Emily punched him in the arm. "No, really. Ratty gray hair turns me on. Ah!" He danced back out of the way as Emily threw a fistful of leaves at him. She chased him through the woods, throwing leaves and twigs. At the stream's edge he came to an abrupt stop and let her tumble into him, holding her up by her waist while she caught her breath.

"Furthermore," he went on, "I have no intention of marrying Caroline. She's already told me I'm not handsome enough for her, so I'm off the hook. And even if she changed her mind, I'm not changing mine. Who wants to marry a girl who thinks he's not good enough for her?"

"You don't have a choice," said Emily.

"Sure I do. Hey, I'm grateful that she broke the spell, and I appreciate all the hard work she put into it, and I know that it's traditional that the girl who breaks the spell marries the frog prince—if it is a tradition. How does something like that become a tradition anyway? There can't be that many princes who have been turned into frogs. But even so, suppose I don't marry her. What can she do about it?"

"You change back into a frog."

"What!"

"Granted," said Emily, "that's still a choice, in an extreme sort of way. But I can't really see a boy rejecting Caroline over—"

"I turn back?"

"No one told you?"

"No!"

"Sorry," said Emily. "I guess girls think about these things more than boys. But it's not a tradition. That's just the way the spell works. The prince is turned into a frog. If he's lucky enough to get out of it, he marries the girl who kissed him. Otherwise, it's back to the lily pad. The spell really isn't broken until the marriage."

There was a stirring beneath their feet, and something slithered into the stream with a quiet splash. The prince looked at the water with horror. His face turned white. He took a step back. "I'm doomed, then. Caroline doesn't want me."

"Oh, that's not a problem. It doesn't count if she loves someone else. If the girl doesn't *want* to marry the prince, he's off the hook. Remember, marriage is supposed to be a reward for her. You know, a commoner marrying into royalty."

"All right, all right." Hal had taken his arm off Emily and was now pacing up and down beside the stream, thinking out loud. "So Caroline marries another man, and that's the end of it. How long do I have for her to do this? Is there a time frame?"

"Um, yes. I think there is. I don't know what it is off the top of my head. I can look it up when we get to the city. But I'd say you've got plenty of time. The people who originally created these spells were usually pretty sensible. They'd have known that a royal wedding isn't thrown together overnight."

"Or I could just make sure I turn her off. Act real mean to her, so she'll hate me. Get drunk and threaten her. I'd never really slap a girl around, of course, but if she *thought* I would . . ."

"Pretty risky," said Emily. "She might be a girl who likes that sort of thing."

Hal laughed, then looked thoughtful. "You don't think?"

"No. I wouldn't try it. Caroline is too smart to be tricked. And spells like these are designed so you can't wiggle out of them. If you don't do your part, it makes things worse."

"And it's bad for you, right?" Hal looked straight at Emily, who looked away. "I can put two and two together as well as the next guy. Caroline is keeping me as a backup prince, in case she doesn't find anyone else she likes. But if she doesn't marry me either, she'll get compensation from your mother's estate. Am I right?"

For a long minute Emily looked so forlorn that Hal was ready to put an arm over her shoulders and tell her not to worry. But then she straightened her spine, turned, and faced him squarely. "True, but so what? There's lots of boys in Melinower, so I'm told. The Council of Lords is there, with all of their families, and the city is full of aristocracy. You know that when a girl looks like Caroline, there are plenty of boys who will forgive her humble origins. What's the problem?"

"One word," said Hal. "Dowry."

"Oh."

He started pacing up and down again. "Anyway, it won't be as easy as you think. The problem won't be finding a boy who's attracted to Caroline, the problem is finding a boy that Caroline is attracted to."

"Oh well, she just wants someone handsome. I'm sure there are plenty of good-looking boys in Melinower."

"Sure," said Hal. "But she's a girl. Who has ever been able to figure out what a girl likes about a boy? One girl will meet a guy and think he isn't worth a second glance. Then the next girl comes by, sees the exact same guy, and thinks he's the greatest thing on two legs. You know what I mean?"

Emily swallowed hard. "Yes," she said quietly. "I know what you mean."

To make up for the delays, the trio rode into the evening, and it was full dark when they reached the outskirts of the city. Here the girls began to slow their horses. Hal was perceptive enough to understand why. Caroline knew little about the world outside Ripplebrook, and Emily's sophistication came only from books and her mother's teachings. It was difficult enough for two young women to ride into a strange city, far more difficult to ride in at night, tired and bedraggled and grimy with road dust.

So the prince turned his horse off the main street and

pointed out a tavern. It was called the Bull and Badger, and the painted wooden sign showed a small furry animal with its teeth sunk into the nose of an angry bull. It was not a friendly sign, but warm light showed from the windows and cheery conversation echoed faintly when the door opened. "I know this place. The proprietor has a couple of rooms he lets out, cheap, and you can get a bath here, and the food is pretty good, if you don't mind pub food."

The girls looked doubtful. The City of Melinower had the full range of taverns, from crowded dockside bars filled with drunken sailors to upscale pubs filled with potted ferns. Here a man would bring a woman so she could sip frothy pink drinks while he drank wine. Even if he didn't like wine, he would drink it anyway because his girlfriend would make it clear that she didn't like beer breath. (Dating can be tricky in Melinower.) And by Melinower law, all taverns were also required to provide food and lodging. Nonetheless, even the best taverns were counted among the sleazier places to lay your head. Hal saw their expressions. "It's not that kind of place," he said. "The rooms are clean, and they're only used for sleeping."

"Pub food is fine with me," said Emily. In the darkness Melinower Palace could faintly be seen, looming sternly over the city. The tiny pub looked all the more enticing.

"How cheap is cheap?" said Caroline.

"I've got a little money," said Hal. "I'll take care of it."

So they stabled their horses and went inside. There was a fair crowd in the pub, but all had left their tables and the bar, and were gathered around a large man who seemed to be having a loud argument with someone unseen. A boy of fourteen was behind the bar. He saw them come in and gave a wide smile.

"Hey, Hal! Your Highness! Welcome back. We haven't seen you in a while."

"Hello, Tommy. Yeah, it's been a long time. I've been busy."

"There was a story going around that you got turned into a frog."

"Was there really?" The Prince shook his head. "Crazy how these rumors get started, isn't it? Is your father around?"

Tommy shook his head. "Mom and Dad are setting up the booth at the fairgrounds. I'm in charge tonight."

"Well, good. These are my friends Caroline and Emily."

"Hi," said the boy. The girls murmured greetings back.

"They want to clean up before going to the palace. We're going to need those rooms upstairs, and baths later, and some dinner."

"Sure," said Tommy, but he looked a bit worried. He bent his head toward Hal and spoke low so only the two could hear. "Uh, Your Highness, you know I hate to ask this, but if my father was here, you know he'd want to see the color of your money."

"I have money back at the palace, Tommy. I'll send a courier with payment as soon as I get back."

Tommy looked really unhappy. "Of course we trust you, Your Highness, but the King . . ."

"My father's debts are not my debts, Tommy. You know I'm good for it."

"Well . . ."

"We'll be gone first thing in the morning. You'll have the money before your father even gets home."

Tommy made up his mind. "Okay, Hal. Give me a couple of minutes to get the rooms ready."

"Great. And while we're waiting, how about a couple of flagons of small beer for the girls?"

"Coming up."

Hal worked his way back across the crowded floor, clearing a path for the two girls, shaking hands and slapping backs as he went. Everyone seemed to know him, and greeted him with a smile. They seated themselves at a rough wooden table and took in the crowd. The big man was reaching the end of his story, punctuating his sentences by waving a copper tankard, splashing beer on anyone who fell within its range. He had a dense black beard, and thick hair showed from the cuffs of his leather jacket. A heavy crossbow was slung over his back. "So the Princess says, 'Well, is your name Gerald?' "

"It's all lies," said an unseen voice.

"She says, 'Then is it Patrick?' "

"Never happened," said the voice.

"So," said the big man, "the Princess puts a finger to her pretty cheek, ponders for a while as if in deep thought, and finally says, 'Could your name—just possibly—be Rumpelstiltskin?' "

The crowd roared with laughter. The big man spread his arms expansively, then brought his mug to his lips and tilted it. He looked surprised. "Where's my ale?"

The crowded parted and through it came a short man. A very short man, in his early thirties, whose chin just reached the height of the tables. He stalked to the bar, climbed up on a stool with catlike nimbleness, and pounded a fist on the wood. "What's a guy got to do to get some service here?" Tommy quickly drew a mug and slid it to him, then brought three flagons to the Prince's table.

The dwarf was standing on the barstool, addressing the crowd. "That's not the way it happened. She was anti-Semitic. She made up that story to make me look bad. She said I demanded her firstborn child—yeah, right. Typical slur against the Jews. Anyone can see that."

"What I see," said the big man, "is that you tried to con a girl with some wild-ass story about a magic spinning wheel, and she turned the tables on you."

"That's not true. Hey, you gonna drink or just keep waving that thing around all night?"

"Well, being as you're buying, I'm drinking." The big man put his mug on the bar and looked around. "Hey, it's Prince Hal."

Hal waved. The big man waited until his mug was filled and came over to the table, gesturing for the dwarf to follow him. "Your Highness, good to see you again."

"Bear McAllistair," said Hal, introducing him to the two girls. "A fine shot with a crossbow. You're in town for the tournaments, I presume?"

"Sure am, Your Highness, and hope to take home a little prize money again. Allow my to introduce my height-challenged friend, who is named Rumpelstiltskin, as you may have heard. Recently run out of his own kingdom by an anti-Semitic conspiracy, to hear him tell it."

"Pleased to meet you," said Rumpelstiltskin. "Although I'm not Jewish, actually. People just think I am. I don't know why."

"Perhaps because your parents were Jewish," said Bear. "I've often found that has something to do with such misapprehensions."

"What makes you think my parents were Jewish? No one knows who they were. They left me on a doorstep."

"They left you on the doorstep of a synagogue. Kind of a dead giveaway, that. Plus they named you Rumpelstiltskin."

"Stiltskin isn't a Jewish name. You're thinking of Rivkin."

"What's wrong with being Jewish?" said Caroline.

"Aside from the persecution? I'll tell you." Rumpelstiltskin put his mug down with a thud, and it became clear to the three young people that he and Bear had been drinking for a while. "It's the food. I don't like the food. I could put up with the prejudice and the slander, but the food is awful. The matzo latkes, the kreplach, the kasha varnishkes. It's bland, it's fatty, and it's tasteless."

"No, it isn't," said Prince Hal. "What about the chopped liver?"

The dwarf pondered this. "Okay, the Jews make good chopped liver, I'll give you that."

"And the corned beef," offered Emily. "And the pastrami."

"Right," said Caroline. "And the bread. A nice pastrami sandwich on rye."

"With a slice of pickle," said Bear.

"Okay, okay, you've made your point," said Rumpelstiltskin. "I just don't like being Jewish, that's all. Do you spin?" He said this to Caroline in a sudden change of subject.

"As a matter of fact, I do," said the blond girl, amused at the little man's question.

"Hey," said Bear. "Don't get started on that again."

"What, what? I'm just asking. So you spin. How good are you?"

"Pretty good, actually. Not to blow my own horn, but I'm one of the best spinsters I know."

"Okay," said Rumpelstiltskin, "but are you fast? Because we only have from midnight to sunrise."

"Aw, leave her alone," said Bear.

"Can she really spin?" said Hal to Emily. That would explain something about Caroline. Spinning wasn't exactly a craft, in the sense that it didn't require an apprenticeship: but a good spinster was always in demand, and it was one of the few ways an unmarried woman could support herself. "I was in her house and I didn't see a spinning wheel."

"She sold it to pay for the frog search," whispered Emily.

"Oh, great. I am really under a serious obligation here. How good is she?"

"She can spin embroidery thread."

"Really?"

"I bought some from her myself."

Embroidery thread. Even Hal knew that spinning didn't get any better than that. Rumpelstiltskin was still explaining to Caroline. "Of course you can spin flax. Anyone can spin flax. The question is, can you spin unretted flax?"

Retting meant soaking the fibers so they wouldn't stick together. "Why do you want to spin unretted flax?"

"I want to keep the natural color."

"Weave it and dye the cloth later. Otherwise, it will take too long to separate the fibers. You won't get much thread in one night."

"Yep," said Bear. "That's what led to the whole fiasco."

"What fiasco?" said Caroline. The Prince and Emily leaned in closer. "What are you talking about?"

"I have a magic spindle," said Rumpelstiltskin. "A wheel that can spin flax into gold."

"He says," said Bear.

"I tell you it will work. It was enchanted by a top-drawer magician. I custom-made it to his specifications. I'm a cabinetmaker by trade," he added by way of explanation. "But he never showed up to take delivery, so the wheel is mine."

"Excuse me," said Caroline. "I'm sure this is a very nice tavern and all that, but I don't think you'd be spending your evenings here if you could spin flax into gold."

"He can't," said Bear.

"I tell you, it will work. I just don't want to waste it."

"Go on," said Caroline.

"The problem is that it will only work once, for one night. And unretted flax is hard to spin. Pound for pound, you don't end up with much gold."

"So," cut in Bear, "my little friend here came up with a swindle. You know what a miser the King of Mathagar is. Unlike our own dear king."

"All right," said Hal. "That's enough of that."

"Um, sorry, Your Highness. Anyway, Rumpelstiltskin finds this girl and works out a deal. He tells the King of Mathagar he's got this girl who can spin flax into gold. If he marries the girl, the gold is his. Of course the King wants a demonstration."

"Of course," said Emily.

"Rumpelstiltskin arranges that he and the girl will be searched and locked in the castle dungeon. The next morning, he'll come out with a bag of gold.

"He went for it," said Rumpelstiltskin. "I had him in my hand."

"Except that the King decides he doesn't trust Rumpelstiltskin. He kicks him out and spends the night in the dungeon himself, with the girl. And guess what? The next morning, there's no gold, but the old boy decides to marry the girl anyway."

"What a romantic story," said Hal. "I feel a sentimental tear welling up in my eye this very minute."

"Some things money just can't buy," said Emily.

"Rumpelstiltskin goes to the girl and demands payment according to the terms of their agreement," Bear went on.

"That seems fair," said Caroline. "Even if things didn't go according to plan, she'd never have married the King if he hadn't brought them together."

"Yes! See! My point exactly," Rumpelstiltskin told Bear.

"And the girl tells the King some wild story and gets our friend here and his spinning wheel run out of town."

"Bigoted jerk," said the dwarf.

"I'm sure it was a good effort," said Caroline, "but I'm sort of retired from the spinning industry just now. Thanks for asking."

"Your problem, my friend," Bear told Rumpelstiltskin, "is that you're going to have to start hanging out with dumber girls."

"Yeah, yeah, look who's talking. What about you and that magic sword?"

Bear's grin froze on his face. "That's completely different."

"It was a great investment, I'm sure. At least I didn't spend cash on my spinning wheel."

"You have a magic sword?" asked Emily.

"Not exactly," said Bear. "Say, it's time for another round. Who wants one? I'm buying."

"Not so fast," said Rumpelstiltskin. "You told your story, let me tell mine."

"I want to hear about the magic sword also," said Emily. "I'm studying to be a sorceress."

"Trust me, you don't want to study this one. Except maybe as a bad example."

"Don't feel bad," Emily told Bear. "You aren't the first person to be fooled by a fake magic sword, and you won't be the last."

"Oh, it's not fake," said Rumpelstiltskin. "It's just that most magic swords are enchanted to help you *win* the fight. Mr. Genius here gets the world's only magic sword that guarantees you'll get your butt kicked."

"I can't understand it," said Bear. "It worked just fine on the docks."

"You bought it at the docks?"

"From a spice ship that came from the Far East. It was their first trip this far west. Just a small ship, with a hold full of nutmegs. Well, I got to talking with the sailors, thinking I could pick up some curios maybe. And one thing led to another, and he sold me this enchanted sword. I mean, it seemed like a really good price for an enchanted sword."

"Now you know why," said Rumpelstiltskin.

"I tried it out before I bought it, of course. He had a couple of unenchanted swords and we sparred for a while. He couldn't get past my guard."

"He was letting you win, of course."

"No, no, it's not like that. I tried it both ways, each of us taking a turn with the magic sword. And I couldn't get past his guard either. Sure, maybe he was really good, but—I don't know. The sword's enchanted all right. But there's something wrong with it."

"Sometimes a spell just doesn't take," said Emily.

"This is great," said Caroline. "Magic swords. I love the city. We never hear stories like this back in Ripplebrook.

"May I see the sword?" said Hal. He had been silent up until now. All the others looked at him. "If you have it with you," he added.

"Sure," said Bear. "It's on my saddle. I'll get it for you."

"No, don't get up," said Hal. "I'll get it. You're still riding that roan? I know your horse." He slid away from the table. "Back in a minute."

"Nice guy," said Rumpelstiltskin, when the Prince had gone.

"Good old Hal," said Bear.

"Why do people treat him like that?" said Caroline.

"Like what?"

"Well, you know." Caroline had to think for a minute. "Here's good old Hal. Call him by his first name, shake his hand. It's like they don't even know he's a prince. Aren't people supposed to be more—I don't know—more deferential?"

"Usually they are," said Bear. "But your typical prince is an upper-class snot. Hal's not that kind of guy. You don't have to do that bowing and sucking up when Hal's around."

"He is more casual than I expected," said Rumpelstiltskin.

"Everyone likes Hal. And he's a good guy. He doesn't forget his friends."

"Mmm," said Rumpelstiltskin. "I'm told he doesn't forget his enemies, either."

"All the more reason to be friendly to him."

"I'm not sure I approve of this," said Caroline. "I think people should be more respectful."

"We don't have room to talk," said Emily. "We've been pretty casual toward him ourselves. She looked curiously at Caroline, who had been anything but respectful toward the young Prince.

"But that was just us." Caroline seemed to be speaking half to herself. "I didn't expect the whole city to act like this."

Bear laughed. "If you two young ladies are looking for a chance to practice your curtseys, don't worry. Once Hal takes you up to the palace, you'll get plenty of chances to be respectful and deferential. There's no shortage of snobs in Melinower. Especially at the palace. Maybe that's why everyone is so easygoing around Hal. I mean, there's Prince Jeff and Prince Kenny, the two handsome brothers, and then there's Hal, the . . . uh . . . um." Bear suddenly realized that both girls were staring daggers at him. His voice trailed off, and he quickly developed a keen interest in the bottom of his mug.

"The youngest brother," finished Rumpelstiltskin for him.

"Yeah!" Bear perked up. "That's what I was about to say."

"Somebody's got to be youngest," said Hal, returning to the table. "Turns out I was the most qualified for the job."

He laid the sword down. They all looked at it, the men with rather more interest than the girls. It was in a slim scabbard of varnished light wood. Strange glyphs were burned into the scabbard. To these natives of Melinower, unfamiliar with the languages of the east, they looked like mystical occult symbols. The handle was a hard stack of compressed leather disks, and there was a simple perforated metal dish for the hilt. Hal slid the blade partly out of the scabbard. It was single-edged, slightly curved, gleaming with a light coat of oil. The men bent over the blade, even Bear, who had examined it many times already, to spot the fine dark lines running through the metal. Satisfied with this indication of quality, they all leaned back again.

"Not bad-looking," said Hal finally. "Kind of pretty, in one of those simple-but-elegant sorts of ways."

"Huh," said Bear. "It looks better than it fights."

"Does it have a name?" said Emily. "Magic swords tend to have names."

"Sure it does. I call it *the sword that I bought from a sailor down at the docks and if I ever see him again I'll twist his head off*."

"Catchy name. Has a certain ring to it."

"It's a singing sword, too."

"Really?" said Caroline. "And what does it sing?"

"Madrigals, mostly. But once in a while it will burst into a few verses of 'Highland Lassie.' "

"He's kidding," said Hal. "A singing sword is one that rings when you pluck it. Here, listen." He snapped the sword with a thumb and forefinger. It responded with a clear, musical tone, like a tuning fork. "It happens when the metal is worked just right, and the edge is ground a certain way. It's pretty rare."

"I'd heard of it," said Bear. "But until this one, I'd never seen it."

"Really good razors do it," Rumpelstiltskin observed. "That's about all this sword is good for."

"I'd like to try it out," said Hal.

The two other men looked surprised. The girls were surprised also, but feeling themselves bound to support Hal, they tried not to show it. Hal hadn't expressed a great interest in weapons on their journey—he didn't seem the type to get into them.

"Now? Here?" said Bear.

"Sure," said Hal. "We've got all evening to kill. It's a fine, clear night, and there's room outside."

"Well, okay," said Bear. "You're the Prince. Whatever you want."

"I've got a sword you can use."

"Hey, wait a minute," said Rumpelstiltskin to Hal. "You can't fight him."

"Why not?"

"He's trying to sell you a sword. Of course he's going to let you win."

"I am not," said Bear, whose expression showed he had exactly that in mind. He gave Rumpelstiltskin a vicious look. "Who said anything about selling the sword? I didn't bring it up. If I was trying to sell this sword, would I have told the Prince it was defective?"

"You didn't. I did."

"Although come to think of it, maybe I wasn't handling it right. I'm a crossbow man myself. This might be a terrific sword in the hands of the right person." Bear added this last a bit hopefully.

"There, see?" said Rumpelstiltskin to the Prince.

"Don't worry about it," said Hal. "I'm not challenging you to a duel. Just try out a few cuts and blocks. I want to see how it handles." He had already gestured for Tommy to bring over some empty grain sacks and was wrapping the heavy cloth around the blade, tying it in place with thick twine. He was wearing his own sword. Now he drew it and laid it before Bear. Bear shrugged and began wrapping that blade also.

"What is he getting at?" whispered Caroline to

Emily. The younger girl could only shake her head.

Few will question the observation that when men are in close proximity, and ale is in quantity, there is apt to be fighting. And if swords are present, there will frequently be bloodshed. The Bull and Badger had certainly seen its share of drunken combat. At the same time, its patrons were equally familiar with friendly wagers and games of skill, where men young and old would batter each other, often to exhaustion, with blunted weapons. So it came as no surprise when the big man, known to his friends as Bear, and the skinny young man, known to everyone as Prince Hal, stepped outside with padded swords. The crowd followed them out, with enough people carrying lanterns and candles to light the scene. Caroline and Emily found themselves on the inner edge of a circle of spectators, while Bear and Hal squared off in the middle.

Hal raised the sword above his head, in the position known as a high guard. As he did so, Caroline saw a surprised expression cross his face. He lowered the sword and looked at it. Bear grinned. "Can you feel it? That's a magic sword, all right."

"I feel it," said Hal. "The sword wants to fight on its own." He made a few experimental cuts through the air, and to Caroline they seemed noticeably different, more flowing, more circular, than the sparring she had seen among the boys in her village. He drew his dagger and brought the sword to high guard again. Bear drew his dagger also, holding his sword to his side in an outside guard.

He nodded to show he was ready, and Hal hesitated not a second, immediately swinging the sword down in a movement so fast that Caroline could barely follow it. Not fast enough, though, for Bear parried it with his dagger and swung his own sword at the same time, striking Hal's side just above the waist.

Hal doubled over with an audible "oof." Emily sucked in her breath and Caroline saw most of the crowd wince. Bear said, "Sorry, Your Highness."

Hal straightened up. He grimaced with pain, then shook himself and smiled. "No problem, I wasn't using that kidney anyway." There was polite laughter from the crowd. "You attack this time."

Bear feinted with a vertical cut, drawing back as Hal leaned quickly in to parry the blow. He swung his sword around to cut from the side, but even then the oriental sword was ready, and Hal expertly knocked his blade aside. Bear was now close enough for Hal to draw a cut, and the oriental blade flowed like liquid: yet before Hal could complete the cut he felt the point of the big man's dagger against the stomach.

He looked down at the knife. "Methinks it's time for a strategic withdrawal," he said, and stepped back. There was more laughter from the crowd this time, and a bit of applause for Bear.

Caroline couldn't understand it. She didn't know how to fence herself, but she had seen enough of the local tournaments to know that Bear's movements were slow. Sure, he was technically good, and he had more reach than Hal, but any competent boy should have been able to get past the man's guard. There was something wrong here.

"One more round," said the Prince; and then, even

before Bear could finish nodding, he leaped forward with a scream, *"Hai!"* and swung the blade full force at Bear's head. Startled, Bear threw out an arm and caught the blade on his dagger, the force of the blow driving him down to one knee, and from there he blindly thrust his sword forward. It passed right between Hal's legs.

"Ooooo," said Hal in a mock falsetto, and mugged a face toward his audience. They burst into riotous laughter, for he did look completely ridiculous, with his comical expression and the sword protruding from between his legs in a bawdy manner. He winked at them, then stepped over the blade and gave Bear a hand up. The big man got a round of applause.

Caroline was furious.

How can he do this to me? she thought. He had just made a fool of himself, and, therefore, his companions, which included her, in public, out in the streets, in front of a brawling tavern crowd. It was her first night in the city, the city where she intended to find a noble husband—as he well knew—so that appearances counted for everything. She knew that Hal was not good-looking, but at least he carried himself well, behaved like a gentleman, and had a quiet, reserved dignity. Now he had showed himself to be a buffoon, and an incompetent swordsman to boot. *For goodness sake, if he wanted to try out the sword, couldn't he test it somewhere quiet and private?*

"What was that all about?" whispered Emily, coming up behind her. The younger girl looked confused, apparently thinking the same thoughts Caroline had.

"I don't know," said Caroline. "I just hope you're a better sorceress than Hal is a swordsman."

They followed the men inside, who were laughing and talking about weapons, and comparing daggers and blades. Inside, they refilled their glasses and were soon seated around the table once again. Bear unwrapped Hal's sword and gave it back to him, and Hal unwrapped Bear's sword, slid it back into its smooth wooden scabbard, and laid it on the scarred wooden table. Bear hardly bothered to look at.

"You see what I mean, Your Highness? The blade itself is pretty nice, and when you hold it in your hand you can feel the power moving inside it. You can practice with it, and make draws, and cuts, and thrusts, and feints, and the sword seems to know what to do and move on its own, which is what you expect a magic sword to do. I'm not a fool. I wouldn't be taken in by just any old magic sword scam. This one seems like the real thing. It's only when you get to actually fighting with it that you find it can't hold up."

The Prince nodded. "I'll take it. How much do you want for it?"

It was a somber group that set out for Melinower Palace the next morning. Caroline was still seething over Hal's performance of the night before, followed by his purchase of the sword, especially as it was becoming clear that the Prince did not seem to have much money. Emily had shrugged it off. "Boys and their swords," she said. "Who knows what's going on in their heads when they get into that stuff? And I don't think you should be so concerned about what the Prince buys. You act like you're married to him already."

"I just don't like to see money wasted," said Caroline, whose upbringing had been quite a bit different from Emily's. But she admitted to herself that it had been more than that. When all you had was your reputation, as Caroline did, you gave a lot of thought to protecting it. Some of the Bull and Badger's customers were still laughing about last night's contest. It bothered her that her companions affected not to notice this.

She was in front of the inn, checking the harness on her horse, when Rumpelstiltskin called her over. The little man had been sitting on a bench by the door, with his elbows on his knees and his head in his hands. He looked thoroughly hungover, and Caroline did not doubt that he and Bear had been up drinking long after the three companions had gone to bed. But he looked up when she stopped in front of him.

"Listen, kiddo," he said, then frowned. "Um, I've forgotten your name from last night."

"Caroline."

"Caroline, right. Listen, you stick close to Prince Hal, okay?"

"Sure," said Caroline, wondering what brought this on.

"No, listen. I mean it. I've seen a lot of kids like you drift in from the farms, hoping to make their fortune in the city. And this place will chew you up if you don't keep your head about you."

"Sure."

"Melinower is a city that is held together by connections. And you don't have any, you see? As long as
you're by his side, you're somebody, and people will
treat you right. Without him, you're nobody, and you
won't get the time of day around here. You see? This
sorceress girl you're with—I don't know about those
types. They've got their own circles they move in. But
for you, Prince Hal is the only connection you've got.
So you stick with him and don't let him shake you off.
You understand what I'm saying?"

"I understand. But why are you telling me this?"

Rumpelstiltskin rubbed his eyes. "I don't know. I just
like your style, that's all. Or maybe you really will marry a
lord—why not, you've got the looks, and determination—
and then I'll have a connection, too. But in any case, I
see you walking around with a sour look this morning,
and I have to tell you, that's not the way to do it. When
you ride into the palace, you better look like you and the
Prince are dearest friends, and don't let anyone suspect
different."

This was such obviously good advice that Caroline
was ashamed of herself for needing to be reminded of it.
She immediately switched on her perkiest expression.
The change was so dramatic, and with her blond hair
swirling around her head and her full lips curved into a
smile, so affecting, that Rumpelstiltskin had to sit back
and laugh. "That's the ticket. Keep that up, and you'll go
far."

Emily and the Prince came out and mounted their
horses. They were a little quiet at first, but Caroline's
cheerfulness lightened their spirits, so all were in a good

mood as they rode toward the palace. Hal had wrapped the oriental sword and its scabbard in oiled cloth and stowed it behind his saddle. He was still wearing his own sword. Emily's head was turning from left to right, taking in the new sights. From her reading and education, she knew what to expect, but to see it all for herself—the paved streets crowded with carts and carriages, people and animals, pie shops with their chimneys puffing smoke, delivery boys staggering comically through the streets with baskets or boxes stacked higher than their heads, couriers in uniform dashing in and out of doorways with missives tucked inside their jackets—as well as all the things she was used to from home; the butchers, bakers, smiths, and such, but many more of them. The streets did not meet in corners but opened up into squares, with statues and fountains and sometimes gardens. School-children in smart uniforms marched double file behind scholars in pasteboard hats and tattered gowns. Down one street a man led a bear cub on a chain and down another she saw a tiny animal with a long curled tail—could that have been a monkey? There were bookstores—she longed to go inside them—and entire shops that sold nothing but sweets.

And every now and then she would catch a glimpse, in a darkened doorway or a half-shut window, of someone wearing a midnight blue cloak or perhaps a pointed cap, that bore the twin symbols of a star and a crescent moon. And she made a special effort to try to remember those places, knowing that in them was someone in the business of sorcery.

Caroline rode by Hal, equally observant but subdued.

She had long planned to travel to the city, but in fact had never really thought about what she would find when she got there. She had vaguely imagined someplace with a gleaming castle rising out of a cloud bank, rows of carriages pulled by white horses, and perhaps a few hat shops. Now, confronted by more people than she had ever seen in her life, she was feeling, if not overwhelmed, at least pretty much whelmed.

Hal, for his part, was not oblivious to the feelings of his two companions—a courtly upbringing had taught him to recognize subtle nuances of tone and gesture—and so he decided to turn off the crowded main thoroughfares and onto the quieter streets of what was known as Gentry Place, along an avenue lined with up-scale shops that catered to the nobility. But his good intentions fell awry, for though the streets were emptier, the shops themselves were even more intimidating than the people.

Emily edged her horse over to Caroline's, and whispered, "Glass windows."

"I see them," Caroline whispered back. She was staring straight ahead, trying to be cool, trying to act uninterested in the objects that filled those windows. Bolts of cloth—silk and velvet and lace, displayed alongside elaborate dresses and bonnets. Glasses of crystal, bowls and dishes of porcelain thin as eggshells, silver cutlery. Chains of gold, rings set with emeralds, and long, long strings of pearls. Carved oak chests, inlaid with cherry and ebony, and finely tanned leather luggage. She reminded herself that she had seen all this before. Ripplebrook was not a poor town, after all. It was just that she had never seen so much of it all at once. Suddenly she felt Emily's hand on her arm.

"Caroline," the girl whispered, "we'll have to change clothes."

"Impossible."

"We can't go to the castle like this. Look at them!" The younger girl gestured at two elegantly dressed women entering a shop.

"They're getting out of a carriage. We're on horseback. If they were riding, they'd be dressed like we are." Caroline was not at all sure this was true. But in her months of swamp work, she had plenty of time to think about what she would do when she finally found her prince and how she would act when presented in court. The two girls were wearing divided dresses, for riding. Once dismounted, Caroline thought they would look formal enough, at least for the first day. She was used to dressing less well than her friends, and they could learn the court customs as they went along. "Listen, the castle is the center of government. All sorts of people go in and out of there all day long. Right?"

"I guess," said Emily.

"So nobody is going to pay much attention to us. As long as we're with Hal, we'll be okay. Anyway, there's no place for us to change clothes. And if we did, we couldn't ride in them anyway."

"Yes," said Emily, a bit reluctantly. She was watching another set of finely dressed women get out of another carriage.

"And we only have a few dresses, so we can't use

them up right away. We have to save them for the right occasions."

"Well, that's true. Like if we meet the Queen."

Caroline laughed. "Even if we cling to Hal, I don't think we're likely to meet the Queen anytime soon."

Meanwhile, Hal had slowed his horse so they could catch up. He drifted alongside. "Everything all right?"

"Fine," said Caroline. "We were just talking about clothes."

"Sure," said Hal, who was not certain that girls ever talked about anything else. He pointed to the left. "That's the main gate where the public enters the palace. By public, I mean the lords, the lawyers, the people who work in the ministries. Not just anyone can walk in." He pointed to the right. "We'll go in through the private family entrance. There's also a big family entrance where we take the carriages out and have a big processional and people line up to see us. But this is the entrance for day-to-day things."

Caroline had a momentary vision of herself riding out in a carriage pulled by a team of six white horses, her handsome prince at her side, waving to a throng of admirers. She pushed the thought aside. The time for dreaming was past. This was the real thing.

They were approaching a high, wrought-iron fence, fronted by a double row of oak trees. A narrow guardhouse was situated next to a narrow gate in the fence. A guard came out of the house and saluted the Prince, who waved to him. Rather glumly, Caroline thought. She expected a boy who had been away from home for so long to be a bit more eager to return. The guard unlocked the gate.

Emily didn't move. She was staring upward. Hal looked at her quizzically. Finally she said, "You live here?"

Caroline could well understand the question. The palace towered over them, and it wasn't just the hill it was built on. The place was huge. Great ramparts of black stone rose from behind the trees. Thick crenellated towers rose from every corner, festooned with banners. Behind the walls could be seen block after block of square buildings, with steeply pitched slate roofs. Everywhere jutted balconies and landings and windows and doors, through which steady streams of people could be seen leaving and entering. Several score of chimneys puffed light brown smoke. And from the tallest building extended a high flagpole, proudly displaying the colors and crest of Melinower.

"Oh no," said Hal. "I mean yes, but this isn't all ours. The Council of Lords meets here and they have their chambers here also. You have to remember that Melinower Palace is the seat of the government. The royal apartments are only a part of this."

"That makes sense," said Emily. "I knew there were big castles around, but I knew they weren't *that* big."

"Well, it's a palace, actually. A castle is a personal residence. We have a castle at our estate in Losshire. The palace is mostly offices. You'll see when we get inside. It takes a while to learn your way around. Even our apartments take some getting used to." By that time they were inside the gate, the horses' shoes ringing on the paved road that led up to the palace walls. A man on horseback was coming toward them. As they reached him he turned his horse sideways, blocking their path, and pushed back his broad-brimmed hat.

"Well," he said. "If it isn't little Hal. The prodigal son returns."

Hal's expression was a study in controlled neutrality. "Hello, Kenny."

"I heard you got turned into a frog."

Hal shrugged.

"Of course," said Kenny. "Being small, soft-bodied, and wet behind the ears probably wasn't that big of a change for you."

Hal sighed and threw back his arm in a gesture that encompassed the girls. "Let me introduce Miss Caroline and Miss Emily, of the village of Ripplebrook. Ladies, this is my brother, Prince Kenneth."

Kenny swept off his hat and gracefully bowed from the waist. "The pleasure is mine," he said, his gaze particularly lingering on Caroline's eyes.

"Oh my," said Caroline.

It was a reaction common to girls her age. Indeed, Caroline might have been more restrained than most, for Prince Kenny dazzled many women. He was tall. Even when he was sitting on a horse you could see how tall he was. But not skinny. For a tall man he was amazingly broad-shouldered. His jaw was square and set off a carefully trimmed and pointed beard. His eyes were piercing blue, and when he swept off his hat a great mass of auburn locks fell to his shoulders.

The hat itself, of brand-new felt, sported three iridescent feathers from a bird of paradise. Every ruffle on his collar had been carefully starched, and the gold buttons gleamed on his deep blue jacket. His shirt was studded with pearls. Every finger, including the thumbs, sported a gold ring, each with a different precious or semiprecious stone. He wore a gold-and-emerald cross around his neck, and from his waist swung a sword in a jewel-encrusted scabbard.

Caroline's eyes were shining. This, she thought, was what a real prince looked like.

But Kenny had already turned his attention back to Hal. "The old man knows you're back. He wants to see you right away. I guess you're going to explain to him how you screwed up yet another mission."

There was a short silence while Hal appeared to be considering several replies and then deciding against any of them. Finally he said, "I'll see him."

"Yeah, well, stop by my room this evening. I've got some flies that need to be cleared out. I've been saving them in case you wanted a snack." Kenny turned back to the two girls, bowed again, and pushed his hat back onto his head. "Good day, ladies."

"Good day, Your Highness," both girls dutifully replied. Caroline looked after him with an awestruck gaze. When she finally turned away, she found that Prince Hal had continued up the drive. The girls hurried their horses after him. "Did you see him, did you see the way he looked at me?" Caroline whispered to Emily. "Isn't he gorgeous?"

"I think he's a jerk," said Emily. "Why is he so nasty to his brother?"

"And did you see his clothes? Weren't they fine?"

Caroline went on. "Why doesn't Hal dress like that?"

They both looked ahead at Hal, who was simply dressed in plain duck cloth. "I think Hal looks just fine," said Emily. "Lots of boys aren't into clothes."

"Prince Kenny is so tall," said Caroline. "He's at least six feet tall. And his hair is beautiful."

"Hal's hair is . . . lots of boys aren't into clothes."

In the meantime Hal had reached the base of the high stone wall, dismounted, and handed his horse over to a stable hand, who led it away. More stable hands appeared to help the girls dismount. While they were getting used to this, servants appeared from various doors in the wall and took their packs from the horses, carrying them inside and disappearing. The girls looked anxiously after them, although neither wanted to be the first to express concern. Hal made a patting-down motion with his hand, and said, "They're getting rooms for you. They'll put your bags in them."

"Thank you," said Caroline.

Hal had drifted over to one of the doors, which looked the same as the other doors but apparently wasn't, for guards stood on either side. He consulted with one of the guards, who opened the door for him. Immediately, a stout man in a formal black coat stepped outside, bowed to Hal, and said, "His Majesty the King would like to see you, sire."

"No doubt, Henri," said Hal. "I'll see him after lunch."

"His Majesty would like to see you right away, sire," the formal man said firmly.

"Food," said Hal, equally firmly. "My guests have not eaten."

"His Majesty is most anxious . . ."

"Then we'd best be served quickly. Because the sooner my friends can eat, Henri, the sooner I can see my father."

"Actually, I'm not all that hungry," said Caroline.

"I can wait, too," said Emily.

Henri favored them with a small smile. Hal shrugged and said, "Okay, then come with me."

They followed him through the small door, which turned out to lead to a wide hallway, whose walls were decorated with exquisite paintings and mirrors with carved and gilded wood frames. Around them, uniformed maids were dusting and polishing, and every time they came to a door someone was there to open it for them. Hal led them down one hallway and along the next, passing countless antechambers, where courtiers waited and consulted one another, while sitting on velvet-cushioned chairs.

"You have a lot of servants," said Caroline.

"Too many. We could get by on half of these."

"Are we going to the throne room?"

"Not quite. Dad isn't hearing petitions now, so he won't be sitting on the throne. He has a private office. That's where I'm going."

"What should we do?"

"Nothing. Wait here. I'll just be gone a minute."

He stopped and consulted with several officers in charge of a small counting room. From here a messenger was dispatched to the Bear and Badger with payments for the sword and the previous night's lodging. He then led Caroline and Emily into a small antechamber with a settee, just big enough for the two girls to sit side by side. Hal walked past them to a door set in the back of the chamber. The door was painted to match the decor of the rooms. It wasn't exactly hidden or secret, but each girl had to admit that she would not have seen the door unless it opened. Hal waited until the girls were settled, then pushed the door and eased himself in.

He was at one end of a long, narrow office, almost a corridor. He stood in gloom, while small windows at the other end cast a glow over his father's desk. In between were tall bookcases that made the room even gloomier. The intended effect was that a visitor would walk deeper and deeper into darkness, then emerge to find the King bathed in mystical light. Hal always thought it was kind of a dumb trick. He wondered if any of the lords and nobles who visited his father were really impressed by this stuff, and was tempted to knock some books off the shelves as he passed, just to destroy the somber atmosphere.

He pushed the thought away as being childish and approached his father's desk. The King, sunlight reflecting off his gray head, dressed in a royal blue robe, dipped his quill in a pot of ink and continued to write. A short stack of books was at his elbow. Hal stood silently. He knew that making people stand at your desk was a way of showing your authority, but he also knew that the two chairs beside him had the legs slightly shortened, just enough so that visitors would find themselves looking up to the King. Hal wondered who first thought of these stupid ideas. He continued to stand. He was not in the mood for a fight, and experience had taught him that the only way to avoid one with his father was not to talk to him at all.

Finally the King looked up and said, "Did you get it?"

Hal took the bag containing the philosopher's stone from his pocket and laid it on the desk.

The King nodded. "Good."

That was it. "Good." Not "Congratulations" or even "Thanks." Not "Excellent work, my boy. Our problems are solved! The whole family is grateful to you." Hal told himself he wasn't disappointed. He hadn't expected gratitude.

He placed his hands on the desk, leaned over, and looked at the two books by his father's side. One was a book of spells. The other was a book of alchemy. He looked at his father's eyes. The King's face was expressionless.

So he knew. Knew that the philosopher's stone was useless. That he had sent his youngest son out to steal an artifact that he couldn't use, that Hal had spent seven weeks as a frog for nothing. Probably he had known for days. He might have learned right after sending Hal out. But Hal knew one thing for certain. There would be no apology, no expression of concern for the risk he had taken on this futile quest. Just "Good."

Hal straightened up, turned, and walked back to the door. He had his hand on the knob when he heard the King's calm voice, "I haven't dismissed you yet."

Hal hesitated with his hand on the knob. Then he released it and walked back down the narrow office. When he was halfway, he stopped before a bookshelf, as though considering a selection. Without looking at the King he put out an arm and swept half a dozen books onto the floor. Then he left the room.

Now it so often happens that when people move from the country to the city, they may encounter an emotional letdown sometimes described as the "small frog in a big pond" phenomenon. To cite a familiar example—a young man may be the best student in his school, winning all the awards, taking all the honors, and developing a pretty high opinion of himself. He finds a patron to sponsor him to a university, arrives at class on his first day—and discovers that every single student in the room took top honors at his or her school.

Or a young woman is named queen of the county faire. She travels to the city with the dream of turning her looks into her fortune, and finds the shops are full of girls who were queens of their county faires. A great beauty in her hometown, she is now totally unexceptional. For the larger the crowd, the more difficult it is for any one person to stand out.

This did not happen to Caroline.

Caroline was, to put it in the plainest terms possible, a major babe. She had bright blue eyes, long soft lashes, flawless skin, and blond hair that grew nearly to her waist without getting split ends. Her figure could not only turn a man's head but unscrew it from his vertebrae. When she was happy, her smile was bright enough to guide ships at sea, and when she was sad, she had the undeniably charming habit of pouting rather than frowning. Pouting in a grown woman is cute only when she has very sexy lips to begin with; otherwise, it must be left to little girls. Caroline could pout up a storm.

When Hal came back out the two girls were still sitting in the antechamber and giggling. He looked around to see what was funny.

"All sorts of young gentlemen have been passing by and flirting with us," explained Emily.

"Ah," said Hal. "Did you flirt back?"

"Oh no."

"No," added Caroline.

"No," said Emily.

"Not really."

"Right," said Emily. "Not really flirting."

"Maybe we smiled a little."

"Smiling isn't flirting. It's just smiling."

"That's all," said Caroline.

"Sure," said Hal, who knew full well what a smile from the right girl could do.

"Did you give the King the philosopher's stone?" asked Emily.

"Yes. He said thanks. Turns out that he already knows that it's unusable. When I went in he had a couple of magic books on his desk. He didn't even touch the stone. So he knew."

"So all your trouble was in vain. I'm sorry."

"Water under the bridge," said Hal. "Let's eat."

The palace contained a number of public dining rooms that served meals with various degrees of formality, as well as a very small dining room for the exclusive use of the royal family and a slightly larger one for their personal guests. This room, paneled in carved oak, with high south-facing windows, had a table that could seat perhaps a dozen people. It was to this room that Hal brought Caroline and Emily, and it was here he found his brother Jeff, seated at one end of the table with a stack of ledgers.

Jeff was a year younger than Kenny, but nearly identical in height and build. He wore a jacket of gray woven cloth, with gold braid on the shoulder and sleeves, not as gaudy as Kenny's, but certainly finer than Hal's, a white linen shirt with a gray silk sash, and one ring, a gold signet with the royal seal. He kept his hair cut shorter than Kenny, but his eyes were just as blue, and a whole lot brighter when he fixed them on Hal.

"Hal!" He jumped up from his chair and pounded his brother on the back. "Am I glad to see you. Mom cried for days when she heard about the frog thing. I wanted to look for you myself, but Dad absolutely forbade it.

Too risky, he said. He didn't want another son being enchanted."

"I understand."

"Have a seat," said Jeff, pulling out chairs for the girls. "They'll be serving in a minute. Tell me about the spell. It must have been awful. But you got kissed and rescued." He looked the girls over. "We have one of you to thank, I take it?"

"Right," said Hal. "This is Caroline. Caroline, my brother, Prince Jeffrey."

Caroline tried to untie her tongue, but before she could say anything, Jeff took her hand in both of his and squeezed. "It's an honor to have you here. Good job on finding and rescuing Hal here. The whole family is grateful to you."

"Oh, it was nothing," Caroline managed to say, keeping her hand in his. "Any girl would have done the same."

Jeff turned to Emily. "And you must be Rapunzel."

Emily looked surprised. Before she could say anything Hal shook his head. "Ah, no. She's still back at the tower."

Jeff looked reproachful. "Hal."

"Give her time. She's running low on supplies. She'll be out of there by the end of the summer, I'm sure of it."

"What?" said Caroline. "What's this about? Rapunzel?"

A waiter came in with a basket of rolls. Hal took one and started buttering it. He looked at Jeff and shook his head slightly. "I did my part."

Jeff looked embarrassed. "We need that fee, Hal."

"What fee?" said Caroline.

Hal said, "Rapunzel's family won't pay the rescue fee until Rapunzel actually returns home."

Caroline looked shocked. "You charged money to rescue that girl? Hal! That is so mercenary."

"Not my choice. The King sets and collects the fees."

Jeff said, "Dad wanted Hal to just stuff the girl in a sack and bring her in. Hal refused. Dad's been kind of cool toward Hal since then."

"Not," said Hal, "that we had a warm relationship before."

"And then Dad got some idea in his head about turning lead into gold . . ."

"Brass," said Emily.

". . . only then he found out it doesn't work, but he'd already sent Hal off. So Hal hasn't been around to do more slay-and-rescues and we lost those fees, too. Which Dad thinks is Hal's fault for letting himself get turned into a frog."

"Wait a minute," said Caroline. She watched a waiter came in with a soup tureen. He set it on the table, then started ladling it into porcelain bowls. She looked at the table. There were four spoons in front of her, and they all appeared to be real silver. She made a mental note to see which spoon Hal used and turned back to him. "You're giving me the idea that money is tight here. I thought the royal family was rich."

"We are," said Hal. "We have plenty of money coming in from our estates, and we get a generous allowance from the Council of Lords. If certain people would just show some fiscal responsibility, we'd be fine."

"Okay, Hal," said Jeff. He tapped the ledger books. "You're preaching to the choir here."

"But," said Caroline, "can't the King raise taxes if he wants more money?" Then she frowned inwardly. Emily and Hal were both eating soup, and she missed seeing which spoon they used. It was annoying. Why put all this silver on the table when they were just having soup for lunch?

Jeff shook his head. "Not in Melinower. The Council of Lords sets the taxes and controls the budget. And they pretty much told Dad that enough is enough. But listen, I don't want to bore you with family matters. Tell me about yourselves." He looked at Caroline. "How did you break Hal's spell?"

"Oh," said Caroline. She flipped her blond tresses back over her shoulders, while returning his gaze, deciding that she liked it when he looked into her eyes just like that. "Well, it was just persistence and a lot of luck." She gave a brief rundown of the grid method for searching the swamp and the ditches she dug for drainage. Hal offered some descriptions of her frog nets and traps. Jeff, when he heard the story, was full of praise.

"That," he said, "was clever. You know, it's probably just as well I didn't go out there myself. I'd have just been tramping around in the swamp, catching frogs haphazardly, then dragging them back to the village trying to persuade girls to kiss them."

"Well, thank you. It just took a bit of planning."

"And netting out the tadpoles. I don't think anyone

has ever thought of that before. That was brilliant."

"You really are too kind." Jeff really did have the most lovely eyes, Caroline thought. Being a beautiful girl, she was used to praise from boys and normally tended to discount it. But when Jeff spoke, she couldn't help doing a little wiggle.

"I'm glad all your hard work turned out to be worth it in the end. Hal's very lucky. I know you'll be very happy together. Have you met our mother yet? When is the wedding?"

"Hey, where are my manners?" said Hal. "Would anyone else like a roll?"

"I'll take one," said Emily.

"These are wonderful rolls," said Caroline, breaking one open. "I love the way the outside is so crispy."

"Yeah, they're great. We don't make them here. We buy them from a bakery in the city."

"What?" said Jeff. "What did I say?" He looked perplexedly from Hal to Caroline.

There was a moment of awkward silence. Then Hal said, "Caroline doesn't want to marry me."

"I haven't made up my mind yet," said Caroline. She looked at the table. There were at least three knives that could have been butter knives.

"She wants someone, um, taller."

"Hal's a great guy," said Jeff, loyally. "But if you don't want to marry him, well, it's your decision. Certainly Dad will be happy."

There was more silence. This time Emily broke it. "Why? Why will the King be happy?"

"Dowry," said Hal. "Don't worry about it."

"Dad's kind of hung up on money," said Jeff. "It takes a pretty stiff dowry for a commoner to marry into nobility. And to marry someone who is in line for the throne, well, it's impossible. That's why the frog spell is so famous. The common girl gets to marry the noble son, no strings attached. She leapfrogs over the dowry requirement, if you'll excuse the pun."

Caroline exchanged glances with Emily. Emily had an I-told-you-so look. A servant came through, took away Caroline's soup plate, and set before her a giant plate containing a whole roasted duck. She looked at it, momentarily distracted, wondering if she was expected to carve this for the group and what knife to use. Then she looked up and realized that each person at the table was getting an entire duck, something that, in her experience, would feed a whole family. Another waiter came through and set beside her a platter of roasted potatoes. And another set down a plate of green beans with slivered almonds. And more servants were coming behind him.

And this was just lunch.

The rich, she thought, were very different from the poor.

She started thinking about dowry.

It was while they were eating that yet another servant arrived to tell Prince Hal that rooms were ready for the two girls, and that their luggage had been stowed in them. Shortly afterward two matronly women in maids' uniforms arrived and offered to show the girls to their rooms when they were ready. Caroline and Emily left rather hesitantly. They were in a strange palace in a strange city, and the only person they really knew was Prince Hal. Now he had vanished, lost among hundreds, perhaps thousands, of strangers in a vast and labyrinthine palace. They followed the women meekly.

Caroline found herself in a small bedchamber. Small by the palace standards—the room was five times the size of her house. A thick rug lay across the stone floor, and the walls were hung with tapestry. A four-poster bed, with heavy ticking and a thick pillow, stoo its headboard against the wall. A bed key hung beside it. Two wax candles stood on a dressing table, on either side of a washbasin. The table also held a pitcher of water, a stack of folded towels, and a silver hand mirror. Her bags were piled by the dressing table. The maid poured some water into the basin and stood beside it, waiting.

Caroline stood in the center of the room and waited for her to leave. When it became clear after a few minutes that the maid was not leaving, she cleared her throat, and asked, "Um, am I supposed to tip you?"

The woman smiled gently. "No, miss. Would you like me to help you undress?"

"Ah, no. I can manage by myself."

"When you're ready to open your bags, I can unpack for you."

"Ah, actually I think I can manage that by myself, also."

"If you prefer, I can leave now. When you need me, there is the bellpull by the bed."

"Ah, great, yes. That will be fine. Yes, thank you."

When she was out of the room, Caroline opened the window and looked out, hoping to see some view of the city, perhaps some glimpse of the countryside beyond it. But the window looked into a wide courtyard, with a sunny garden, and a fountain, and a steady stream of people walking to and fro. For some reason this made ___ __d, and she turned away and lectured herself sternly.

"___ hold of yourself," she whispered. "So you're ___ couldn't see Ripplebrook from that win- ___ thinking about a dowry. You've come ___ g to be stopped now."

She washed her hands, splashed water on her face, and resolutely set to unpacking. Untying her bundles she took out three dresses, donated by her girlfriends. Two of them were almost new. The women of Ripplebrook had held a hurried meeting, then presented Caroline with their verdict. "Keep it simple," they said. "We can't keep up with the fashions in Melinower, and they won't expect you to. They'll know you're from the country, whatever you do, so don't try to look like you're not. Just be yourself." The dresses they chose—one white, one pale pink, and one pale blue—were simple and unadorned, but very well made and of quality material. Each had short sleeves, leaving the arms bare in the country style, and a loose waist, with neither stays nor sash. Caroline unfolded them and hung them in the wardrobe. Just looking at them gave her new confidence.

At the bottom of her pack was a small wooden box. Caroline pulled it out and looked at it curiously. It had no lock. In fact, it appeared to be one of those oriental puzzle boxes. After a bit of pushing and pulling she got the lid to slide out. Inside were two tiny parcels of folded paper.

She unfolded them both and laid them on the dressing table. The first one contained a set of gold earrings with tiny diamonds. Caroline recognized them. They were the proudest possessions of her friend Ashley. Printed on the paper, in neat block letters, were the words, "Well, we can't let you appear in court without proper jewelry, can we?"

The second paper had been wrapped around a coil of thin gold chain, from which was suspended a small sapphire. It was the most cherished possession of her friend Brenna, and the paper held the girl's loose scrawl. "Don't shame us, lassie. And write and tell us *everything*." The word everything had been underlined three times.

Her friends. Now truly homesick, Caroline held the papers to her breast and let a tear well up in each eye. Then she blinked them away, stowed the jewelry back in the tiny box, and placed it on the bed, beneath the pillow. She lay back on the bed and stared at the ceiling, trying to will her mind to become calm and logical.

Dowry, she thought.

Prince Hal's room was on the southeast corner of the palace. To the south, large French windows faced the harbor, always bustling with merchant ships, naval vessels, and fishing boats, and the wharf itself, with its shipyards and ropemakers and sailmakers and sailor's pubs and, of course, the fish market. To the east another set of windows faced the common market, the last stop for many of the goods that came in on those merchant ships before they were dispersed among the populace, and on a hill beyond that, the broad greens and ivy-covered towers of Melinower University. A wide stone terrace ran around the outside of the rooms, so that Hal could throw open a set of windows, step outside, breathe the fresh air, and look out over the city. He did this sometimes, and most often it was to the south, over the harbor and out to sea, to the distant horizon where adventure beckoned young men, as it has since the first boy gazed seaward, lo those many years ago.

But there was no time for woolgathering now. Hal pushed the French doors open with one foot, climbed onto the terrace, and walked along it until he came to another set of French windows. He rapped twice with his knuckles by way of announcing himself, pulled the doors open, and stepped down into the spacious quarters of his brother, Prince Jeffrey. He looked around and gave an admiring whistle.

"I've got to hand it to you, Jeff. This is amazing. I can see what you've been doing since I've been gone. I didn't think you'd be able to get it all together."

Jeff was sitting behind a leather-topped desk, with sheets of foolscap, a blotter, quills, sealing wax, and two big pots of ink—one black, one red—in front of him. The desk was wide enough that it took up nearly the width of the room. Extending forward from each side of the desk were two long—very long—narrow tables. It was these two tables that elicited Hal's comment, for when he last saw them they were piled high with box upon box of bills and invoices, some of them nearly crumbling with age. Now the boxes were gone and in their place the bills and invoices were in orderly stacks, held in place by metal spikes, and next to each pile were one or more leather-bound ledger books, their columns filled with neatly penned numbers.

"Thank you," said Jeff.

"I mean it. I'm really impressed. This was one hell of a job."

"You don't know the half of it. Every time I thought I had a grip on it, more bills would come in. Or they'd find another box somewhere. There must be twice as much here as when you left. Dad, of course, just denied everything. Kenny took his side, as usual."

Hal opened one of the ledgers, winced slightly as he saw that it was marked mostly with red ink, and closed it again. He opened another one. This time his pained expression was more perceptible as he noted that nearly all the numbers were in red. He closed it and turned to Jeff. "So how bad off are we?"

"It's not good," said Jeff.

"Whom do we owe money to?"

"Hah. Better to ask if there is anyone we *don't* owe money to. Then I could give you a simpler answer. No."

"Fill me in on what I missed. Are we bankrupt, then?"

"No. Not quite. Not yet, anyway. I've talked to the biggest moneylenders about some of Dad's debts, and they're willing to stretch out the payments. He's owed some of these debts for years, so they're willing to wait a bit longer. In fact, it's kind of a prestige thing to them, having the King on their books. With the money from our estates and the royal allowance, we can meet our interest payments, our expenses, and still pay a little on the principal. So if Dad and Mom and Kenny would just control their spending—"

"Dream on. Is it my imagination, or do we have even more servants than when I left?"

"We have more. And more horses. To pull the extra coach we bought. And more stable hands to take care of the horses. And we've pretty much bought more of everything else also."

Hal just shook his head.

"Of course," said Jeff, "we've got the tournaments coming up, so that will bring in some cash. But then if Dad is forced to abdicate—"

"What! What? Someone is suggesting that Dad abdicate the throne?"

"Oh yeah," said Prince Jeff. "I guess you wouldn't have heard about that. We've managed to keep it in the family and in the Council. Apparently the Council has been checking their own records, back to a dozen years or so. And they've raised a question of—how did they put it—'misappropriation of funds' was the term they used."

"How nice to be King. I suppose for anyone else this would be called embezzling."

"Possibly. Anyway, the Council is putting pressure on Dad to name his heir and move on. They really want him out of here. So they're hinting that if he abdicates, he'll avoid the charges and the scandal."

Hal opened another ledger and flipped through the pages. The number of entries in red ink seemed to far outnumber the entries in black. Once again he closed the book and returned it to its neat stack. "I'm starting to think I was better off staying in the swamp. I've got an idea that might help. I'll tell you about it after I see Mom."

Emily welcomed the opportunity to wash up and get out of her traveling clothes. Like any young woman of Melinower, she thrilled at the opportunity to stay at the palace. Unlike Caroline, however, she didn't plan to stay more than a night and therefore saw no need to completely unpack. She brought out *The Book of Shadows* and made a halfhearted attempt to study it, then found herself setting out her makeup kit before the mirror and studying the contents of that instead. Emily didn't normally wear makeup, except for special occasions. Now she eyed her reflection critically in the looking glass and wondered if she should put some on. She told herself that being in the royal palace counted as a special occasion and that it had nothing to do with Prince Hal. Or Prince Jeff, or any other sort of boy. Emily was not like Caroline. She had an apprenticeship. She was destined for a successful career as a sorceress. She didn't have to worry about what boys thought of her. She nodded at her reflection, perhaps a trifle smugly. All that glamorous stuff could be left to girls like Caroline. Emily was a professional.

Having decided that, she picked up her book again and opened it to a chapter that described some seventy methods of breath control that had to be mastered before uttering an incantation. This was every bit as fascinating as it sounds. It was easy to understand why sorcerers often locked themselves in isolated towers to study, away from the distractions of the world. (It was also easy to understand why some sorcerers went mad.) For a young woman spending her first day in the big city, not to mention the palace, there were far too many distractions, and they were far too close at hand.

So she was glad that there came a knock on the door and that she opened it to find Prince Hal. She hadn't been completely sure that she would ever see him again. Hal had changed clothes also and was wearing a white shirt with a navy blue waistcoat. Behind him Caroline wore a simple pink dress with her long blond hair tied back with a bit of ribbon. She thought the outfit gave her an innocent country-girl look, and she was right. Emily was clad in a severe black dress with a black cape lined in red. She thought her clothing gave her a professional sorceress look. It did—sort of. She was clearly too young to be more than an apprentice.

Hal was quiet and subdued, even more so than when he had entered the palace, so the girls followed him without saying much. Emily, in fact, didn't even ask where they were going as they traveled along lushly decorated hallways and down wide, carpeted staircases. It wasn't until they got to an elegant door, gleaming with white lacquer and gold fittings, that Hal said to her, "Of course, she really wants to talk with Caroline, but I'll introduce you anyway."

"Who?" said Emily.

"Who?" said Caroline.

Hal looked surprised. "My mother, of course. Didn't I say that at lunch?"

"Your mother?" said Caroline. "The Queen?"

Hal pondered this. "Hmmm. My mother. The Queen. You may have hit on something there. Why yes, I believe there *is* a connection."

"I have to go back to my room," said Emily. "And put on some makeup."

"So do I," said Caroline.

"You don't wear makeup," said Hal.

"I have to . . . brush my teeth again. And my hair. And buy some makeup. And then put it on."

"Me too," said Emily. "Why don't you go ahead without us?"

"Quit fooling around. She's waiting to see us."

"She's waiting to see you," Emily told Caroline. "You're the one who kissed her son. I really shouldn't be intruding." She turned and walked down the hall. Caroline grabbed her arm before she got a dozen steps.

"Where are you going? I thought you *wanted* to see the Queen?"

"Of course I do," said Emily, as Caroline dragged her

back along the corridor. "At a reception or something. In a receiving line. Maybe make some small talk. Not go in and actually *meet the Queen*. Let me go! She's going to think I'm some small-town pudding head."

"What will she think of me? I'm from the same town you are. At least you lived in a castle."

"It was a little castle. In fact, it was more like a mansion."

"It wasn't a shack. Emily, help me." Caroline took both of the younger girl's hands. "I can't go in there alone. I'll have to talk with her. What if I choke up? I need you to fill in the gaps."

"Hal will be with you."

"Hal, yes!" Caroline glanced back down the hall at Hal, who was waiting patiently out of earshot, and dropped her voice to a whisper. "You like Hal, right?"

"Well, yes. So?"

"Okay, so Hal was turned into a frog. For a long time he hasn't seen his mother. And all this time the Queen, his mother, has missed her son. Her youngest son. Her baby. All she knew was that he was missing in action. And this is their reunion. Don't you understand what a tender, touching, emotional moment this is going to be for them? And that Hal wouldn't have brought us here if it wasn't important to him?"

Emily looked at Hal. He was leaning up against the door, looking off into space. His face showed he was lost in somber thought. She thought of her own mother, gone so recently, and of the special bond mothers have with their children. She thought of Hal in the swamp, the dark, wet, lonely nights, wondering if he'd ever see his family again. She nodded to Caroline. "You have a point. Okay, I'm right behind you."

The two girls approached Hal again. He raised his eyebrows quizzically. "Are you ready now?"

"We're ready," Caroline told him. "Just an attack of butterflies. We're fine."

"Then let's go." And with that, Hal kicked the door open, stepped inside, and yelled at the top of his lungs, "Hi, Mom! I'm home! What's for dinner?"

A pleasant voice wafted out from inside the room. "Wipe your feet!"

Emily looked at Caroline. "Tender, touching, emotional. Yeah, right."

Caroline was looking at the carpet, searching for a place to wipe her feet. Hal touched her on the arm. "That was a joke. We were joking. Relax. Come on in." He led her into a large sitting room with very high ceilings. The walls were done in white-and-gold lacquer, as was the furniture, while the carpet was an intricate pattern of gold and light blue. Huge, sunny windows overlooked a cobbled courtyard where small fruit trees grew. The windows were draped with lace, more lace than Caroline had imagined could exist in one place. Even stranger was a large glass bowl beneath one window, where tiny, finely marked fishes swam around a water lily. A maid was laying out a tea table, under the supervision of a tall, elegantly dressed woman. *This must be Queen Helen.* The maid was dismissed. In a daze, Caroline saw Hal hug and kiss his mother, heard herself being introduced. She managed to curtsey, then found herself sitting in a chair with a small plate containing a thin slice of cake in her hand. She struggled to bring her thoughts into focus, and realized the Queen was speaking.

". . . tremendously worried," said Queen Helen. "You can't imagine how relieved I was to hear that the spell had been broken." She gazed fondly at Caroline. "Young lady, we are tremendously in your debt."

"Oh . . . no . . . I . . . it was . . . yes . . . not at all," said Caroline.

"Hal, do be a dear and pour the tea." The Queen switched her gaze to Emily. "I believe Hal mentioned you are here to resume an apprenticeship. And I judge by your clothes that you are a student of sorcery, is that correct?"

Emily managed a high-pitched squeak.

"That can be an honorable profession, although so many people in that line of work indulge in the most unseemly behavior. This woman who enchanted poor Hal, for example. By all accounts she seems to have been quite, quite wicked. I do hope you will not resemble her in any way."

"Tea!" said Hal, pressing a cup into her hand. "Nice hot tea. Two sugars, right, Mom? And here you go, Emily. And pass this one to Caroline. Sugar, Caroline? Try one lump. Say, this is good tea, Mom. Did you switch shops?"

Caroline now had a plate in one hand and a cup and saucer in the other. She watched Emily lean forward and set the plate on the table, then balance the saucer on one knee and lift the cup to her lips. Caroline did the same. So this was tea. She'd never had it before. (Five pence to the pound! Injurious to body and spirit!) The taste was not unpleasant, and the hot liquid seemed to clear the haze from her head.

"My great-uncle Alphonse was turned into a frog," the Queen was saying. "Although, family loyalty aside, I must say that it was not done without provocation. He was something of the black sheep of the family already. He led this poor woman down the garden path, then treated her in a most ungallant manner. Certainly he should have foreseen that something of the sort was coming. You cannot ride roughshod over the feelings of a sorceress and expect her to overlook it."

"That's true," said Caroline.

"However, she did not turn him loose in a trackless swamp where all hope was lost. She dropped him off in a small fountain in the garden where we were able to find him the next day. That's the way the thing is properly done, as we've always considered it. You can teach the offender a lesson without being malicious about it. Not like that—what was her name—Amanda? Not like that Amanda woman."

Caroline could not help enjoying this a little. She gave Emily a wicked smile. The younger girl was showing a great deal of interest in the bottom of her teacup.

"Then what happened to your great-uncle?"

"Well, Caroline, the family found a young woman from a good family who was willing to kiss Alphonse and break the spell. So they lived happily ever after, as the saying goes."

"How nice."

"We were so fortunate to have a girl of your determination and loyalty living near that swamp. I honestly feared we had lost Hal forever. I'm sure the two of you will be very happy together."

"Oh," said Caroline. "Yes. Well, I've been meaning to talk to you about that."

"Hal is such brave boy," said Helen. "His father sends him on quests all over Melinower, and Hal never complains. Such awful scrapes he gets into. Of course, he's always been that way. Once when Hal was a little boy, I took the whole family down to the seashore. Well, Hal had eaten beans for lunch and—"

"Mom!" interrupted Hal in a warning tone of voice.

"But perhaps I'll tell you that story some other time."

"No you won't," said Hal.

"Would anyone care for another cup of tea? Well then." The Queen's voice suddenly took on a brisker tone. She opened a drawer beneath the table and took out a quill, a pot of ink, and some foolscap. "We have a lot of planning to do. Caroline, they tell me that the wedding must take place fairly promptly, or Hal will turn back into a frog. So we must get down to work, and you'll have to be fitted for a wedding dress very soon. Of course, the girls will need time to prepare their bridesmaids' dresses. I think we should come up with a simple design, so they'll be able to wear them again. Hal, this is all going to be girl talk from here on, so you may as well run along. Emily, you may stay if you wish."

"Oh, please stay," said Caroline. The moment of truth had arrived, and she was suddenly finding out that, while it may be easy to criticize a boy to his face, and even easier to criticize him to your girlfriends, it is quite a different thing to tell a mother that her son is not good enough for you. Particularly if the mother happens to be the Queen.

But if she was counting on having Emily in her corner, she was quickly disappointed. The younger girl said to Helen, "I'd love to, but I have so much to do in the city. And I'm sure you and Caroline have so many things to talk about." It was now her turn to give Caroline a wicked smile. Caroline glared back at her.

Hal stood as Emily did. "If you're going into the city, I'll escort you. I have a few errands to run myself."

"Then here," said Helen to Emily, leading her to a cabinet. "You'll need a sweater."

"Um, no, thank you, Your Highness" said Emily. "I'm fine for clothes."

"It's chilly outside."

"It's warm, Mom," said Hal. "She doesn't need a sweater."

"Take a sweater with you in case it gets cold later."

"Mom!" said Hal, in that same warning tone.

"Well, if you think you'll be all right." She hugged Hal again, accepting another kiss on the cheek, and Emily managed to slip through the door, sweaterless. A few minutes later Hal joined her outside. Emily was glad to see him, for she really did not know her way around the city. And exploring it with Hal seemed the ideal way to learn the streets. She followed him down a flight of stairs to a broad, busy hallway. Large doors at one end led out of the palace, but Hal took her instead to a quiet, tree-filled courtyard.

"First things first," he said. "What were you planning to do in Melinower?"

"I need to get started on my apprenticeship," said Emily. "Apprenticeships in magic are very complex. There are papers to sign and arrangements to make. Where is he, by the way?"

"Who?"

"The wizard."

"What wizard?"

"The sorcerer. You know, the one that kidnapped Rapunzel. What did you do with him? Is he in jail?"

"Ah, no."

"What, is he locked up here? You have dungeons?"

"No, he's . . ."

"You didn't banish him, did you?"

"He's dead," said Hal.

Emily stood quite still. "He's what?"

"I had no choice. He attacked us just as I was getting Rapunzel out of the tower. He had some sort of magic where he was able to hurl these wicked balls of flame. It was only by the merest chance that I was able to dodge the first one and get my blade into him before he could let loose with another. A moment more, and I'd have been toast."

"I see," said Emily. There was a broom leaning against the wall. Someone had used it to sweep leaves from the cobblestones. "Do you happen to remember his name?"

"Um, no. Kind of a long, foreign name. It escapes me right now."

"Was it Gerald, do you think?" Emily reached for the broom handle and picked it up."

"No, it was an unusual name. It will come to me in a minute."

Emily made a few experimental sweeps with the broom. "It wasn't Patrick, then?"

"No, it was a foreign name, as I said. Let me think. It was something like . . . like . . ."

Emily stopped sweeping and held the broom handle tightly with both hands. "Was it something like . . . Torricelli?"

"Yeah! That was it."

Her scream could be heard throughout the palace.

"It's just that I don't think Hal and I are compatible," Caroline told Queen Helen. "I mean, I've only known him for a few days. Marriage is such a serious thing. I don't want to rush into it."

The Queen eyed her doubtfully. "I must say that shows admirable restraint. Most girls your age would do exactly that, given a chance to marry into royalty. In fact, I'm rather under the impression that most of the girls in this kingdom dream their whole lives of marrying a prince."

"Oh, I don't doubt it, Your Highness. I feel the same way. It's just that I'm not sure that Hal is the right prince for me. Or that I'm the right girl for Hal."

"How odd you should say that. I'm told that Rapunzel said almost the same thing?"

"Really?"

"I'm afraid I understand you even less. Do you intend

to go about kissing even more frogs? Until you find a prince that's right for you?"

Caroline looked into her cup, noticing a few specks of leaf in the dregs of her tea. She swirled them a bit. She had once heard that some women could read the future in the bottom of a teacup. She put the cup down and looked at Queen Helen.

"Your Highness, you do have two other sons."

"Prince Jeffrey and Prince Kenneth," said the Queen proudly. "Have you had a chance to meet them?"

"Yes, Your Highness. They are both quite handsome."

"I am grateful to be blessed with three handsome sons." The Queen said this with pride and absolute sincerity.

Caroline pushed on anyway. "I was talking with Jeff—er—Prince Jeffrey, and he seemed really nice. And I thought that if I perhaps had a chance to get to know him better . . ."

"My dear girl, surely you are not considering marrying Prince Jeffrey?"

"Or Prince Kenneth. Well, it just seemed that if they turned out to like me and, well, I wouldn't want Hal to be unhappy so . . .

"Oh dear. It's just out of the question, Caroline. There's the dowry issue, after all."

"Yes, dowry," said Caroline. "I was thinking about that after lunch. If I hadn't broken the spell on Hal, the royal family would collect a dowry on him also, right? On all three of the boys?"

"That is correct."

"But now you're only collecting it on two sons. You've lost Hal's dowry potential."

"In exchange for having Hal restored to me," said the Queen. "I certainly have no complaints about that. And I do think you'll make a lovely addition to our family, dear. I hope you don't mind, but I had some inquiries made, and they have returned nothing but praise for you. Also, I must say you are uncommonly well-spoken for a girl of your class."

"Oh, thank you. My friends were kind enough to lend me books, and I've always tried to better myself."

"Did you have trouble with the silverware?"

"Um, yes I did."

"The secret is to start with the outermost set and work in. But don't worry. There are finishing schools that will teach everything you need to know about court etiquette. How to speak and how to walk and how to reply to an invitation to a garden party. Of course, you'll also have attendants to guide you through all that."

"Attendants? You mean the maids?"

"Oh dear me, no. I mean your ladies-in-waiting. Girls your age from the best families, here to put in a few years at the palace, get some court experience, and of course do a little husband-hunting of their own."

All her life Caroline had heard of ladies-in-waiting. She hadn't considered the possibility that she would actually have some. None of her plans had gone farther than the altar.

"Courtly life is not nearly as complex now as when I was a girl," the Queen went on. "So many of the old traditions have been dropped, the old rules ignored. The pace of life is so much faster today, you see. No one has time to change clothes six times a day. Everyone is so intent on making money."

"Yes, money," said Caroline, struggling to get back to the subject. "What I was trying to get at is that you're expecting to receive dowry from two sons. Does it really matter which two? If, merely as an example, I married Prince Jeffrey, you'd still collect dowry on Prince Hal and Prince Kenneth."

"My dear girl, you make it sound as if the boys were being auctioned off."

Caroline rolled her teacup between her palms. "Please believe me, Your Highness, when I say I mean no disrespect, but isn't that pretty much what is happening?"

The Queen gave her a stern look, then relaxed. "I suppose there is some truth in that. But not all dowries are equal. A prince who is in line for the throne commands a higher price than a prince who is not."

"But Prince Kenneth is the oldest son, isn't he? Prince Jeffrey isn't in line for the throne."

"Oh no. By Melinower law and custom, the King chooses his own heir. So he can pick either Kenneth or Jeffrey, depending on who he thinks would make the better leader."

"Then he could pick Hal?"

"Well, I suppose so," said Queen Helen, a little sadly. "But he won't. Hal and his father do not get along."

"Yes, I gathered that."

The Queen rose and crossed over to the window. She spent a moment looking at the trees in the courtyard below. "You may as well know the truth, Caroline. The royal family is in no small amount of debt. The King has already declared that the girl who marries Jeff or Kenny has to bring a substantial dowry. I don't think he cares too much who Hal marries."

Caroline, who knew enough to stand when the Queen stood, came up beside her. "That's good actually. Because Hal doesn't care too much for me. He's really in love with Emily."

The Queen faced her. "Emily? Your friend who was just here?"

"Oh yes. I've been watching them the whole trip here from Ripplebrook. They get along very well together. She's bright and she's educated, and she has property and some money. I'm willing to guess that she could put together a nice little dowry. And he's definitely in love with her."

"I do want Hal to be happy," the Queen mused. "And since he was going to marry a commoner anyway . . . do you know for certain that she loves him?"

"Absolutely. She's crazy about him. No question about it."

No sooner were the words out of her mouth than they were interrupted by a scream from the courtyard below. The Queen threw open the window and leaned out for a better look. Caroline leaned out with her.

A very upset Emily was chasing Hal around the courtyard, whacking him with a broom.

Queen Helen looked at Caroline and raised her eyebrows.

"Also," Caroline blurted out, "I can spin flax into gold."

Kenny took off his helmet. "You know what your problem is, Jeff? Girl-wise, I mean."

"I suppose that, once again, you're going to expound on your theory that the best girls are attracted to the biggest jerks."

Kenny was outside the stables, letting his squires remove his armor. As each piece came off it was given to one of the armorer's boys for cleaning and polishing. Beneath the armor he wore not only a linen shirt and trousers, but also pads of wool felt over his shoulders and at other pressure points. All in all it had been hot workout, and the prince's face and hair were wet with perspiration. A squire handed him a cloth, and he began toweling off.

"Or the biggest dweebs. I've had to refine my theory. Every time we send Hal off on a quest, he finds a different girl. Last time it was Rapunzel. This time he comes home with two. Before long he'll be bringing them home in bunches, like grapes."

"He didn't bring Rapunzel home."

"Of course not. He's keeping her stashed away in that tower, where he can tap her at his leisure."

"Now that's ridiculous," said Jeff. He thought for a minute. "You don't really think that Hal . . . no. No way."

"Think what you like. My point is that certain girls go for weeds like Hal. They call it the harmless look, the nonthreatening male. The girls who are intimidated by a strong, virile man—"

"You're referring to yourself, no doubt."

"Exactly. The girls who can't handle a guy like me will go to the opposite extreme."

"But most girls, you think, fall for arrogant jerks."

"You call it arrogance, the girls call it confidence. But you, my brother, try to have it both ways, and it just doesn't work. Too big and too strong to appeal to the ninnies. Too smart and too generous to appeal to the bimbos. Your style might get you in good with the Council of Lords, but it won't get you anywhere with Caroline." Kenny threw the towel aside, letting one of the squires pick it up. He inspected his lance, then handed it off for cleaning. "I'll be using this one for the tournaments. Polish it up well and set it aside," he told the squire.

Jeff was preparing for fencing practice of his own. He had his sword with him and pretended to inspect the scabbard. "Caroline?"

"The girl that released Hal from the spell."

"Oh, was that her name?"

"If you haven't seen her, you have to get a look at her, Jeff. I tell you, Hal knows how to get himself rescued. That girl is one great piece of ass."

Jeff had his back to Kenny. He gritted his teeth, then he forced himself into a look of unconcern before he faced his brother. "Now, don't be disrespectful to the girl, Kenny. She's going to be a princess soon, remember."

"Oh, come off it. Don't tell me your blood didn't start pumping when you saw that blonde. A great pair of knockers, lips that can suck the—"

"Kenny!"

"Hey, calm down, Jeff. I just want to tell you that after the jousting tournaments that girl will be mine. She's exactly the type that goes for good-looking guys. The only thing they like better than a handsome man is a handsome man on horseback."

Jeff considered a few remarks about the back end of a horse, but couldn't put anything together in time to make it sound snappy.

"They like it when a guy is a winner," Kenny continued. He sat down and let a squire pull off his riding boots. "Especially when the other girls in the crowd are cheering him on. Women always want what other women have. Even Hal knows that. Did you know he put himself in the lists for the tournaments this year?"

"The girl has no dowry, Kenny. You marry her, you've given up the throne as far as Dad is concerned. Leave her to Hal."

Kenny grinned again. "Who said anything about

marrying her? I'm still working on that rich little duchess who has the hots for me."

"The fat one? You're not even promised to her, and already you're planning to cheat on her."

"It's not like I love her. And she doesn't love me. She knows it would be a political marriage. Women expect that sort of thing."

"You know, Kenny, that would almost sound reasonable, coming from anyone but you. If you found a wife who was beautiful, loyal, and desperately in love with you, you'd still cheat on her."

Kenny buttoned his tunic. "Fortunately for you, Jeff, you will be able to marry anyone you want. And so will I. I have a plan to get us out of debt."

"Uh-oh." Jeff leaned against the wall and regarded his brother suspiciously. "I think your last plan to get us out of debt was to go to war. You talked Dad into going before the Council of Lords and asking for a declaration."

"War is the standard solution for a country in financial straits."

"The *country* isn't in financial straits. Just us."

"As you unnecessarily pointed out to the Council. But Jeffrey, my lad, I have another idea, and the laws back me up a hundred percent on this one. It is the most traditional way for a royal family to dispose of its debts, and the Council can't do a thing about it. Dad will name *me* his heir. Then *you,* Jeffrey, can marry anyone you want, with or without a dowry. That will be my gift to you. But don't pin your hopes on that blonde. I have an eye on her myself."

"I'm overwhelmed by your generosity. And just what is this traditional method by which the King can absolve himself of debt?"

"We expel the Jews," said Prince Kenny.

Jeff stomped up the outside stairs that led to the Meli-nower Palace royal suites. He had spent an hour working off his anger by hacking at padded equipment with a sharp sword and battering away at sparring partners with a blunt sword. But he still burned with an inner fury, a fury caused by the knowledge of an upcoming injustice. An injustice, Jeff thought, that he would be powerless to prevent.

Not that he wouldn't try, of course. He'd go to the Council of Lords. If anyone in the family had influence with the Council, it was Jeff. But Jeff knew he didn't have all *that* much influence. Mostly the Council trusted him to try to keep the King from getting deeper into debt. That didn't mean they'd be willing to overrule an expulsion order against the Jews. Especially, as Jeff suspected, if his father and brother were willing to cut the Lords in for a piece of the action.

So he was preoccupied with dark thoughts as he went up the stairs and thus he didn't see Caroline coming down until he nearly bumped into her. This did have a cheering effect. For most men, getting close enough to bump into a girl like Caroline would be the high point of the afternoon. Actually bumping into her would be cause for a holiday.

"Hi," said Caroline, giving Jeff a cheery smile. She slid to one side, giving Jeff room to pass her. But not as much room as she could have, letting him brush her as he went by.

"Hello," he said, and debated whether to say more. Jeff had discovered at lunch that, the more he spoke to Caroline, the better he liked her. And that was not a good thing to feel about a girl who supposed to marry one's brother. He decided to keep walking up the stairs.

Caroline, who had been coming down, turned and followed him. "I was looking for Prince Hal's room," she said.

"It's up here," said Jeff. "The big windows on the other side of the terrace. He's not here, now. He went into the city with Emily."

"Oh, that's too bad. I wanted to talk to him."

"You can come back later, if you don't see him at dinner. He likes to come out in the evening and look at the ships in the harbor." Jeff took another step up the stairs. Caroline took one with him. She seemed in no hurry to end the conversation. Jeff stopped and looked at her.

In the world that Jeff lived in, there were only two kinds of princes. You were either a noble prince, or an evil prince. Later generations would have to deal with things like antiheroes and situational ethics, but these were simpler times, and Jeff had long ago made up his mind that he was going to be the noble prince type. And noble princes did not steal their brother's girlfriends.

Okay, it was true that Caroline hadn't seemed too

enthused about marrying Hal. Nor did it seem to bother her that he was on his way into town with another girl. It was pretty clear that she didn't think Hal was handsome enough for her. Jeff could understand that. A lot of girls felt that way about Hal. Most of them, in fact. All of them, actually, at least so far as Jeff knew. But to Jeff, that was all the more reason he shouldn't steal his brother's girl. Being better-looking was just an unfair advantage. On the other hand, she never said she *didn't* want to marry Hal. Not to Jeff, anyway.

Besides, there was nothing he could do with her, even if Hal wasn't an issue. Marriage was out of the question: She was just a commoner, and there was the dowry issue. Sure, he could attempt to have a fling with her— there were plenty of girls in the kingdom who would jump at the chance to have a fling with a prince. But Caroline had made it pretty clear she was in for the long haul. To mislead her would definitely not be noble.

So the best thing to do was to bid her good day and continue walking away. But that plan had a flaw also. Caroline had the loveliest eyes that Jeff had ever seen. They were big, they were wide-open, she was looking right at him, and Jeff could almost feel the various lobes of his brain shutting down. He tried dropping his gaze away from her eyes, but that meant he was staring at her breasts, which were no less appealing, albeit in a different way. And staring there was ungentlemanly besides, so he looked at her face again. A breeze was coming in off the harbor, causing her hair to ripple, and waves of light shimmered on the soft strands.

"Is something wrong?"

"No," said Jeff. For a moment he considered telling her about Kenny's plan. He knew, from her stories about finding the frog, that she was a clever and practical girl, and she was easy to talk to. But he wasn't ready to divulge state secrets to her. "Nothing's wrong."

"In that case," said Caroline, "I wonder if I might ask you a favor?"

"Go ahead."

"Last night we stayed at an inn called the Bull and Badger. I need to return there, but I don't think I can find my way through the city."

"I don't know it, but I can find out where it is."

"Could you possibly see your way clear to escorting me there?"

This, Jeff knew, was impossible. It was not good to spend time with his brother's beautiful girlfriend. It was certainly not good to spend time with his brother's beautiful girlfriend when Jeff felt the way he did about his brother's beautiful girlfriend. It would certainly not do to be seen going into an inn with his brother's beautiful girlfriend. Jeff could snap his fingers, and any one of a dozen servants would appear who could be counted on to prepare a coach and take the future princess anywhere she wanted. There was no need for Jeff to get involved and risk causing trouble.

"I'd love to," he said.

The afternoon sun was warm and bright, the tournaments were bringing visitors into the city, and the streets were crowded with shoppers. Emily and Hal sat on the second level of a tea shop, whose open windows let them enjoy both the sights and sounds of the busy street below. They each had a glass of wine. Emily did not particularly like wine, but her mother had taught her it was an upscale thing to drink, and she had better get used to it.

She sketched out her plans to Hal. "It's common for sorcerers to loan out their apprentices for a year or so. It gives the apprentice experience that maybe he couldn't get with his own master. Torricelli was very big on alchemy, and Mummy wanted me to learn it. She thought chemicals were the wave of the future."

"Sorry about that."

"It's okay. I think Mummy would have changed her mind about him anyway if she'd known he was kidnapping girls. Anyway, while a sorcerer might take you on loan, it's a lot more difficult to find one who will take over your apprenticeship. Generally they want an apprentice who has been with them right from the beginning. And even when they do let you into their program, there's always a hassle about transferring all your credits."

It was her first time alone with Hal since the night in the forest. Of course, they were surrounded by people now, so she wasn't really alone with him, but that was not important. The important thing was that Caroline wasn't there.

Emily was on her way to see another sorcerer. Hal had offered to show her a bit of the city first, and Emily had accepted. It had been one of the most pleasant outings she could remember—Hal seemed to know everyone, from the richest lord to the humblest dishwasher, and everyone seemed glad to see Hal. They had gone to the wharves, where Emily admired the elegant tall ships with their webs of shrouds and lines. She watched the sailors in their loose canvas trousers, held up with elaborately knotted belts of rope. "I just noticed," she told Hal. "You dress sort of like a sailor."

"I was a naval cadet," said Hal. "Melinower tradition. We all have commissions. The first son joins the Royal Guard, the second son joins the army, the third son joins the navy."

"So that's why Kenny and Jeff wear those jackets with the gold braid."

"Yep."

"What if there's a fourth son? No, let me guess. He enters the clergy, right?"

"Nope. He signs on with a discount travel agency. Very handy guy to know, especially for those last-minute deals on cruise ships."

"No doubt." Emily had toured the university, with its vast and fascinating library. She had been to a print shop and seen glowing ladles of molten lead poured into the molds, and the printer's devils, hands and faces black with ink, setting type as fast as she could read.

They had passed a deserted building, austere but elegant. "The Assassins' Guild," Hal explained.

"You're kidding," said Emily, who had heard of the Assassins' Guild, but didn't believe it.

"Why do you say that?"

"I always thought the Assassins' Guild was a legend. I mean, it just seemed ridiculous, that people would tolerate a bunch of murderers in their midst, openly soliciting business."

"You're right, it is ridiculous, and it didn't exist for real. The King set that up, and staffed it with a bunch of Guards. Whenever someone came in trying to hire an assassin, or join the assassins, the Guards would beat the stuffing out of him, warn him to stay out of trouble, and throw him out on his ear. The crime rate plummeted for a while, until word got around. I have to admit," the Prince finished, a little grudgingly, "Dad does have some good ideas."

They passed a wig shop, where she looked at wigs made of horse hair and camel hair, and even human hair, the most expensive kind. The wigmaker offered Emily three shillings for her hair. Emily respectfully declined. He shrugged.

"Best I can do, I'm afraid. Brunette is not so popular these days."

"It's a fad," said Hal. "Bald men have started wearing wigs. Some men even shave their heads before they go bald, so they can wear a wig and be in fashion."

"Do the women in Melinower wear wigs?"

"Of course not. Women don't go bald. Why would a woman need to wear a wig?"

Most amazing of all, Emily had seen a dress shop. Not a seamstress, who measured you and made dresses for you, but a room with racks and racks of dresses in every size. The owner explained to Emily that you tried on dresses until you found one that fit, then you bought it, all ready to wear that very same evening. She selected a dress and showed Emily the dressing room, and Emily gave Hal her purse to hold, but Hal grabbed her wrist instead and dragged her back into the street.

Now she looked at the throng below. "Look how excited they all are," she told Hal. "It's like a big party. Is it because of the tournaments?"

"Hmm?" said Hal. He seemed a bit distracted. Emily hoped he wasn't thinking of Caroline.

"I said, 'Are people in Melinower always this happy?' "

"Seem a bit tense to me," said Hal. "Like they're under a strain. Especially the shopkeepers. I wonder . . ." His voice trailed off, and he absently tapped a coin on the table. Then he suddenly tossed the coin into his cup, stood up, and took her hand. "Let's go."

"Where?" said Emily, but Hal merely led her down the stairs and back into the crowd, until they turned into a long storefront with many display cases. Its wooden sign showed it was a branch of a well-known chain of magic shops. Emily looked around and frowned in distaste.

Junk, she thought to herself. *Cheap imitations. Strictly for the rubes.* There were racks of incense and gaudy incense holders, stacks of scented, colored candles and carved candleholders, paper symbols to paste above doorways—all with charts and instructions to show which incense to burn, which candle to light, and which symbol to paste to achieve the desired degree of good luck. There were shelves of medicinal soaps, poultices, bundles of dried herbs, bottles of elixirs, and one entire table devoted to ointments that purported to restore male potency. Another displayed products that promised to increase the size of a woman's bustline. Emily looked at these and rolled her eyes.

Most of the shop was devoted to charms. They hung on racks in long aisles, charms of every description. They were variously made of gold, silver, copper, brass, crystal, carved stone, ivory, horn, whalebone, mother-of-pearl, narwhal tusk, and scented woods, and they ranged in size from pealike beads to round medallions as big as a barrel lid. The shop seemed to be doing a steady business. Emily counted a dozen people going through in just a few minutes.

She caught up with Hal, who was purchasing a small

charm and talking with the proprietor. She waited until he was finished, then followed him into the street. "You see," she said. "That's why it's so important to get a good apprenticeship. The last thing I want is to end up in the kind of spell mill that produced that charm, where they've got a dozen apprentices cranking out cheap magic for the masses." Hal just nodded. "What did you buy, anyway?" she finished.

Hal opened his palm and showed her a small charm carved from a wolf's tooth. "For luck in the tournaments," he said. "Actually, it's a charm for speed and aggression."

"Oh, Hal. If you want a good luck charm I can find a dozen people in this city who will give charms with better-quality luck. Talk to me before you waste your money."

"It wasn't much money. I really wanted to talk to the man who runs that shop. He takes bets for the tournaments."

"And you're asking about your brothers? Did you buy the charm for one of them?"

"For me," said Hal. "I've entered my name in the lists."

"Oh." Emily found it hard to imagine Hal in any sort of physical competition. Granted, the tournaments had plenty of events that didn't involve combat—juggling, tumbling, and such—nonserious, carnival-type games. But she didn't think the royal family would compete in one of those. It would be too undignified.

They walked farther down the street. Hal said nothing more. Emily decided he wasn't going to volunteer the information, so she had to ask. "What did you enter?"

Hal looked her in the eye. "Swordfighting."

"Uh-huh."

They walked some more in silence. Emily glanced over every now and then to see if Hal was smiling, if he was joking with her. He looked dead serious.

"Swordfighting," she said.

"Right."

"Um. You are, uh. Last night at the inn, you really got your—I mean—you seemed to be having an off night."

"Right."

"Have you ever done competition fencing before?"

"First time for everything."

"Have you ever taken lessons?"

"I don't have to. I'm a natural athlete."

"Hal! Are you joking with me?"

Before he could answer they were interrupted by a door opening in a nondescript building. There was a flash of uniform cuffs, and a scrawny man, battered and bruised, was flung across the sidewalk to land with a thump in the street. The door slammed shut.

Hal jerked a thumb at it. "Thieves' Guild. Word hasn't gotten around on that one yet." He turned a corner and led her down a narrow street, then stopped. He had to. They were at the end of a cul-de-sac. Brick walls rose on either side, and a windowless stone building sat in front of them. A single iron door was set into the center. "This is it," he said. "Bungee, right. This is the man you wanted to see?"

Emily switched her attention to the door. "Bungee, right," she said. "One of the finest sorcerers in the Twenty

Kingdoms. I've written to him. Actually, he would have been my first choice, except my mother had already made arrangements with Torricelli."

"He does a lot of work for the nobility," said Hal. "Although Dad prefers our court magicians. If you want to apprentice to one of them, I'm pretty sure I could arrange it."

"Top-ranked magicians don't go into government work," said Emily. "Bungee is the best."

"Will he take you on?"

"I guess I'll find out now. But I've got something to sweeten the pot." She dug into her handbag and brought forth a scroll of cracked, grayish leather. She showed it to Hal, but without letting it out of her hands. "The *Book of Djinn*," she said. "The ancient Persian book of spells, once the sole property of the Caliph of Baghdad, said to be written by the wind itself and transcribed onto human skin. Extremely rare and valuable."

"Huh? No it isn't. I don't know much about sorcery, but I know you can buy copies of the *Book of Djinn* at magic shops. They're expensive, but they're not all that hard to find."

"This one is," said Emily. "There are only three like it in the world and none other in the Twenty Kingdoms. This is the *Book of Djinn Teacher's Edition*."

"Teacher's Edition?" It took a moment for the meaning of this to sink in, then Hal let out his breath. "Wow! You mean with the answers in the back?"

"Exactly. Can save you weeks of work on a complex spell."

"I don't believe that's really human skin, though."

"Sure it is." Emily flipped the scroll over and showed Hal a small blue heart dyed into the back cover. Inside was the word "Mom." "See? He had a tattoo." She put the scroll away and looked at the door. "What do you think of this?"

The door was impressive. The frame seemed to merge seamlessly into the wall, gray stone blending into darker iron. It was free of rust, with the slick black surface that came from being painted with linseed oil. It positively bristled with rivets, yet there was no knob, no knocker, and not the slightest sign of a lock or keyhole. In the center of the door, just at eye level, was a spot of bright gold. Hal walked up and looked at it. It was a small brass plaque, about the size of his thumb, and engraved with the sign of a star and a crescent moon. There was no name.

"Looks intimidating," he said. "Maybe there's another way in."

"Push on it."

"Ah, better knock first." Hal was in no hurry to enter the wizard's castle, which was understandable, considering what happened the last time he entered a sorcerer's castle unannounced.

Emily laughed. "Don't worry about it. It's a test."

Hal said, "Mmm?"

"You know the sort of thing. The door looks impossible to open, so no one even tries. I'll bet we just have to give it a push and it will come right open." She leaned on it with the palm of her hand, and sure enough, it swung back silently on massive but perfectly balanced hinges. Inside was a small entranceway and a curved staircase leading upward. Emily stepped inside and turned around. "You see, magicians love tests like these. They want to know if you're the type who can be fooled by appearances, or if you're persistent enough to seek out the truth. Or something like that. Kind of silly, I think. If they—"

The door slammed shut, instantly cutting off her words. No matter how hard Hal pushed, it stubbornly remained closed.

Rumpelstiltskin bought two mugs of ale and paid for them with a small silver coin. "I always like to tip big," he explained. "I hate it that people think Jews are stingy."

"I thought you weren't Jewish," said Caroline.

"I'm not. But people think I am. So I tip big." He settled himself into his chair and looked over the scarred wooden table, past Caroline, out the front door of the Bull and Badger, where he could see Prince Jeffrey waiting in one of the royal coaches. A liveried driver held the reins to four glossy black horses. A pair of footmen stood on either side of the door. The dwarf shook his head admiringly. "A coach and four, eh? I gotta admit, you work fast. From Hal to Jeff in one day. You made a play for Kenny yet?"

"I've met him."

"Be careful. They say he's bad news."

"He didn't seem so bad to me."

Rumpelstiltskin shrugged. "Well, women see men differently. So which one is it, Jeff or Kenny?"

"I don't know," said Caroline. "I don't know how they feel about me, yet. And there's another thing. Apparently it hasn't been decided yet who is going to inherit the throne."

"Yeah, I heard that, too," said Rumpelstiltskin. "Here in Melinower the King chooses his heir. Must make for a lot of family friction." He sipped his ale and eyed her over the rim of his pewter tankard. "You're still going for the whole ball of wax, eh? The handsome prince and the throne? You know that being married to the King doesn't give you any right to rule. It's not the same as being a regent Queen."

"I will be perfectly happy with the title of Queen. I'm not greedy."

"Of course not."

"Then let's get down to brass tacks. You've got a magic spinning wheel. You need someone who can spin."

"Right."

"You know for sure this thing will spin flax into gold? You've tried it?"

"No," said Rumpelstiltskin. "It's a one-shot deal. You can't try it out. The magician said a spell over it. It will work for one night, unless he says the spell over it again."

"Presumably there's more to it than that."

"There must be: Otherwise, every magician would have one, and there would be piles of spun gold everywhere. But that's not our problem. I have this wheel, and it is definitely enchanted. Wait until you sit down at it. You can feel the power coming out of it."

"All right, for now we'll say it works. What's the deal with this flax? Why flax? Flax is awfully hard to spin. You get a strong yarn, but it tends to lump. Only the best can get it smooth and even."

"The best meaning yourself?"

Caroline just tossed her hair.

"Smooth I don't care about. I'll settle for lumpy gold. Are you fast, that's the question?"

"I'm fast but . . . it has to be flax?"

"Unretted flax."

"Oh dear."

"It's the Law of Similarities."

"The what?"

Rumpelstiltskin didn't understand it completely either. But he explained it as best he could. "Turning flax into gold isn't really magic. It's alchemy. See, magic is symbolic, but alchemy is allegorical."

"What's the difference?"

"Actually, I'm not sure. But I do know that whatever is turned into gold has to *look* like gold to begin with. That's why you can't turn lead into gold. It has to be brass. And a particular type of brass that is the right color."

"Virgin brass," said Caroline.

"Right. And you can spin flax because the stalks are golden to begin with. At least until they are retted. Um, what is retting anyway?"

"Soaking the stalks in water so the fibers separate more easily. But some of the color washes away."

"That's why it has to be unretted, then. Can it still be spun?"

"Yes, just barely. But it will be slow going. I don't think I can do more than a couple of spindles in a night. My half won't be nearly enough for a dowry."

"That's what the girl in Mathagar said. That's why we have to work a deception. Show the King the first bag of gold, then tell him the rest will follow."

Caroline thought about this. "I don't know," she said. "I've been honest my whole life. I *earned* the right to marry a handsome prince. I don't think I want to start off the relationship with a lie."

"Okay, take the gold you have and invest it. You're in tight with the royal family. People will be offering you all sorts of lucrative partnerships so they can get in tight with you."

"Hmmm, maybe. I'm under a time constraint, though. It's either marry Hal, or marry someone else. Otherwise, Hal turns back into a frog."

"Yeah," said Rumpelstiltskin. "I can see that would be a problem for you. Not to mention for Hal. Still, I think it's time to cash in on this. A bag of gold might not help you much when you go back to the castle, but certainly it isn't going to hurt things."

"Yes," said Caroline. "And then there's that issue of the firstborn child."

"What!" said the dwarf.

"There's a story going around that you demanded the firstborn child of that girl in Mathagar."

"I told you that was nonsense," said Rumpelstiltskin.

"That ditz just likes to make trouble for Jews. Why would a guy want to raise a child that wasn't his own? Women are always telling each other that someone is going to steal their children—gypsies, or fairies, or pirates, or whatever. If I wanted a kid, I'd get married and have my own."

"Sure," said Caroline. "It's just that maybe a man might want a child that wasn't . . . um."

Rumpelstiltskin stared at her. "Wasn't what?"

"Well, you know what I mean."

"No." Rumpelstiltskin looked blank. "What are you talking about?"

It seems to be my day, Caroline thought, *for getting into uncomfortable conversations*. "Well, it was just an idea. I meant that because you're . . . you are . . . and if it carries over to your children . . . so you'd want one that wasn't . . . you know . . . deformed."

"Deformed? Oh!" Rumpelstiltskin slapped his stubby legs. "You mean these? These are because of a childhood illness. They're not hereditary. Nothing to worry about—my kids will be fine."

"Good, good," said Caroline, deciding to change the subject anyway. "When do you want me to spin the gold?"

"Might as well do it tonight, if you can."

"Here?"

"No, I've got a room on the edge of the quarter. It's over a goldsmith's shop, in fact, so we'll be able to change the spun gold for coin right there. I want to make some money and clear out of here. The word on the street is that there is going to be trouble for the Jews. Nothing to do with me, but I don't want to get caught up in it."

"Here in Melinower?" Caroline frowned skeptically. "I thought we were above that kind of thing."

"It can happen anywhere if the ruling class thinks it's being squeezed by the bankers. Although, actually, I was thinking it was time to move on anyway."

"Will the rest of your people—um—*those* people be leaving?"

"It's not so much a question of leaving as being driven out. But no one is going anywhere before the tournaments—there's too much money involved." Rumpelstiltskin produced a scrap of cloth and was sketching on it with a stick of charcoal. "Here's a map to my place. We've got between midnight and dawn, but I'd say get there well before midnight so we can get set up."

"I'll be there."

"Great. And don't be nervous. I'll be really gentle."

Caroline shrugged. "It's spinning. What's there to be gentle about?"

Rumpelstiltskin stared at her. There was a long silence. Finally, he said, "Didn't anyone tell you?"

"Tell me about what?"

"Dammit." Now it was Rumpelstiltskin's turn to be uncomfortable. "I thought everyone knew about this."

"What?"

"And your friend is a sorceress. I figured you must have heard."

"What?"

The dwarf looked around the room, as if seeking help. None was forthcoming. He said, a little desperately,

"Remember you're getting a bag of gold out of this, maybe more. This is a really good deal, no matter how you look at it."

"Rumpelstiltskin, what *are* you talking about?"

Rumpelstiltskin drained his mug and stared down into the empty tankard. "Um, when you're working a spell of transformation like this, there has to be—uh, there is always—it must be accompanied by a loss of virginity."

There was a clank as Caroline set her mug down on the table. There was a scraping noise against the stone floor as her chair slid back. When Rumpelstiltskin looked up she had drawn herself to her full height and was giving him a look that could have frozen the brine in a pickle barrel. "I think, sir," she said icily, "you need to find yourself a nice Jewish girl." And she walked out.

⤐

"It's good to be King," King Jerald of Melinower said once. He was younger then. He hadn't thought anything like that in many years. Now he thought it would be good to be retired.

The Council of Lords had been hinting at it for some while. At first the King had resisted. But lately it was beginning to seem like a better and better idea. He would try to concentrate on the papers in front of him, but in his mind's eye he could see the cool green woods that surrounded the family estates in Losshire, and the trickling streams, and the spacious hunting lodge. He hadn't been there in years. There had been no chance to get away.

Money! That was the problem. No. Actually, it was the Council of Lords that was the problem. Smart men, most of them, but they had no idea what it cost to run a monarchy. A king had to live like a king, after all, to command the people's respect. There had been those wagers, but his run of bad luck would have ended eventually. If they'd just let him raise taxes again . . .

He pushed the thought away. That wasn't going to happen, and dwelling on it just gave him heartburn.

Retirement. It sounded so much better than abdication. Let Kenny take over while he was still around to give advice. Kenny and the King saw eye to eye on most things. Kenny would make a good king. But there was still the question of money.

He looked at the papers on his desk. They were the orders for the expulsion of the Jews and the confiscation of their assets. The orders were waiting for his signature and seal. Of course, not all the Jews were wealthy moneylenders. Most of them were not. And not all the bankers were Jews. So it was unfair, but that's the way these things were done. It didn't have to be violent, either. As long as the Jews didn't resist, it was possible the whole thing could be done without injury.

And it had to be done. He couldn't turn the crown over to Kenny with a mountain of debt loaded onto it. Jeff, yes. Jeff was good with accounts and budgets. The Council of Lords liked Jeff. The truth was, if he gave the kingdom to Jeff, there wouldn't need to be an expulsion.

Except it wasn't that easy. There were certain of the

nobility that had to be accommodated. Those who were as heavily in debt as he was. They wanted this expulsion.

It was a question of national security, they told the King. There was too much money owed to too few people. What if the moneylenders were to suddenly call in their loans? A lot of businesses would go bankrupt. Trade would suffer. Melinower would be weakened.

King Jerald wasn't sure he bought into this argument. The others had charts and numbers to support their positions, but the King hadn't really followed them. Jeff could have explained it all, but the Lords didn't want him to bring Jeff to the meeting—which told him, right there, that the arguments for the expulsion weren't that strong.

He brought Kenny to the meeting. Kenny wanted the expulsion even before the Lords heard about it. King Jerald figured that if he gave the crown to Kenny, Kenny would go ahead with the expulsion on his own. That, at least, would free Jerald from making the decision.

But that would be unkingly. Jerald was not the sort who shirked from decisions. Certainly not when he was about to retire. He didn't want to pass into history as a weak king.

He sat down at his desk, picked up the sheaf of orders in front of him, and shuffled through them quickly, although by now he had read them so many times he knew them by heart. He couldn't avoid the decision. But he could put it off for a few days. The tournaments were about to start, and that was always a moneymaker for Melinower. Obviously you couldn't have the expulsion disrupting the tournaments. Afterward?

He put the papers carefully back down on the desk.

Bungee pushed back the sleeves of his robe and stared nearsightedly at a brazier. He sprinkled a pinch of black powder over the coals, then nodded approvingly as a thin sheen of blue flame appeared and spread itself across the fuel. Over it he placed a small cauldron of black iron. When the liquid inside began to bubble and roil, he stirred in two measures of finely ground gray leaves and watched with satisfaction as the water turned a deep orange-red.

"You don't mind making the tea, I hope," he called to Emily, who was sitting in a straight-backed chair in the center of the room. "So many girls today object to making the tea. They say it's unfair—I don't know why. When I was serving my apprenticeship they always had us boys make the tea. As well as constantly sending us down to the shops for jam and muffins."

"I don't mind making the tea," said Emily, accepting the cup he handed her. Inwardly she noted that this was the second time today she had been served tea, and there was the concept of too much of a good thing. How often did city people drink this stuff?

She looked around. Bungee, she knew, was a successful sorcerer, and his laboratory showed it. His books were kept in glass-fronted cases. Candleholders were on every wall and shelf, with drips of wax showing they were used often. Wax candles, too, not the cheaper tallow. Half a dozen very finely wrought brass balances, of differing sizes, were on the table. One side of the room held a pendulum clock of good quality, while the other held a clock that showed the phases of the moon—it surely had been custom-made. Next to the window was an expensive telescope, and an astrolabe, and a precisely calibrated compass, all for taking the positions of stars. Copper bowls and stoneware pestles were neatly stacked and arranged according to size. Pinned to the wall was a Periodic Table of the Elements, showing all four of them—earth, fire, wind, and water.

"Of course that's only when we have clients," continued Bungee. "When we're at work just make what you want." He was poking among the tall cupboards that lined his workshop and eventually produced a small pitcher of cream and a pot of honey, which he set on the table before her. When he sat down across from her she saw that his eyes, under thick white eyebrows, were very bright, and she suspected the nearsighted fussiness was a bit of an act.

"I know there are still a lot of magicians who won't

take a girl as an apprentice," said Bungee. "Too much trouble."

Emily was surprised. "We are?"

"Oh, girls don't *cause* more trouble than boys. But you worry about them more." He pointed to a portrait of two pretty girls on the wall. Emily had already noticed it. "I have two daughters myself. I just managed to get the youngest married off last year. I thought the dowry would drive me to penury, but I do find I sleep easier now that they're someone else's problem."

"Congratulations."

"Never managed to get them interested in the business, though. Too many books, they said."

"Some people feel that way."

"Not Amanda," said Bungee. Without warning, he suddenly switched to Chaldean. (In the same way that Latin was the *lingua franca* of priests and scholars, Chaldean, the ancient tongue of Babylonia, was the language of sorcerers.) "A very smart woman, your mother. I admired her greatly. Inclined to be a bit short-tempered, I understand. But did excellent spellwork."

"She taught me a lot," said Emily. "And yes, her spellwork was very precise." She spoke in fluent Chaldean. Bungee gave an approving nod.

"She was ahead of us in so many ways. Calling forth spirits from the darkness, for example. Sure, we can all communicate with the other side, one way or another, but only Amanda could do it for forty percent off the standard rates."

"She saved even more on evenings and weekends."

Then the old sorcerer shook his head. "Still, I must say I did not agree with her decision to get involved with a man like Torricelli. That was a bad business with the girl. Kidnapping, mmmph, bad for the reputation of the profession. I don't blame our Prince for having to whack him. You made the right choice, coming to me. You'll get an apprenticeship in real sorcery. None of that newfangled alchemy nonsense."

"They were trying to make brass into gold. My mother prepared a philosopher's stone."

"Hmmph. Our King sent for me not a month ago and quizzed me on philosopher's stones. I told him he was wasting his time. Can't rely on alchemy. Not like a good solid spell of real magic."

"Well," said Emily. "It sounds like you've decided to accept me."

"Hmmm? Oh yes. I'm delighted to have you. You seem to be an entirely sensible young lady, and of course your references are impeccable. I'll have my so-licitor start drawing up the paperwork tomorrow, and when it's ready, we can review it."

"That's wonderful."

"And, ummm." Bungee let his eyes fall on the book that Emily had left on the table. He had made a great ef-fort not to pay attention to it during their conversation, and had succeeded reasonably well. Now that the matter was settled, he tapped the scroll on the cover. "Now, let us discuss the matter of your mother's library. Which, of course, is your library now."

"That's correct," said Emily. "And of course, it will be at your disposal for the term of my apprenticeship."

"Splendid, splendid. How soon do you think you can have it delivered here?"

"I'll start making arrangements as soon as the papers are signed."

"Ah. You are being sensibly cautious. I approve of that. Now then. There are some matters that remain to be discussed." Bungee poured them each another cup of tea. Emily took the opportunity to look over his shoulder at the mantelpiece. There were statues there, Golden Pentacle awards, given out each year by the Sorcerers' Guild. She saw two large ones, for Best Spell and Best Potion, and a smaller statue for Best Curse in a Foreign Language. Emily was impressed.

"Do you have a boyfriend?" Bungee was saying.

"Oh no," said Emily quickly. Immediately she felt the color rising in her cheeks. "Not at all. No."

Bungee, who hadn't raised two daughters without learning a few things, smiled inwardly, fiddled with his teaspoon, and pretended not to notice her blushing. "That's fine," he said, stirring his tea. "Because if you did, you would have to explain to him that a sorcerer's apprentice must maintain his or her chastity."

"Oh that's no problem," said Emily. "We've already discussed it."

"Good, good. So you've discussed it with this person who is not your boyfriend?"

"Uh . . . yes."

"Fine, fine. I won't pry any further. Now, we need to talk about your clothing allowance."

Clothing allowance? Emily managed to refrain from speaking aloud. *What clothing allowance?* Instead she said, "My mother always insisted that a sorceress should dress like a sorceress."

"Quite right, quite right." Bungee rose from the table, crossed his arms behind his back. "There are some areas where it doesn't pay to cut corners. Before a man buys passage on board a ship, for example, he wants assurance that the craft will convey him safely to his destination. If he sees a slovenly crew, and officers in unkempt uniforms, he worries that the ship itself might also not be well kept up, and fears for his own safety. Thus it's important that the crew and the officers look smart.

"Similarly, a woman who is seeking a banker with whom to entrust her savings will want one who looks prosperous. For who will trust a banker who is losing money?"

"I understand," said Emily.

"Good, good. You see, my dear, we weave complex and precise spells here, carefully laid, and when ingredients are called for, we use only the finest. Consequently, my fees must be proportionately high."

"Of course," said Emily.

"It therefore follows that our clients must be among the well-to-do. Although I occasionally do some pro bono work for a worthy cause, we will spend most of our time dealing with the nobility and moving in Melinower's circle of elite."

"I have no problem with that," said Emily, who could not think of a more desirable job description.

"As part of your lessons, I will instruct you in the gentle art of self-promotion. For now, suffice it to say that you must wear clothing of fine quality, from dressmakers of good reputation. We will establish accounts with several shops who will provide your clothes. It is very important that, outside of these walls, you never appear in clothing that is patched, stained, or even slightly worn."

"Yes, that makes sense," said Emily, who was outwardly calm but inwardly ecstatic. This was going far better than she dared hope. An apprenticeship with a top-echelon sorcerer, that involved hobnobbing with Melinower's nobility, and to top it off, he was virtually ordering her to buy new clothes at his expense. What more could a girl ask for?

Bungee went on. "It is quite likely that you will encounter some of our clients while at these shops, or at other social occasions. They may invite you to lunch or tea. When that happens, you must never accept an invitation for that same day, or the next. You must always protest that you are too busy, but can make time for them later in the week. It is important that you do so even during slack times, when we are not busy. In fact, those are the times that it is especially important."

Emily considered his words. "Because we are maintaining the impression that we are in demand?"

"Quite so."

"Even for the King?"

"Well, no. For the King or Queen we drop everything and give our immediate attention. Good point. I'm glad you brought that up."

"You're welcome."

"It may also occur," Bungee said, "that our clients will

want to gossip with you, especially if they are young women close to your own age. As a sorceress in training, you should maintain a professional detachment. Listen attentively, try to empathize, but do not share information about our clients, or, especially, about yourself."

"I understand," said Emily. "My mother often spoke along the same lines. She said that to be most effective, a sorceress must carry an aura of mystery about her."

"She was quite right," said Bungee. He carried the teakettle back over to the brazier and began filling it with water from a porcelain jug. "To maintain the client's respect it is necessary to be somewhat unpredictable, perhaps even harsh. It keeps the layman from taking us for granted."

"My mother said the same thing after she used the frog spell."

She was unprepared for the reaction to this simple remark. There was an explosive hiss of steam as Bungee spilled water on the hot coals, and a clang as he set the iron teakettle hard on the grill. He spun around to face Emily. "Amanda used the frog spell?"

"Well, yes. There was this boy . . ."

"Surely not . . . she didn't . . . not our Prince Hal?"

"He was trying to steal the philosopher's stone."

"Dear me, dear me." Bungee began pacing up and down rapidly. "My dear girl, this puts quite a different light on the whole situation, you understand."

"Um, no."

"Emily, my clients consider me a trusted professional. When they bring a sorcerer into their lives it is nearly always for delicate assignments requiring the highest degree of confidence. They do not want to deal with someone whose associate may transform one of them, or their children, into an amphibian."

"But *I* didn't put the spell on Hal! It wasn't me!"

"Yes, yes, I understand. But rightly or wrongly, some people will attribute the sins of the parent to the child. For others, your very presence will remind them that it *could* happen to them and shake their confidence. The social stigma is impossible to avoid. Good Lord, what could Amanda possibly have been thinking?"

"But he's not a frog now!"

"Yes, thank goodness. Was it you who kissed him?"

"No," said Emily, with the tiniest sigh. "It was a girl from the village."

"Hmm. A good-looking girl, of course. Magicality demands it."

"Yes. Very. The most beautiful girl in the village, all the boys say."

"That certainly helps. And now she becomes a princess. Very good. This turns the story from a cautionary tale into a romantic fairy tale. We may be able to salvage the situation yet, indeed, garner some good publicity from it. When is the wedding?"

"They haven't set a date yet."

"No?" Bungee glanced at the clock, the one with the moon phases, grabbed a quill and a sheet of foolscap, and scribbled some numbers. He pulled up an abacus, did some hasty calculations, then threw down the quill. "Without knowing the exact details of the spell, I can't begin to work this out with any sort of precision. But I shouldn't think there is room for delay."

"The problem is that Caroline—that's the girl—doesn't want to marry Hal. She says he's not handsome."

"What! That's absurd! Prince Hal is a fine young man. My daughters think he is quite good-looking."

"They do?" Emily was surprised. "They said that?"

"As I recall, they said he was cute. It's the same thing, isn't it?"

"Um, no."

Bungee put his hands on the back of a chair and leaned over it, looking at her intensely. "My dear girl, I regret very much having to tell you this, but I must withdraw my offer to take you on as my apprentice. I simply cannot let this sort of shadow fall over my business."

"But it's not my fault!"

"Yes, yes, I know, but I have no choice. If our Prince reverts to a frog, the damage to my business could be severe. I simply could not afford to be associated with you." His shoulders sagged. "And Emily." He hesitated. "Emily, no other magician of good reputation would do so either. That's why the frog spell is so rarely used."

"I understand," said Emily glumly. She realized he was right, and her hopes of a good apprenticeship were sinking like a stone in water. But she kept her features composed, determined not to cry in front of this man. She slid her book off the table and put it back in her handbag. Bungee watched it go with reluctance.

"Wait, now. Of course it's not as bad as all that. I'm speaking about only if our Prince reverts to a frog. Once this affair is all settled, I'm sure we can deal with it."

"But what can I do?"

"This girl is from your village, isn't she? You must

know her—all people from small villages know each other. Talk to her. Try to influence her to make up her mind. She's a commoner, isn't she? Really, I should think there would be no problem persuading her to marry Prince Hal."

Emily made no reply at first. Indeed, she seemed so distant, so lost in thought, that Bungee was about to call her name, when she finally spoke. "You would think so, wouldn't you?"

She gathered up her belongings and turned to the door. "Master Bungee, thank you for your time. I hope we will have the opportunity to discuss this again."

"I am optimistic that we will, dear girl. And I look forward to it very much."

Emily was about to start down the stairs when she stopped and turned around. "Ah, Master Bungee."

"Yes?"

"I was wondering—in your opinion—since we would be meeting with so many nobles—is it possible—would there be a chance – that one would propose to me?"

"To a commoner? Of course not. Why do you ask?"

"No reason," said Emily, and left.

❧

"So what's the problem with Emily?" said Jeff. "She looked kind of upset when she got back."

"I don't know," said Hal. "She went to set up her apprenticeship with a master sorcerer—a man named

Bungee—and she's been kind of distracted ever since. You know, like when you talk to her she's listening to you, but she's not listening to you?"

"Bungee is supposed to be pretty good. She didn't say anything about him?"

"She said he wants her to make tea."

"Oh that. Yeah, a lot of girls get upset about that."

They were back in Jeff's quarters. Hal was clearing ledgers and account books off one table and stacking them on another. When he had the table cleared he took a bundle, wrapped in oiled cloth, from under his arm. It proved to be a wooden scabbard. He laid it on the table and pulled the oriental sword partway out.

"What's this?" asked Jeff.

"It's a sword."

"No kidding. A sword, eh? So that's what a sword looks like. Wow, I'd never have guessed. Well, thanks for sharing this with me, Hal, but I'm kind of busy and . . ."

"I'm entering the tournaments with it."

Jeff tilted his head back and looked at Hal. Hal was a capable swordsman, in a rough street-fighting sort of way. The youngest prince had, in the course of his assignments, defeated his share of bandits and thugs. But real-life swordfighting was nothing like tournament swordfighting, and Jeff said as much. "It's all technique, and those guys are masters, Hal. You don't stand a chance."

"This is a magic sword. And it sings."

"I've got a razor that sings, but it won't help me win a shaving contest. Hal, if you want to start getting into tournament swordfighting, I'll back you all the way, but you can't start with the annual Melinower games. You want to find some small-town tournaments and work your way up."

"Jeff, I've got an angle on this. Listen to me. You've fought in tournaments, right? You're pretty good?"

"Well . . . yes."

"And you've gone up against men with magic swords?"

"Yes, and that's just what I mean. There's nothing special about a magic sword, aside from the fact that it's magic. All you need to make one is a swordsman and a really good wizard. The wizard transfers the swordsman's skill into the sword."

"So any sword can be made into a magic sword?"

"Uh, no. I guess there are only a few wizards who can do it. And it has to be a specially forged sword to take the spell. And you need a whole bunch of other ingredients to work the spell, I think."

"Uh-huh."

"But if you've got all that stuff, any swordsman can have his skill transferred into the sword. So the sword is only as good as the person who gave it his skill. If it came from an expert, Hal, it will help you fight like an expert. But if you're going up against another expert, you'll get your butt kicked. And in the Melinower tournaments, they're all experts."

"All the better for my plan," said Hal. "Jeff, when you fight, do you parry with a dagger or with a buckler?"

"A dagger, of course. No one fights with the buckler any more, even in tournaments."

"Okay, let's try it. Take the magic sword." He passed it over to Jeff.

"What, here?"

"Sure. We've got room." Hal was bustling around the room, taking one of Jeff's swords down from the wall and moving chairs and tables out of the way. "Just a couple of lunges."

"We'll have to get padding."

"No need. We'll do it theatrical style. I just want to show you how it works."

Jeff was examining the scabbard. "I wonder what these runes mean."

"They're not runes. This swords comes from the Far East. Those little pictures are their style of writing. I looked them up in the library this afternoon."

"What do they mean?"

"Near as I can figure, they translate into 'Danger, hold by handle only. Keep pointed end away from you.' "

"Sage advice, I'm sure." Jeff slid the gleaming blade out of the scabbard. "There are more of them on the blade. Stamped into the steel."

"They say, 'Made from steel.' "

Jeff gave him a look. "Hal, are you *sure* this is a magic sword?"

"Stand back, and I'll show you."

Theatrical swordplay has a tradition that is nearly as old as theatre itself. The intent is to look exciting without risking injury, and for that reason the techniques are often used by real defense instructors to demonstrate moves to students. So Hal and Jeff both knew the positions to assume, standing far enough apart so the blades could clash, but their bodies were out of reach, keeping one foot anchored firmly to the floor so they could not move closer. Hal started with his sword held back in a rear guard, dagger in his left hand. Jeff held a dagger also, the magic sword above his head in a high guard.

"It's got power in it," he admitted. "I can feel it."

"Right," said Hal, and slashed upward with his blade. Jeff moved instantly to parry with the magic sword and found the blade caught by Hal's dagger.

"What the hell?" he said.

Hal was smiling. "What did it do?"

"I don't know, but that wasn't me. It was the sword."

"Right. Now, let's change swords." The two men switched. Hal feinted with the magic sword and Jeff attacked. Once again Hal parried with his sword, then counterattacked with a draw cut that had the edge of his blade whistling mere inches from Jeff's chest.

Jeff stepped back and looked at Hal. "Well, that was strange. What is it doing?"

"It's an oriental sword. Over here, we attack with the blade and parry with the dagger. But in the east, it's different. They use the blade for both attack and parry. They don't use daggers or even bucklers. So the person whose skill went into this sword couldn't deal with dagger parries. Asian pirates fight this way. We only ran into a few when I was in the navy, but I saw enough of the technique to figure it out."

"Hmmm." Jeff considered this. "But he could parry with the blade, and he had that fast, slashing counterattack, so . . ."

"So I combine his skill with the blade and my skill with the dagger, and I've got an unbeatable combination of attacks and parries."

"Okay." Jeff shrugged. "You've got a chance. I'll help you brush up on your dagger work and teach you some tournament skills. If that's what you want to do . . ."

"Also," said Hal, "we bet everything we have on the outcome."

"Actually," said Emily, "he seemed like quite a nice little man."

Caroline gave her a withering look. "Oh, you'd have done it with him, I suppose."

"No, of course not. Besides, it wouldn't have worked anyway. Someone should tell him."

Caroline was surprised. "You think the magic spinning wheel is a fake?"

The two girls were in Emily's room, which was a bit smaller than Caroline's. In the back of her mind, Caroline was secretly pleased to see this. She was going to be a princess, after all. It was only right that she should get a bigger room. In the front of her mind, she knew this was petty and didn't mention it.

"Not a fake," said Emily. "Just incomplete. He can't do anything we can't do. That spinning wheel just means some wizard knew the spell for transforming brass into gold. He bound the spell up in a spinning wheel, so it can be used even when the wizard isn't around." Emily was sitting on the bed, with her books scattered around her. She wasn't trying to study now.

It just gave her a reassuring feeling to have them around, to feel their solid weight, and to know, in a strange palace in a strange city, that they were her own.

"Fine," said Caroline. "If the wizard knew his stuff, then the wheel ought to work."

"Nope. You still need the philosopher's stone and red mercury and the virgin brass."

"Oh. Right. Well, not the virgin brass, anyway. He said you could do it with flax."

"Flax. Hmmm. Maybe flax. I don't know about flax." Emily stretched out on the bed and grabbed another book. She spent a minute searching it, then put her finger on a page. "Flax, right. Gold stalks with purple flowers. It's the Law of Similarities."

Caroline was brushing her hair and looking in the mirror. "I can't believe how smooth the looking glasses are here. I've never seen a reflection like this. I wonder if I really look like this."

"What? What else would you look like?"

"Well, just because it's a better-quality looking glass doesn't mean it gives a more accurate reflection. Maybe my looking glass at home is right, and my face is actually a little wavy and bumpy."

"If your face was wavy and bumpy," said Emily, "I'd have mentioned it."

Caroline turned away from the mirror and sat down on the bed with Emily. "Rumpelstiltskin mentioned the Law of Similarities"

"Yep. To do a transmutation, the stuff you start out with has to have similarity to the stuff you want to make. That's why you can turn brass into gold, but not pewter."

"That's why he specified unretted flax. When you soak the flax in water, a lot of the gold color washes out."

"There are probably other things you can turn into gold, under the right conditions."

"Unfortunately, we don't know what they are. So where does that leave me, dowry-wise? I still have to find a way to marry Prince Jeffrey."

"Oh?" Emily rolled over onto her stomach and looked at Caroline through cupped hands. "You've pretty much decided on Prince Jeffrey?"

"He rode with me in the royal carriage back to the Bull and Badger. He's very nice. Did I tell you I rode in the royal carriage? Also, the Queen says that when I'm a princess I'll have ladies-in-waiting."

"Really? That's great. Um, what are ladies-in-waiting anyway?"

Caroline frowned. "I'm not sure. I think they're like bridesmaids, except they do it full-time. Oh, and I have to approve a design for their dresses. I think Queen Helen is right. It's such a shame if they can only wear them once."

"Prince Jeffrey," Emily prompted her.

"Anyway, Jeffrey is just so fine. I just love to look at his eyes. And he's very smart. He knows a lot about money and taxes and stuff. I think that's good. And he really cares about the people. I'm sure he doesn't go out drinking with them the way Hal does, but he cares about the schools, and the tax rates, and things like that. I respect that. When I become a princess, I'm going to care about the people also and not think so much about myself."

"That's good," said Emily, "since I'm still going to be one of the people."

Caroline frowned. "Of course, I'm talking about myself right now."

"Well, you don't have to change overnight. And you're not a princess yet."

"Right. Jeff has to become king first. If he's king, he can marry anyone he wants, dowry or no dowry."

"That's a big if."

"Right. Kenny could still become king."

"Oh, come on!" Emily sat up suddenly. "You wouldn't marry Prince Kenneth, would you?"

"Why not?"

"You know perfectly well why not! He's a jerk, that's why."

"How do you know? We only met him for a few minutes."

"And he was a jerk. And Hal doesn't like him. And neither does Jeffrey."

"He's very good-looking. Of the three brothers, Kenny has the best chance to be king. And he is the handsomest."

"Oh, you!" Emily turned away from her.

"I'll have to get Kenny interested in me, but without making Jeff angry. That will be tricky. Don't look at me that way. I don't have a whole lot of options here."

"You could just marry Hal," Emily said. Or at least, that's what she thought she said. Somewhere between her brain and her mouth, the words got lost.

Caroline gave her a questioning look. "What? Did you say something? You were mumbling."

"Oh?" Emily gave a small cough. "Sorry, something caught in my throat. I was just saying that—um—you could still marry . . ." Her voice trailed off. She found it again. "You could still marry Hal."

"We've been through all that," said Caroline dismissively.

"Is it really so important that a boy be handsome?"

"Of course it is. Haven't you ever thought about having children?"

"Certainly."

"Well then, you're going to have to do it with your husband. Now can you imagine waking up next to Hal in the morning?"

Emily felt her cheeks grow hot. She ducked her head into a book. "I hadn't really thought about it."

"And what about the children? You want good-looking children, of course. To have good-looking children, you need a good-looking husband."

"You're not breeding cattle!"

"I'm being practical. And I know what I want and how to get it. I want girls who look like me and boys who look like Jeff or Kenny."

"What if the girls look like Kenny, and the boys look like you?"

"You're not being at all funny, you know. Why are you trying to push Hal on me again? I thought you liked him yourself?"

"Me?" said Emily. "Not at all. I just don't want to see you lose everything by waiting too long, trying to improve a situation that is already pretty good." She put down her book and took up another one, examining a page carefully, not meeting Caroline's eyes. "I mean, I like Hal myself, of course. But after all, I have an apprenticeship to finish. It's not like I can get involved with a boy at this point in my life, even if he was interested in me."

"Aha!" Caroline turned around. "There! That's exactly what I was talking about."

"What?"

"Selfishness. I'm going to have to be careful. I've been thinking about nothing but myself, and I didn't even ask you how your apprenticeship meeting went."

"Um, fine, thanks for asking. We just have some—um—details to work out. Oh, and Hal showed me around the city for a bit."

"Is Hal back? I need to see him. The Queen wants us to set a wedding date. I need to give Hal some excuse to stall her while I work on Jeff."

"Not Kenny?"

"Or Kenny." Caroline collected her hairbrush and left. Emily waited until the door closed before she looked up from her book. And made a face.

❧

"No," said Jeff. "No, no, and no! Hal, how could you even ask this? It was Dad's gambling that got the family into this mess to begin with."

"This isn't gambling. It's a sure thing."

"Oh right. How many times did we hear Dad say that?"

"Okay, so it's still something of a gamble. But it's a gamble we've got to take.

"The hell we do! No." Jeff turned away from Hal and

stalked back to his desk. "I'm in charge of the finances, and we're going to go to the Council of Lords and work out a payment scheme—"

"And one hell of a lot of innocent people will suffer, just so a handful of wealthy deadbeats can get out of paying their debts. I've heard."

Jeff stopped with his back to Hal. Then he crossed to the other side of his desk, turned around, and lowered himself slowly into the chair. "When did you hear about the expulsion? Kenny just told me today. And Dad hasn't mentioned it at all."

"Guys talk, you hear things. The Royal Guard is making preparations for something big. The Jews can tell they're being watched, and they're nervous. And I know the way Kenny thinks."

"I tried to talk to Dad. He wouldn't say anything one way or another."

Hal sat down in front of Jeff and rested his elbows on the desk. "Jeff, the word has gotten around about this magic sword. Everyone thinks it's a joke. They haven't figured it out. That means the odds will be tremendous. I'm thinking we can get thirty to one on our money. Maybe fifty to one. Enough to get the family out of debt. With that kind of money, the Council of Lords will demand that Dad name you his heir."

"My personal ambition is not enough justification to . . ."

"I'm not talking about your personal ambition. It's you or Kenny. Either we gamble on the tournaments or Kenny starts driving people out of their homes. Can you think of any other way to stop it?"

Jeff thought for long minutes. Finally he said, "No."

"Besides," said Hal, "if you're the king, you can marry Caroline."

Jeff scowled at him. "Now don't you start. Kenny made me the same offer, if I play along with the expulsion. What makes you both so sure I want to marry Caroline?"

"Two reasons. One, you've seen her. Two, you're a guy."

"Caroline is not the only beautiful, doe-eyed, slim-waisted, full-breasted, personable young woman with perfect skin, a dazzling smile, and a sharp mind in town, you know. There are other girls like her around."

"Name them."

"Never mind. Let's say we had enough money to bet on the tournaments, a big enough bet to clear our debts. We don't, but even if we did, why should I back you? Give me the sword and let me win with it. I have more tournament experience than you."

Hal shook his head. "Won't work. You're too good, Jeff. You won't get the odds that I will. I had a street fight with this sword last night, outside of a local inn. I was soundly thrashed."

"I get it. And you made sure everyone saw you lose, of course."

"It was all over town today. The best part was that the girls were there. Nobody thinks a guy would throw a fight in front of his girlfriend."

"Let's see." Jeff reached back behind his head, where there were half a dozen bellpulls located near his desk. He selected one and rang for his valet. The man appeared in a few minutes. "Good evening, Winthrop.

"You rang, sire?" Winthrop was thin and balding, and always seemed to have a few beads of perspiration on his high forehead, even though his features were usually calm and composed.

"I did indeed, Winthrop. My brother here tells me he has entered his name in the tournaments. He wishes to compete in the swordsmanship contest."

"I have heard the same thing, sire. Should I instruct the royal physician to lay in an extra supply of ointment and bandages?"

"Hey!" said Hal.

Jeff hid his smile. "A capital idea, Winthrop. But first, answer a question for me. I understand that you have been known to place a wager or two."

"In my salad days, sire. Alas, Mrs. Winthrop tends to keep a tighter grip on the purse strings. Such bets as I place now are for purely nominal sums."

"But you're aware of the odds?"

"Yes, sire."

"And what are they offering for Prince Hal?"

"When I left the city this evening, sire, the odds on Prince Hal were one hundred to one, against."

Jeff's mouth dropped open, but he recovered quickly. "Thank you, Winthrop. That will be all."

His valet turned to exit. He stopped when Hal called his name. "Hey, Winthrop."

"Yes, sire?"

"Did you bet on me?"

"No, sire."

"Oh, come on. Not even at a hundred to one? Not even sixpence?"

Winthrop hesitated, then cleared his throat. "It is my experience, sire, that bookmakers tend to know their business. They would not offer such long odds without good reason."

"I see. Thanks, Winthrop."

As soon as the servant left, Jeff bounced out of his chair. He began to walk back and forth over the length of the room, thinking out loud. "Okay, we've got a chance with this, but we'll have to keep it quiet. I'll need to train you on your parries, but we can't let anyone see us. Especially not Kenny."

"Right."

"Too large a bet will change the odds. The book-makers will get wise. We'll have to get proxies to place the bets for us. Lots of small bets. But no one from the palace. The servants will certainly talk too much and so will the courtiers."

"Right."

"The Royal Guards are all under Kenny's thumb. I'll use army officers. They'll be discreet if I tell them to."

"Right."

Jeff grabbed some of the ledgers from where Hal had stacked them. He selected two out of the pile and tossed them on his desk, lit an extra candle, and produced an abacus.

"I never could figure out how to use one of those," said Hal.

"Shush," said Jeff, pulling a stick of chalk from his

desk. He began doing sums on a slate. For a long time there was only the clicking of the abacus, the scratching of chalk, and the occasional quiet whisper of pages turning as he riffled through the ledgers. The more he worked, though, the more his enthusiasm waned. Eventually he threw the chalk aside and sank back in his chair. Disappointment showed in his face. He said, "It's no use, Hal. I've tapped every discretionary fund we have. Even at a hundred to one, we don't have enough to cover the bets we're going to need."

"Yeah, I figured that," said Hal calmly. "We need to hock the family jewels."

For Prince Jeffrey, the day had wrought one emotional blow after another. It had started at lunch with Caroline, and the sudden realization that love at first sight was by no means a myth. He had plunged from passion to helpless anger when he learned of his brother's conspiracy against the Jews. This had been replaced with excitement when he accepted Hal's plan to gamble the family out of debt. But now Hal had tossed yet another burning brand in the air and expected Jeff to catch it.

"What! Sell the crown jewels? Impossible! No!"

"Not the crown jewels. Of course not. What kind of dolt do you take me for? The crown jewels belong to the kingdom, not to us personally. I mean Mom's jewels."

"Good Lord! That's almost as bad."

Hal shrugged. "It's not great, but it can be done."

"Mom's jewelry. Hal, some of those pieces have been in the family for six generations. Diamonds, rubies, emeralds. They're priceless."

"They're far from priceless. You'll be surprised at how quickly the jewelers will be able to put a price on them." Hal picked up the magic sword, examined it, and slid it back into the simple wood scabbard.

"We can't do it. These are—"

"Diamonds, rubies, emeralds, I know. Jeff, they're worthless chips of glasslike material that are only valuable because people *think* they're valuable. Anyway, we'll get them back after the tournaments."

"You've got a lot of confidence in yourself and that damn sword."

Hal said nothing to this.

"Anyway," Jeff went on, "it takes time to sell pieces that valuable. We've got to act tomorrow."

"We don't have to sell them. We just have to borrow against them. We can get quick cash with them as collateral."

"We'll only get a fraction of their worth." Jeff got to work with his slate and abacus again. "Still, yes. We can do it. That still leaves one major problem."

Hal nodded. "Mom has to agree to it."

"Right," said Jeff. "How will you get her to agree to this? Mom is pretty easygoing about a lot of things but still—we're talking about a woman and her jewelry."

"Ah, well," said Hal. He pushed aside some papers to clear a space on a table, then sat down on it, resting the sword in his lap. "Actually, Jeff, you're going to have to be the one to tell her."

"What? Why me? This is your idea."

"Because Mom will hit the ceiling if she finds out I'm entering the tournaments. She'll never agree to the plan if I propose it. You're going to have to do the big brother thing and convince her I'm not going to get killed."

Jeff blew out his cheeks and exhaled. "This is going to be tough. Next to jousting, the swordfighting events are the most dangerous. And she still thinks you're the baby of the family."

"I know. Ideally, I'd also like to sell those gold chains that Kenny has, but we can hardly ask him to help us out."

"I don't know." Jeff shook his head. "Mom is going to scream."

As if on cue, they both heard a distant scream coming from another part of the castle. Both boys cocked their heads. "Was that Mom?"

No further noise ensued. Hal shrugged. "Maybe one of the maids saw a rat?"

"Well, whoever it was has stopped now." Jeff listened a bit more, then laughed. "It certainly was perfect timing, though."

And then they did hear something. It was the sound of running feet. The feet rushed in closer, skidded to a stop, and then the door was flung open. Winthrop was outside, panting and disheveled. "Prince Jeffrey, Prince Hal, come quickly. It's the Queen!"

By the time Jeff and Hal reached the Queen's suite, there were already a dozen or more anxious servants clustered outside the door. The door itself was firmly locked. "She won't let anyone in," said Winthrop. "She just asked for you."

"Then," said Jeff, "there's no reason for all this hanging about. I'm sure you all have plenty to do."

It was clear that he intended them to move along, and they did so, casting backward glances toward the Queen's chambers. Jeff rapped on the door with his knuckles, at the same time holding Winthrop back. "Stay here by the door. Don't let anyone in until I say so."

"Yes, sire."

They heard the key turn in the lock, and the door opened a crack, just enough to let them see Queen Helen's eye peering nervously out. Then the door opened just enough for Jeff and Hal to slip in. Once inside, Helen locked the door again and stood with her back to it.

"It's your father," she said. "He's gone mad."

"Where is he?"

"In the bedroom."

Jeff and Hal exchanged glances, then walked to the royal bedchamber and opened the door. The King was lying on the bed, clothed in loose trousers, a flannel shirt, and wearing a battered straw hat. He had a candle in one hand. With it, he was attempting to light what appeared to be a pipe made from a corncob.

"Ah, hello, boys," he said, and waved to them. His fist was closed, and he was holding the pipe between thumb and forefinger. "Let me give you some advice. You can lead a horse to water, but you can't make it drink."

"Say what?" said Jeff.

"Remember what my daddy used to say, 'Just 'cause a cat has her kittens in the oven don't make 'em biscuits.' "

"I don't remember Grandfather saying that."

"What's he talking about?" Hal whispered to his mother.

"I don't know," she told him. "I came back from dinner, and he was in here, dressed like a farmer. I asked him about it, and he's been rambling like this ever since. I sent all the servants away. I don't want them to start talking."

"Take care of the pence," said the King, "and the pounds take care of themselves."

"The servants are already talking," said Jeff.

"They haven't seen your father. I sent them out right

after they heard me scream. I couldn't help myself. I thought he had gone insane."

"You can't teach an old dog new tricks," said the King.

"Sure, Dad," said Jeff. "Let a smile be your umbrella." To Hal he said, "We definitely can't let the Council of Lords find out about this."

"We can't let Kenny find out about this," said Hal. "Or he'll want to take power right away."

"You don't suppose he's drunk, do you?"

"Your father never gets drunk," said Helen.

"Maybe we should get him drunk," said Jeff. "Maybe he'll snap out of this after a good long sleep."

"It ain't the things we don't know that get us in trouble," said the King. "It's the things we do know that ain't so."

Suddenly Hal started laughing. "I've got it, I've got it," he said between chuckles, leaning against a bedpost.

"What?"

"It's the philosopher's stone. He's giving us cracker-barrel philosophy."

"I've never met a tax collector I didn't like," said the King.

"Yeah, I'm not surprised," said Hal. He hopped up on the bed, grabbed his father's wrist, and pried open his hand. "Give me the stone, Dad."

"I've never been a member of any organized political party," said the King. "I'm a monarchist . . . ow." The philosopher's stone dropped out of his hand and rolled across the carpet. He looked at Hal, and at Jeff, and at Queen Helen. Then he rubbed a hand over his face. "That was certainly strange."

Kenny came through the door, flinging it back against the wall. "Dammit, Jeff, that stupid servant of yours tried to keep me out. What the hell is going on here?"

Helen sat on the bed and put her arms around the King. "Are you all right, dear?"

"I'm fine now, Helen. Just an attack of philosophy." The King pulled off the straw hat, looked at it with distaste, and threw it and the corncob pipe onto the floor. "Thank you for your assistance, boys. You may leave now."

"No problem," Jeff told Kenny. "False alarm." Kenny wasn't listening. He had picked the philosopher's stone off the floor and was staring at it with a surprised expression.

Hal took it out of his hand. "Just some magical stuff, Kenny. I'll take care of it."

Kenny didn't seem to notice. "What does not kill me makes me stronger," he murmured.

"I don't doubt it," said Hal. He followed Jeff back out of the bedchamber. Jeff closed the door and Hal wrapped the philosopher's stone in his handkerchief. "I'm giving this back to Emily. We can't use it, and we don't know what other kind of trouble it can cause."

"I agree. It's a bit of sorcery. Let a sorceress handle it."

"When Mom comes out, will you talk to her?"

Jeff exhaled, then nodded. "All right, I'll do it. But she won't like it."

Caroline was wearing a white dress. She was following a simple rule of fashion: wear colors during the day, white at night, so you stand out more in the darkness. She ran along the outside wall, up the stairs that led to the terrace, where the three Princes had their apartments. A puff of wind disturbed the warm night, and ruffled her hair and the hem of her dress. An observer below, seeing the fair young woman, shining in reflected moonlight, rising against the dark stone, might be forgiven for thinking he was watching an angel ascending heavenward.

But Caroline was thinking down-to-earth thoughts. Although she hadn't mentioned it to Emily, she had decided to take her case directly to the King. She had, in her own opinion, an ironclad case. She was entitled to marry a handsome prince. Prince Hal, for all his sterling qualities, was not handsome. There were handsome princes available—why not switch? It was simple justice as far as she was concerned, and she couldn't see why people had to keep muddying up the issue with questions of dowry.

The King, she thought, could straighten everything out. It was better to give decisions like this to a man. The Queen was a very fine woman, but you couldn't explain to a mother that her son was not handsome. And even among women in general, there were far too many who seemed to think every man who came along was attractive. Whereas a man, on the other hand, never thought another man was handsome. Himself maybe, but not other men.

Getting to see the King would be a problem, she knew. There were people who had waited for years to get an audience with the King. But Caroline was sure she could figure out a way. She would start by getting Hal to explain the protocol to her. She was already in the royal apartments, so she was pretty close to start with.

With these thoughts on her mind she reached the top step and entered the terrace. As she rounded the corner toward Hal's windows, the bright moon illuminated the stones in front of her. Caroline stopped. Her hand rose to her mouth even as a scream rose in her throat.

There are few experiences quite so chilling as a horrified scream. Queen Helen's shriek of anxiety, earlier in the evening, was not the kind to send shivers down the spine. A wounded soldier's cry of pain does not raise the hairs on the back of the neck. No, the combination of a dark castle, a bright moon, and a scream of horrified despair coming from a young woman, splitting an otherwise silent night, is unequaled for sheer, unadulterated bone-chilling.

So it was just as well that Caroline did not scream. She thought she did. She certainly felt like she was screaming. But in truth she was so paralyzed with shock that the muscles in her throat constricted, and all she could utter was a long, drawn-out, "eeeeeeeep."

For seated on the stones in front of her was a frog.

It sat on top of a loose pile of clothing, but Caroline was sure who it was even before she recognized Hal's sailcloth shirt. She ran forward and scooped it up, cradling it against her breasts. "Oh Hal," she whispered. "I am so sorry. I am so, so sorry."

The frog wriggled in her grasp. She stroked its back. "It's okay, Hal. It's me, Caroline. Don't worry. I'll get you out of this."

It was obvious what she had to do. Kiss the frog. She knew that the minute she saw it. But Caroline was afraid.

For nothing in Amanda's tales, or Caroline's own experience, had told her that a kiss from the same girl would break the spell a second time. She feared that if the spell could be broken at all, the frog would have to be let loose in a swamp and found again. Perhaps by a completely different girl.

Perhaps the spell couldn't be broken.

It would take but a second to find out. But she hesitated. For if she kissed the frog, and it didn't change, she was facing disaster. It was natural to want to put off the moment of truth.

But Caroline was a girl of strong resolve. She delayed only a few moments before bringing the frog up to her face and looking it in the eyes. A moth flitted over-head. She saw its eyeballs follow the flight. "Try to stay focused, Hal," she told it. "Pucker up. It's changing time. Are you ready?"

"Rrrrrrbbb," said the frog.

"That's the spirit. Okay, one, two, three, change!" And she kissed the frog.

Nothing happened. The frog continued to stare at her.

"Oh no," said Caroline. "Oh my. Oh no. Oh no no no nooooooo." She kissed the frog again. "Come on, Hal. Change!" She kissed it again. "Change!" And again. "Change! What do you want, Hal? Tongue? Change!" Her breath came in short gasps, and she knew she was hy-perventilating, but she couldn't stop. (Kiss) "Change!" (Kiss) "Change!" (Kiss).

Dizziness eventually stopped her. She put the frog down on a parapet and leaned over the wall with her head down, trying to get her breath back. When she came up again her face was wet, but she wiped away the tears and put up a brave front. "Hal," she told the frog sternly, "you're just not trying. Come on, Hal. Concen-trate. You can do this. Think manly thoughts."

She kissed it again. The frog obstinately remained a frog.

From the corner she heard a snicker. She whirled around, quickly hiding the frog behind her. It was Prince Kenny, looking at her with amusement. She gave him a nervous smile and managed to curtsey while keeping her hands behind her back. "Good evening, Your Highness."

"And good evening to you, Miss Caroline. A lovely night to be outside, isn't it?"

"Oh, yes. I was just—just—looking at the moon." Since the moon was behind her, Caroline could only attempt to point to it by twisting her head awkwardly. She realized, correctly, that doing so made her look like an idiot.

"I was looking for Hal. Have you seen him?"

"Hal? Prince Hal?"

"Yes. Prince Hal. My brother. Your fiancé."

"Oh, you mean *Hal*. No. No, I haven't seen him. No. Not tonight. No."

Behind her the frog went, "Rrrrrrrbbb."

"Excuse me," said Caroline. "It must have been something I ate. All that rich food."

"You get used to it after a while," said Kenny. "So you haven't seen Hal? I see his clothes are here."

Caroline looked down at the pile of clothing lying at her feet. "Yes, I noticed those, too. Very strange, isn't it?"

"It's certainly not like Hal to undress out here . . . ah, I see." Kenny gave Caroline a knowing smile. "I apologize if I interrupted a romantic moment."

"Interrupted what? Oh! No, nothing like that. We weren't doing anything."

"Are you sure?" Kenny moved a bit closer. "I thought I heard kissing."

"Kissing? Ha-ha-ha. How absurd. Why, there's no one else here. Who could I be kissing?"

"A frog, perhaps." Kenny reached behind Caroline and took the frog out of her hands. He held it up to his eyes and examined it critically. "Hmmm. Small, flaccid body. Soft, damp skin. Receding chin. Yes, the resemblance to Hal is unmistakable."

"Give him to me." Caroline made a grab for the frog. Kenny held it out of her reach.

"Oh, I think its served its purpose." Casually, Kenny tossed the frog over the parapet.

Caroline shrieked and ran to the wall. Kenny laughed. "Relax, my girl. It's not Hal. It was a joke. Hal is fine. It's just a frog I picked out of the grass this evening. Hal and Jeff are downstairs. I got some of his clothes from the laundress."

Caroline was leaning over the parapet. Down below, the frog lay spattered against the flagstones. Kenny continued. "It was just a gag. Although I must say, you've never looked lovelier than when you were kissing that—"

WHAP.

There is nothing quite like a lifetime of spinning for building up the wrist muscles. Caroline's slap made Kenny see stars, and he held his jaw to make sure it had not been dislocated. With his other hand he grabbed her wrist in case she drew back for another round. "Now now," he said. "Don't get excited. That's no way to treat your future husband."

"What? Yeah, you wish." Caroline snatched her hand back.

"Oh, I think so. You've made your desires pretty clear. You want to marry a handsome prince. And you want to be Queen someday, so you'll have to marry the future king. And there's only one man who qualifies on both counts."

"I don't need you, Your Highness, to tell me my own mind, thank you very much. And anyway, I believe Prince Jeffrey has an equal chance of inheriting the throne.

In fact, I've been told that the Council of Lords favors him."

"Very true. The Council does favor him, for now. But that's because they think Jeff can keep the family out of bankruptcy and avert a financial scandal. Fortunately, I've come up with a plan to solve our crisis, as well as avert all that tedious thrift and responsible spending that Jeff keeps preaching."

"Oh really? Frankly, Your Highness, you haven't struck me as being all that clever. No disrespect intended."

"I have hidden depths," said Kenny. He smiled. "And I like a woman with spirit, as trite as that old line may seem. Sets a different tone from the girls that are always fawning over me."

"You should go back to your little fawns. Besides, I thought a prince of Melinower was sold to the woman with the highest dowry, sort of like a male prostitute, isn't that correct?"

"Careful," said Kenny. "Now you're getting nasty. Try to remember you're still a commoner. I could have you flogged for a remark like that."

"I bet you'd enjoy it, too."

"Possibly I would. All the more reason to watch your place."

Caroline knew that Hal and Jeff would not allow Kenny to hurt her. Still, she was treading on dangerous ground. "Very well, Your Highness. I apologize."

"Accepted."

"In any case, I could not possibly come up with the dowry to marry you. And unless you marry a girl with an enormous dowry, you will not become king. And if you do marry a girl with an enormous dowry, then you cannot marry me. And that, Your Highness, is that." Caroline turned and started for the stairs. "Good night."

"Not so fast." Kenny grabbed her wrist again. Caroline pulled away. He held up his hands. "I'm still going to be king. And as the king, I can set the dowry requirements, or waive them completely. In fact, I've already told Jeff he could marry you, if you were willing."

"Really?" This was interesting. "Prince Jeffrey wants to marry me?"

"If you want to marry him. But remember, Jeff will not be king. I will be king."

Prince Kenneth, thought Caroline, *has taken too many jousting blows to the head.* "And how, may I ask, do you intend to manage that?"

"A simple redistribution of wealth. The worst of my father's debts are owed to Jewish moneylenders. As the Jews have accumulated too much wealth and power in any case, it is high time they were relocated to some other kingdom."

"You're going to expel them?"

Kenny beamed. "Smart girl. Exactly. We'll wait until after the tournaments are over, of course. So as not to hurt the tourist trade."

"That's horrible!"

"Oh, it won't so bad. We're just moving them. We won't be hurting them. Unless they try to resist. I expect some will try to resist, and they'll have to be injured, perhaps seriously. But I don't expect any to actually die. Mostly they'll just be roughed up a bit."

"You really have no idea what a tyrant you sound like, do you? Destroying people's lives like that."

"We won't be destroying their lives. The Jews have been wandering the Earth for two thousand years. This will be just one more wander for them."

"Leaving everything behind for you to loot."

"Of course not. They can take their possessions with them."

"Not everything. Not their homes."

"Oh well," said Kenny. "Can't be helped. The main point is to make it impossible for them to collect on the debts owed them. Think of it as a sort of mandatory refinancing."

"I can't believe you can be so unjust. You'll make a terrible king."

Kenny looked down at her with a fond smile, as though he was explaining something to a bright child. "Justice and honor are for knights to worry about. A king will have to put his name to far dirtier deeds than this before his reign is through. And," he went on, "I'm glad to see you're so upset with me. It shows you've been thinking of marrying me all along, haven't you? If you weren't, you'd just ignore me."

The fact that what he said was true made it all the more infuriating. "I wouldn't marry you if . . . if . . ."

"Yes?"

Caroline took one more look over the parapet, at the smashed body of the frog lying below, and said, "I don't know. But I won't." And she ran from the terrace.

Hal exited the palace and started up the outside stairs
that led to his rooms. It had been a long day and he was
ready for bed. He planned to be up early tomorrow,
practicing his guards and parries with the magic sword.
Tonight, after leaving Jeff and his mother, he had gone
to Emily to return the philosopher's stone. He had been
glad to get rid of it. The stone was connected to the
whole frog experience, and that was something Hal was
trying to push out of his mind. Seven weeks of water
and clammy mud, hunted by snakes and owls, the taste
of insects—most of it was just a blur now, but not yet
blurry enough. He woke each day from uneasy sleep,
knowing that he'd had a nightmare, thankful that he
couldn't remember it.

Still, it was never far from his mind that, frog-wise,
he was still in hot water. The spell obligated him to

marry Caroline unless she married someone else, and Hal couldn't help feeling that she was setting her standards a bit too high. Of course every girl wanted to marry a handsome prince, but the dowry issue seemed pretty much insurmountable. There was a whole city of wealthy merchants and nobles out there. Surely Caroline could find a young man to make her happy if she was willing to make the effort.

You wouldn't, Hal considered, find Emily getting hung up over whether she could marry a prince. Girls like her were too sensible.

In the end, the whole thing came back to the magic sword. If Hal won the tournament, the family debt would be eliminated. Jeff would become king, cancel the expulsion, marry Caroline, and Hal would be off the hook. All he had to do was win one tournament.

Talk about pressure.

Not that Hal was going to try to coerce her. It was up to Jeff to win her over. Caroline was very obviously a girl who made up her own mind, and if she needed advice, she asked for it. Trying to push her toward any particular man might just make her dig in her heels. Hal knew that women were inherently unpredictable. The only thing he was sure of was that Caroline definitely wasn't going to marry him.

At which point his reverie was interrupted by the sight of Caroline flying down the stairs. She flung her arms around him, kissed him on the lips, and said, "I'll marry you, Hal."

Well, Hal told himself, *I've been wrong before.*

Aloud he said, "That's great, Caroline. Why did you

change your mind? I thought you wanted to marry—have you been crying?"

Caroline's face was wet. She had started crying when she saw Hal, and now she began to hiccup. Hal patted her on the back, then led her up the stairs to the next landing and sat her down on the wall. "What's wrong?"

Caroline hiccuped one more time, then said, "I saw a frog."

"Ah."

"I thought it was you. I thought you had turned back into a frog, and it was all my fault."

"I'm fine. I'm not a frog. Nothing's your fault."

She buried her face in his neck. "I don't want you to turn into a frog."

"That makes two of us."

"I know I've been selfish. I didn't want to marry you. I wanted to marry someone who was tall, and broad-shouldered, and good-looking, and you're none of those things, but still . . ."

"Okay," snapped Hal, "Don't do me any favors. I can take care of myself."

Caroline pulled her head away from his shoulder and gave him a narrow look. "Do you want to revert to a frog?"

"Um," said Hal. "Maybe just this one favor."

"Well, okay then."

"Okay," said Hal, wondering if he should get down on one knee. But Caroline was over her tears and had gone from sad to visibly depressed. "I know you'd rather marry Jeff."

Caroline hesitated, then nodded. "Yes. But it just isn't going to happen. By marrying you, at least I'll get into the royal family. I'll never be the queen, but I will be a princess."

"And you'll have ladies-in-waiting."

"Oh yes, I can't forget the ladies-in-waiting. Also, Hal, I kind of feel responsible for you. Since I was the one who got you out of the swamp, I can't help but think that I should see the whole thing through."

"Mmmm," said Hal, a bit distractedly. Now that the emotional crisis was over, another factor had come into play, specifically adolescent male hormones. Caroline was still in Hal's arms and there was no ignoring the fact that this was a beautiful girl. A really beautiful girl. His arms were around her slim waist, her firm breasts were pressed against his chest, and her soft pink lips were only inches from his face. As far as young men go, Hal was a pretty self-controlled sort, but there are limits to what any teenage boy can stand. He cleared his throat. "Um, as long as we're engaged now we might as well— ah—see if we're physically compatible."

Caroline shrugged. Her response was meant to indicate casual disinterest, but since the movement caused her breasts to shift against him, the actual effect was quite the opposite from what she intended. "What did you have in mind?"

"Well, I just thought . . ." But before he could finish the sentence Caroline had kissed him again. It was a short kiss, but she let it linger just enough to give a hint of future possibilities.

"Was that what you had in mind?"

"Yes," said Hal. He let a moment of silence fill the space, then said, "Well, how was it?"

"Kissing you? Not that great, actually."

"Oh."

"I mean it wasn't bad. I'm sorry, Hal. You're kind of cute in that harmless sort of way—I can understand why Emily is attracted to you—but you just don't do much for me."

"Emily is attracted to me?"

"Of course. It's obvious. What did you think of my kiss?"

"Hmmm?" said Hal, who seemed to be lost in thought.

"I asked you what you thought of my kiss."

"Oh. Well, like you said, it wasn't that great for me either."

There was another moment of silence. "Oh really?" said Caroline.

"It was okay, though. Did Emily say anything else about me?"

"What's wrong with the way I kiss?"

"Nothing. It was fine. I mean, did you actually hear her say she liked me?"

"Fine as in really good, or fine as in just okay?"

"Um, really good. It was terrific."

Caroline stood up and faced him, hands on hips. "A moment ago you said my kisses weren't that great."

" 'Great' is a relative term. Under certain circumstances, a kiss might not be that great and still be excellent."

"Don't play word games with me, Hal! Just what makes you such an expert that you can critique a girl's kisses? Don't forget it was my kiss that saved your little froggy butt. You weren't nearly so picky about who kissed you when you were sitting on a lily pad."

"Not bad," said Hal. "We've been engaged a whole five minutes, and we're having our first fight."

Caroline sat down again. "Well, you started it." She let him put his arm around her waist. "Bridesmaids. Six will do, I think."

"Don't worry about it, Caroline. You don't have to marry me. I'm going to win enough money in the tournaments for you to marry Jeff or anyone you want."

Caroline blinked several times. "Is that a joke?"

"No."

"I have a hard time believing you can win big in the tournaments. Unless you're betting on the other guy."

"Of course not. I'm entered in the swordfighting competition."

Caroline blinked. "Satin pumps."

"What?"

"Satin pumps. For the bridesmaids. They can dye them to match their dresses. With all due respect, my prince, I've seen you swordfight. I think your technique needs a little work."

"This will be different. I've got a magic sword."

"I've seen your magic sword, too, remember? I can't think that it will be much use in a tournament, unless they give you a really big, big letter to open." Caroline brightened. "Bring it to the wedding. We can use it to cut the cake."

"No, really. Jeff and I have a way to beat the odds."

"I'm going to bed," said Caroline. She stood up again.

"Your mother is right. There's a lot of planning to do. Here." She leaned over. "Here's a good-night kiss. And I better not hear any complaints."

"No complaints," said Hal.

It was only a short kiss, but it lasted long enough that neither of them saw Emily approach from the shadows, observe them for a split second, then discreetly turn away.

Emily went back to her room, latched the door, and threw herself facedown on the bed. She pulled the pillow over her head. *That went pretty well,* she thought. *Caroline took my advice after all. Tomorrow I can tell Bungee that I can accept his apprenticeship. Everything is working out for the best and I'm not unhappy.*

Really, she told herself, *I'm not.*

"No!" said Queen Helen. "Absolutely not! I forbid it!"

"Mom," said Jeff, "I don't think you can forbid it. In fact, I don't think you can forbid Hal to do anything, anymore."

The Queen was sitting in her favorite chair, which was upholstered in burgundy damask and had elaborately carved mahogany arms. Right now her arms were folded against her chest, and she was sitting up very straight. In the candlelight it was difficult to make out her expression, but her voice was firm and authoritative. "Hal in the tournaments? How absurd. I will have a word with the registration clerks. How could they possibly put him on the lists? He's just a little boy."

"He's only a year younger than me. Kenny and I have been entering for years."

"Well, I don't like you and Kenny entering tournaments either. Swordfighting! It's dangerous. Even with armor. Why with one of those things you could . . ."

"Put your eye out," Jeff finished for her. He was leaning back into his armchair, trying to be casual, with his thumbs tucked into the pockets of a kerseymere waistcoat. "You used to tell me the same thing. Mom, Hal has already been in real street fights. The tournaments are just games."

"Oh yes, that's what you boys always say. Fighting with swords. Jousting with sticks. Don't worry, it's all just fun and games, until—"

"Until someone gets hurt, I know."

"Yes, you go ahead and make fun of me, Jeffrey, but wait until you have boys of your own. And you don't need to lecture me on the tournaments. Your father used to fight in them, before we were married, and I would go to see him."

"Did he get hurt?"

"No, but he could have."

"Totally convincing," said Jeff. "There, see, it's normal for men our age to want to fight in the tournaments, in some way or another. All the guys do it if they can."

"Certainly. And I suppose if all the other boys—"

"Jumped off a cliff, would we do it, too? Mom, it has to be Hal. The odds on him are tremendous. It's the only way we can win enough money to get out of debt."

"Oh Jeffrey, please! Tell me you're not betting on the tournaments. That's just the sort of thing that got your father into so much trouble to begin with."

Jeff had the feeling his own words were echoing back to him. Worse, they made sense. He tried to remember the arguments that Hal used to talk him into this. "I can't explain it now, Mom. You're going to have to trust me. Hal and I have an angle on this. You know how I feel about gambling. I wouldn't do this if the outcome wasn't certain."

"You and Hal have an angle? Jeffrey, you boys aren't doing anything illegal, are you?"

"Illegal? Of course not. Unethical? Maybe. Sneaky, dishonest, disreputable, and underhanded? Perhaps. But not illegal. I mean, if we were commoners, we could be in big trouble. But we're royalty, so it's okay."

"Well, that's good. I don't want you being a bad influence on Hal."

"Perish the thought. Now, Mom, here's the kicker." Prince Jeffrey paused and took a deep breath. There was no way to ease into this, so he decided to just come straight out with it. "To get the money to lay the bets, we're going to have to hock your jewels."

Helen's answer came back swiftly. "No."

Jeff held up his hands as if to forestall argument. Although in truth, the single word "no" could not exactly be considered an argument. "It's not what you think, Mom. We're not going to sell them. No no no. Absolutely not. We're just going to borrow against them. We'll get them back for you right after the match."

"Jeffrey, you cannot sell my jewels."

"Not *sell* them. Use them as security. Sure, I know that they're family heirlooms, handed down from generation to generation and all that, but really, they'll only be out of your hands for a few days. I've already talked with the major auction houses. They'll take good care of them . . ."

"I'm sure they will."

"No, really they will. They know the gems are of good quality . . ."

"They certainly do."

". . . and I'll get them bidding against each other to give us the best rate for the loan. The stones alone . . ."

"Are paste," said the Queen.

". . . are worth more than—what?"

"Are fakes." Helen refilled her teacup and very carefully added hot milk. She didn't look at her son while she spoke. "Jeffrey, it's very common for rich families to have duplicates made of their most expensive pieces. We wear the duplicates under normal circumstances and keep the real ones under lock and key, bringing them out only for special occasions, such as weddings and coronations and such."

"Uh, okay. They're duplicates. So where do you keep the real ones? Is there a strongbox in here? Or at the estate?"

"There are strongboxes both here and at the estate. But the family jewels are gone. I sold them. I haven't told this to you boys, or to anyone else. I quietly sold them off years ago, to pay some of your father's debts." This time the Queen did look at Jeff, and there was a tear in the corner of each eye.

"Um," said Jeff.

"I made the auction houses agree that they would not put them up for sale until after your father's death, so as not to embarrass him."

"Ahhhh, good thinking," said Jeff. "Okay then. It was just an idea, really. You know, Hal and I were brainstorming this bankruptcy thing and we just thought—well, it doesn't matter. We'll think of something else."

The day of the tournaments dawned bright and sunny and clear and warm. To be precise, the tournaments had been going on for three days before Caroline and Emily got there, with the most popular matches—the jousting, archery, and swordfighting—being saved for last. And the first two days had been partly cloudy. But today was definitely clear and warm, and the sod of the fairgrounds was dry and firm. The playing field was an oval one hundred yards long and fifty yards wide, with wooden stands erected around it. The royal box was situated at the fifty-yard line. The King and Queen were already seated inside, and the boxes of lesser nobles were spread out on either side. But the princes had their own box on the opposite side of the field, and it was here that Jeff led the girls.

"Just show these passes to the guards," he said, giving them tickets embossed with gold print. "And they'll let you into our box without any problems. I have to get ready for my match now, but you can look around for a while and take your seats whenever you're ready."

"So many guards," said Caroline. "Jeff, they're everywhere. Are they expecting some kind of trouble?"

"Hmmm? The guards? Oh no. They're mostly here to keep people from bringing outside food and drink into the fairgrounds. The King gets a cut of the concessions. Okay, I'll see you in a little bit."

He strode off quickly across the fairgrounds. Caroline watched longingly until he disappeared into the crowd. Emily nudged her.

"Hey, girl. You're going to marry Hal, remember?"

"I remember," said Caroline, glumly. "I hope he doesn't get hurt."

"Me too."

"I didn't put him up to this. He's not trying to impress me. I just want you to know that. I don't think he is, anyway."

"I know," said Emily. "Hal told me he was entering a match, before we went to see Bungee. I don't know what possessed him."

Both girls maintained an unhappy silence for a minute or so. Then Caroline pointed, and said, "Look! Isn't that Twigham?"

It was indeed the eldest of the village elders. The old man, dressed to the nines in a brown velvet jacket and high-collared shirt, was leaning on his walking stick, waving his peaked cap to get their attention. Emily ran over and hugged him. Caroline followed close behind.

"Twigham! What are you doing here?"

"One of their judges, an old friend, had to cancel, and

asked me to sit in for him. And I thought it was a good excuse to see the city again, and see how our girls were getting along. The invitation came just a day after you left, but I was never able to catch up with you. Old men don't travel fast, you know."

"We're fine," said Caroline.

"We're sitting in the princes' box," said Emily. "Can you believe it? Shall we also try to get you in?"

"No, that won't be necessary. I'll be in the judges' box at the other end of the fairgrounds. I'm afraid I'll have to put off our talk until later. I'm supposed to meet with the other judges before the contest. This will be a particularly difficult field to call."

"What are you judging? Archery? Wrestling?"

"More serious than that. We'll be judging the prettiest baby contest."

"Ouch."

"You said it. They try to choose judges from out of town, so we can skedaddle back there and avoid the wrath of the disappointed mothers."

They were still walking as they talked, and Twigham paused in front of a row of heavy tables, staffed by bearded men in black gabardine. Behind each table was a large chalkboard, where other men were furiously writing and erasing numbers. In front of each table was a tight throng of fairgoers, all with coins, or even bags of coins, in their hands. Most looked eager, some looked desperate. Twigham took his pipe out of his mouth and pointed with the stem. "The betting tables. Doing a particularly good business this year, I see."

"What are they betting on?"

"Everything. Including the baby contest. Prince Kenneth is the favorite for jousting, I see. The odds favor Prince Jeffrey for swordfighting, too. He's not really at the top of his class, but he's popular with the crowd."

"What about Prince Hal?"

Twigham scanned the chalkboards. "Your Prince does not seem to be a serious contender."

"Are you going to bet on him?"

Twigham shook his head. "I am not a betting man, my dear. And if I was, I'm afraid our youngest prince would be too long of a long shot for me."

"I knew it," said Caroline. "He *is* going to hurt himself."

"Emily," said Twigham, "I believe that man is waving to you."

Emily looked. The man in question wore sorcerer's robes. "It's Bungee. I'm about to apprentice to him. I'd better see what he wants." She excused herself and walked toward him. Bungee in turn, excused himself and separated from his own companions, taking her arm and speaking quietly in her ear. "The young woman you are with. The tall, blond one. Is that her?"

"Is that who?"

"Sorry, I should have made myself clear. Is that the girl you spoke of? The one who kissed the frog?"

"Yes. Her name is Caroline. She is going to marry Prince Hal. So everything is set."

Caroline had resumed talking to Twigham. She didn't see Bungee give her a long hard look. "No," he said. "She is beautiful."

"I told you she was beautiful."

"I didn't know she was *that* beautiful. No, there is something wrong."

Emily was immediately alarmed. Was her much-valued apprenticeship about to fly out the window? She was too good a negotiator to let her anxiety show, and her next words were carefully unconcerned. "Well, if there is a problem with the apprenticeship agreement, I'll be happy to—"

"No, no, not the apprenticeship. Everything is fine. It's your mother's spell. I'll have to check it. It shouldn't have worked. It lacks magicality."

Bungee had mentioned magicality once before. Emily had never heard the term, and she said so. "It lacks what?"

"It's a word I made up myself. A theory of my own. Never mind for now. Go off and have fun. But come by after the tournaments are over, and I'll explain."

"Okay."

"And don't count on Caroline marrying Prince Hal."

Emily turned to look at Caroline and when she turned back, Bungee was gone, having disappeared into the crowd. She shrugged and went back to Caroline and Twigham. "That was Bungee. I'm apprenticing to him."

"What did he want?"

"Um, he wanted to give his best wishes to you and Hal."

"Oh, well that was nice." Caroline looked for the sorcerer's robes and hat. But he had vanished.

The girls extracted elaborate promises from Twigham to meet them later, then continued with their tour of the fairgrounds. They passed the chained bear, the fortune-tellers, and the puppet shows; the jugglers, fire-eaters, and strolling musicians; the booths selling sausages and sweetmeats; and, of course, the numerous tents selling ale and wine. They watched footservants help highborn women out of their carriages, noted their clothing, and reassured each other that much of this city fashion was absurd frippery—the people back home dressed far more sensibly and looked just as good.

"I can't believe how women dress here," said Caroline. "Look at those bodices."

"I agree. They seem so tasteless."

"Why even get dressed if you're going to show all that?"

"I think it indicates a lack of confidence, to draw attention to yourself that way."

They studied the women some more.

"Of course, we'll have to get something like it."

"It's the fashion. We have no choice."

"It would look good if it was accessorized properly. Perhaps with a light jacket."

"Or a scarf."

By and by they worked their way back to the princes' box. "We should go up now. The jousting is about to start."

Caroline handed the passes to the guard. "I just wish . . ." she said, and stopped.

"I know," said Emily.

"What?"

"You were going to say that you wish our friends in Ripplebrook could see us getting into the princes' box. I know it's awful of me, but I feel the same way."

"Yes. It's silly, but it would be kind of nice to show off a little. Here we are, hobnobbing with royalty."

"Mmm." Caroline was studying the people around her. To the left was a box belonging to the Duchess of Momerath. The duchess was not around but her three daughters, who ranged in age from late teens to early twenties, were present and talking among themselves in excited whispers. They carried parasols to shield their complexions from the sun. To the right was another box whose owner she could not identify, but which held half a dozen occupants, all young women or adolescent girls. It seemed odd, then Caroline realized that Melinower's nobility, of course, would take pains to seat their fairest daughters next to the princes' box.

Some of the girls carried parasols, and all were fanning themselves against the heat. When Caroline turned away, the girls cast sidelong glances at her.

"Wine, ma'am?" She turned around. A waiter in a white linen jacket was offering a tray with two goblets. Caroline took them and tasted one. It was chilled, sweetened wine. She gave the other one to Emily. "You know, I think I'm going to like being a princess."

"I can see it has its points." Emily took the goblet and settled herself into a chair, at which point everyone in the stands, including Caroline, suddenly stood up. "Why are you . . . oh." Across the field, the King and the Queen were climbing into the royal box. The crowd stood in respectful silence until they sat down. Then the Queen leaned forward, looked around, and waved. The viewers gave her a round of applause. The King sternly stared straight ahead.

"That's got to be Kenny," said Caroline. The jousters were coming onto the field, riding their mounts past the royal box and saluting the King and Queen. They were inside their armor, and the only way to identify them was by the colors of their silks.

"How can you tell? Have you learned all the crests and insignia already?"

"No, but that one has the most elaborate silks. I'll bet that's Kenny." Her voice held a distinct edge of disdain, quite different from the admiring tone she had used when speaking of Kenny previously. Emily wondered what had happened to change her mind about him.

The jouster in question was indeed Prince Kenny, and he acquitted himself well. A jousting match is exciting, even to the uninitiated. Caroline and Emily soon found themselves caught up in the spectacle of huge horses thundering toward each other, hooves pounding, dirt and sawdust flying, riders leaning forward in their saddles; then the crash of wood on metal, as the blunted lances found their targets, and an armored man was thrown from his mount, to hit the ground with a bone-jarring thump.

Kenny raised his helm and took a victory lap around the field, raising his lance again to salute his parents as he rode by. The crowd applauded, except for Caroline, who seemed to be studying the sky and sun. The three girls to the left were watching him with rapturous eyes, as were the six girls to the right. One of them, a girl with very black hair, leaned over. "Hello. I'm Amy. Would you like to borrow my fan?"

"I'm Caroline," said Caroline. "Thank you. It is rather warm."

"That's Prince Kenny," said Amy. "Isn't he handsome?"

"His hair is so beautiful," said another girl.

"And he dresses so fine," said a third.

"He looks all right," said Caroline. "I can't say I really noticed him, myself."

"But you're in the princes' box. Don't you know him?"

"We're with Prince Hal and Prince Jeffrey." Caroline handed back the fan. "I believe I may have met Prince Kenneth once or twice."

"What?" said Emily.

"I suppose you can meet him now," said Amy. "He's coming over."

Prince Kenny had indeed left the field. Attendants had quickly stripped off most of his armor, and supplied him with a broad-brimmed hat with a long plume and shoes with long, pointed toes that curled back. From the approving looks that the other girls gave him, Emily gathered that this was the epitome of style. He approached the box with his helmet under his arm, tossed it in, and vaulted over the rail. "Wine," he snapped to a waiter.

"Yes, sire."

The prince sank into a chair and accepted a goblet. Then, seeming to notice Caroline and Emily for the first time, he raised it to them in a mocking toast. "To success on the field," he said. "For myself, and for my brother Jeffrey."

Caroline ignored him. "What about Hal?" said Emily.

"Two out of three isn't bad. And it's simply a waste of breath, not to mention good wine, to toast to Hal.

Swordfighting? What does that little twerp know about swordfighting?"

Caroline remained silent. Emily had heard her say much the same thing, several times that afternoon. Now she saw the blond girl's fingers tighten around the railing. There was nothing she could say. Emily was in the same position. Caroline might be *almost* a princess, but at the moment she was still a commoner, and she could not talk back to a prince, at least not publicly, and certainly not in his own box. Emily, too, was here only as a favor from Prince Hal, and was about to start a career that depended on receiving royal favors. So she kept her voice mild. "What is it about Prince Hal that upsets you so, Your Highness?" she asked.

"I don't like his taste in clothes," said Kenny, not looking at her. He was watching Caroline.

Caroline turned to him and smiled sweetly. "You fought an excellent joust, Prince Kenneth."

"Okay," said Kenny. "You won't be baited. Clever girls." He tossed off his wine. "Much as I'd like to stay and see Hal get beaten like a rug, I've got other things to do. See you later." He disappeared without waiting for an answer. The three noble daughters on Emily's side and the six noble girls on Caroline's side all looked after him with longing eyes.

"That's Prince Kenny," one whispered to Caroline. "Isn't he handsome?" Caroline shrugged.

"I still say he's a jerk," said Emily.

"He was trying to provoke us."

"Why? Did he want some sort of incident that would force the King to call off your engagement?"

"So Hal would turn into a frog? Eh, maybe. But I think he just likes being mean. I'm glad you didn't say anything out of place."

"Give me some credit. What did you two quarrel about?"

"Quarrel? We didn't quarrel."

"I still have to say I'm surprised. I thought you were attracted to Kenny. Yesterday you were telling me how handsome you thought he was."

"Prince Kenny? Handsome?" Caroline appeared to think about this. "I suppose so. I can't recall that he ever struck me as anything special. If I said otherwise, I'm sure it was just out of politeness."

"Say what?"

"Naturally, since I've been engaged to Prince Hal all along, I really haven't been paying attention to other boys. It wouldn't be right."

"What?"

"In any case, I've always said that looks are not that important in a man."

"What?" Emily's voice rose an octave. The other girls looked at her.

"What matters most is . . . oh, here's Jeff! Isn't he fine?"

Prince Jeffrey was wearing a brightly colored tunic with a ruffled collar and a silk sash. His hair was brushed back from his face and fell down his back, out from under his hat, which sported a fancy ostrich plume. Like Kenny, he eschewed the stairs into the princes' box and vaulted the rail. He gave Emily a smile and a shoulder squeeze, and Caroline a brief hug. It would have been briefer, but Caroline seemed reluctant to let go. "Aren't you in the games this year?"

"I didn't make it into the finals. Too much time working on the books and not enough time practicing. I came up to watch Hal."

Emily was watching Caroline, and Caroline was looking at Jeff with shining eyes. The younger girl had to admit that she had no idea what was going on in Caroline's head and gave up speculating about it. She said to Jeff, "I'm amazed that Hal got so far. He didn't seem so skilled with that sword the night we saw him fight."

"Yes," said Jeff. "Ah, a lot of people are surprised by Hal."

The girls in the adjoining boxes were looking at Prince Jeffrey with admiration and at Caroline and Emily with more than a little jealousy. Their attention was distracted when the first contestant in the magic sword division took the field. A short, slight figure moved into the circle of sawdust. It was Prince Hal.

A shout and a roar went up from the crowd. It was a friendly roar. It was a roar containing applause and a good deal of laughter. It was a roar of friendship. It was not, however, a roar containing respect or admiration. It was the kind of acknowledgment that a well-liked clown might receive. And there is nothing wrong with that, if you are a clown.

But Hal accepted the applause in good spirits, bowing to the spectators on either side and bowing more deeply to his parents in the royal box. Amy whispered to Emily, "There's Prince Hal. He's sort of cute, don't you think?"

Emily scowled.

Caroline was still talking to Jeff. "So the jousting, archery, and swordfighting are the three big events?"

"Four. The magic swordfighting is a different event, separate from the real swordfighting."

"How much is the prize money?"

"I don't know," said Jeff. "It's not bad. It's a nice piece of change, but mostly contestants do it for the honor and glory and that sort of stuff. Of course, we don't get any money out of it anyway."

Caroline frowned. "You don't?"

"Kenny and I always decline them, and so will Hal. The royal family supplies the awards, so it would just be giving money to ourselves. It would look tacky. So we always turn it down. The people then think that we're just doing it for the sport, and that's what we tell them. But of course, it's our own money we're declining, so it's just the same thing as awarding to ourselves anyway."

"But Hal said—"

"The prize money comes out of the gate receipts, but we still make a profit on them. So it works out well for everyone."

"But Hal is expecting to win money," said Caroline. "He told me that. He's expecting to win a lot."

Jeff looked uncomfortable. "Oh that. That's, um, something else."

Caroline looked at him in puzzlement, then shrugged. She edged up closer to Jeff. "Tell me about your sword-fighting. How far along did you get in the preliminaries? Did you win any tournaments last year?"

"Excuse me." Emily interjected herself, both into the

conversation and physically between the two friends. She pulled Caroline to the back of the box and hissed in her ear, "Caroline, what are you doing! You can't flirt with Prince Jeff. Not when you're engaged to Hal! He's right there on the field in front of you."

"I'm not flirting! I never flirt. I'm just being friendly. Jeff has been friendly to us, I'm being friendly back. You should be, too."

"Okay, I'll start talking to him right now."

"No! I mean, don't interrupt me. Um, it will make you seem rude. Just watch the tournament."

She turned away and stood beside Jeff again. Emily glared at her back, then stood on the other side of the Prince. Jeff was watching the field. "Here comes Hal's first opponent. A man by the name of Terence Aviral. He uses a sword called Destiny. About a hundred and twenty years old. A very good knight named Peregrine had his skill put into it."

Although Hal had gotten cheers, Aviral got steady applause. It was obvious he was the crowd's favorite, at least for serious betting. He had red hair and was a little over six feet tall.

"He has a long reach," said Jeff. "That's a big advantage over Hal."

"Hal isn't going to get hurt, is he?" Emily looked over the two contestants carefully. Hal was wearing a light armor breastplate and leather gauntlets. It seemed like very little protection. Across the field the King was leaning back in his chair. Hal's mother was leaning forward, anxiously twisting a handkerchief.

"He'll be fine," said Jeff, not sounding at all convinced.

"I just hope he doesn't make a fool of himself again," grumbled Caroline. "Where's everybody going?"

In the other boxes, the girls were getting out of their seats, picking up their pocketbooks, and making final adjustments to their hair. "A good time to take a break," said Amy.

"Aren't you going to watch the fight?"

Amy glanced back over her shoulder. "What's there to watch? We'll be back in time for the real match."

All through the stands the spectators were getting out of their seats and trickling toward the food wagons and the beverage booths, while people in the upper rows took advantage of the opportunity to slide down to lower, better seats. "It doesn't seem right," said Emily. "They shouldn't walk out on Hal like that. I think it's very rude."

Caroline was also watching the crowd. "I'm staying. Although I really don't want to see Hal get clobbered. It was embarrassing enough the last time. I just hope this is short."

"He's out!" said Jeff. "Aviral's out!"

"What!" Both girls turned their heads. Hal had already sheathed his sword and was tucking his dagger back into his belt. His tall opponent was leaning over to pick up his sword, where it had been knocked from his hand. He straightened up and shook Hal's outstretched hand with an expression of pained incomprehension, the look of a puppy that chased a wagon when the wheels suddenly reversed direction and backed over his tail.

The girls who were leaving their boxes had done an about-face and rushed to the rail. The scene was repeated all around the fairgrounds. The noise level rose,

but Emily could discern a string of repeated queries—
"What happened? "Prince Hal defeated Aviral?" "How?"
"Did you see it?" Somewhat belatedly a smattering of
applause started in one corner of the stands and was
briefly picked up by the rest of the crowd, but most people were more surprised than excited.

"Well," said Emily, "that was short."

Caroline was hopping up and down with excitement
and clapping wildly. "Yes! Yes! That's my Hal," she
shouted. "Did you see him?" she asked Amy. "The
Prince and I are engaged, you know."

"I expected this to be a pretty tight match," said Amy.
"I was going to place a small wager on him myself, but
I didn't have time."

"Wager," said Emily. She thought for a minute, then
looked back in the direction of the betting tables. "Jeff,
did Hal bet on himself to win the tournament?"

"Well, kind of."

"Kind of? How do you *kind of* place a bet?"

"He asked me to place the bets for him."

"All right. So he is gambling on himself."

"Not exactly."

"Jeff!"

Hal's next opponent was coming onto the field. He
was not a particularly tall man, but he certainly had a
longer reach than the Prince. He had dark hair that
gleamed with oil and a waxed and pointed mustache of
the style favored by Melinower's serious duelists. His
name was Sir Timothy Bournesse, a young nobleman of
moderate wealth. But wealthy enough to hire masters in
the art of defense, and with the leisure time to practice

it. He bowed to the King and Queen, then he bowed to Hal, but with watchful and suspicious eyes.

The King was leaning forward in his chair.

Hal bowed back.

"It won't be so easy this time," said Jeff. "Bournesse has been warned."

"What's his sword?"

"It's called the Spirit of Amagon. Amagon was the site of a big battle where Sir Timothy's ancestors fought and were awarded their lands and title. The sword has been in his family for a long time. It may not be that good a sword. I can't think that anyone did much with it before Sir Timothy. But Timmy's pretty damn good even without a magic sword."

"How did Hal win the first match? Was it luck?"

"No," said Jeff. "Watch and see."

The two swordsmen were standing in a circle of sand some ten paces in diameter. Leaving the circle meant you lost the match. So did striking your opponent below the waist or above the neck. In the latter case, of course, your opponent might not live to appreciate your losing. But killing your opponent in the ring was frowned upon. Good sportsmanship was taken seriously in Melinower.

Which was not to say accidents didn't happen.

A solid stab to the torso could win the match, if the referee decided so. A slash gained you points. So did a hit on the arm or shoulder. Contestants could pick up some nasty wounds in a Melinower sword match. Some people claimed that the spectators came to swordfighting tournaments hoping to see blood drawn, that they secretly rooted for an accidental death. These people were considered spoilsports. The spectators all assured one another that they were there to admire the technical proficiency of the combatants. They had not the least desire to see one of them injured. And certainly not killed. Of course not. Not at all. That would be tragic.

They also agreed that it was certainly exciting when it did happen.

Sir Timothy stood balanced on the balls of feet, his dagger in front of him and the Spirit of Amagon pointed up in a high guard. Across the sand Hal stood much the same way, except the Asian sword was pointed down in a low guard. Jeff nodded approvingly. Hal did not have the upper body strength of Sir Tim and was conserving his energy. The referee circled the sand ring and rang a bell to start the round.

"Go Hal!" screamed Caroline.

Hal's eyes flicked to her. Instantly, Sir Timothy saw his opening and made his thrust. Just as fast, Hal's blade parried the Spirit of Amagon, while Hal drew a cut with his dagger. There was a distinct metallic scrape as the point scratched Sir Timothy's breastplate, then the two men leaped apart.

"Point for Hal," said Jeff, watching the referee. "Not a kill strike."

There was a round of applause from the crowd. "Good job, Hal," shouted Caroline.

The two opponents circled each other. Sir Timothy was watching Hal warily. He hadn't seen a parry like that before, but he wasn't going to be taken by surprise again.

This time Hal made the first move. He feinted with his blade, Sir Timothy moved to parry it with his dagger, but Hal shifted the blade fluidly and slashed it across Sir Timothy's chest.

"Another point," said Jeff.

"Hal should be the winner," Caroline pouted.

"Not for a slash. You need a stab for that. Or one more point."

There was more applause from the crowd, sustained this time. Sir Timothy was scowling. Caroline beamed. "The slash is one of my fiancé's favorite moves," she told Amy. "I remember when the Prince was challenged to a duel—this was only a few nights before we became engaged—they were using padded swords and . . ."

"Here they go again," said Emily.

The round started, and Sir Timothy made his move immediately, hoping to catch Hal unawares. It was a classic overhand attack. Hal parried it with his dagger and simultaneously made another of his shifting, slashing attacks, so fast Sir Timothy had no hope of deflecting it. Metal blade rang on metal armor, and the match was Hal's.

Once again there was a smattering of applause. The Queen was standing up, and even the King was slowly putting his hands together. But the stands were still pretty much empty.

"Where is everyone?" asked Caroline. "Don't they want to see this?"

Amy shrugged. "It's magic swordfighting."

"So?"

"Well, you know, it isn't really a sport. It's basically just sort of a gambler's thing. I know this is when all the big money changes hands, but most people think it's a bit—um—sleazy, I guess."

"Oh, for goodness sake," muttered Caroline. "Doesn't that boy ever do anything a girl can be proud of?"

Prince Kenny suddenly appeared in the box again. He elbowed aside the two girls and leaned over the rail. "What the hell is Hal up to? Dammit, I had money bet on Bournesse."

"He's been practicing," said Jeff.

"Yeah, right. Where did he get that sword?" Kenny stalked back out without waiting for an answer.

"Don't go away mad," Caroline called after him. Emily was laughing behind her hands.

There was a break while groundskeepers came out and raked the sand. Hal bounded over to the box. "What do you think?"

"You're doing well," Caroline assured him. She gave him a hug. Emily looked away. Jeff looked away also.

"Well, thanks." Hal separated himself from Caroline. "Jeff, did you place the bets?"

"Yeah, sort of."

"Yeah, sort of? How do you *sort of* place a bet?"

"It's kind of a long story. Just stay focused on the next match."

"Right. Did Mom give you any trouble about the jewels?"

"You could say that, yes."

"But she went along with it?"

"I'll explain later. You better get back to the ring."

"All right. One more match, then we celebrate."

"Don't get overconfident. You still have to win this one."

"Relax." Hal pulled the sword halfway out of the scabbard and snapped it back in. "I've got it taken care of."

Caroline frowned. "That isn't the sword you bought at the tavern, is it?"

"The very same."

"But how did you—"

"Practice," said Hal. "Plus natural talent, of course."

"Of course," said Jeff. "Now if Mr. Natural will get his butt back to the ring, we can finish this thing."

"See you later," said Hal, and trotted back to the ring.

"What's this about bets?" said Caroline. "Jeff, tell me."

Jeff sat down and placed his fingertips together. He looked from one girl to the other. "The odds against Hal are very high. So high, in fact, that a large number of bets, judiciously placed, would resolve our family's financial problems." He said this in a very pragmatic tone of voice, trying to convey the impression that gambling your way out of debt was a reasonable thing to do, not an invitation to disaster.

"But he has to win! How did Hal come to be such an expert swordsman?"

"He has a magic sword."

"They all have magic swords," said Caroline. "Jeff, we were there the night Hal bought that sword. We saw him fight with it. And Jeff, he couldn't hack his way out of a paper bag with that thing."

"There's a trick to using it. Hal figured out the trick."

"What about the bets?" said Emily. "Did you place the bets?"

Jeff let out a long breath and nervously rubbed the back of his neck. "We didn't have the money to place the bets we needed. Our financing kind of fell through. So I—uh—borrowed the money from the army officers' pension fund."

"They let you do that?"

"Well, I'm a prince, after all. And an army officer myself. And I told them I'd pay them back by tomorrow."

"All right," said Emily. "Hal wins this match, you get the money, and you pay back the officers' club out of the winnings. As long as Hal does his part . . ."

"No," said Jeff. "That's the problem. I have to pay back the pension fund before I can collect the winnings."

"Ouch," said Caroline.

"The officers placed the bets. They also kept the chits. We have until tomorrow to return the money to the pension fund and collect the chits. Otherwise, the army officers cash in the chits, and the pension fund gets the money."

"Nice deal for the pension fund," said Caroline. "How do you intend to get the money, Jeff?"

"I don't know yet. I was buying time, hoping something would come up. I'm going to think of something."

"Did you tell Hal?"

"Not yet. I didn't want to discourage him."

"Right," said Emily. "Let's keep a positive outlook. Something *will* come up. The first thing is that Hal has to win the final match."

"Right. But actually, I don't think that will be a problem. He's just fought two very good swordsmen, and neither one could touch him."

"Oh dear," said Caroline. She pointed. "Is that who he's fighting next?"

The other two looked. Approaching the ring was a large man, muscular and very broad-shouldered. He had shaggy black hair and a thick dark beard, and carried a cut-and-thrust sword in his hand.

"Don't you recognize him?"

Jeff looked at the man carefully. "No. I've never seen this guy before."

"He looks familiar," said Emily. "But I can't place him."

"It's Bear McAllistair," said Caroline. "He's the man who sold Hal that magic sword."

Emily leaned out of the box, as far over as she could, trying to see Hal's face. The youngest prince was completely without expression. "I think he's worried," said Caroline. "He looks worried. Does he look worried to you?"

"No," said Emily, who wasn't sure.

"There's nothing to worry about," said Jeff, who definitely sounded worried. "Who is this guy? You say he sold Hal the magic sword?"

"Yes," said Caroline. "And he beat Hal when Hal was fighting with it."

"Oh that. Uh, don't worry about it."

"Right," said Emily. "Caroline, Hal is fighting much better that he did at the tavern. There's a trick to using this sword, remember, and Hal figured out the trick."

"Unless Bear knew the trick all along and was setting Hal up."

"No. No, I don't believe it. How could he know Hal would enter the tournaments? Hal never entered before."

"Look!" snapped Caroline.

Emily looked. The two men had come together in a clash of ringing steel and flashing blades. Cut, thrust, parry, counterthrust, parry again, and the two men drew apart.

"No hits," said Jeff. "No points."

"But look how fast Bear was," said Caroline. "Emily, doesn't he seem much faster than he was at the tavern?"

"Yes, you're right. Oh no. He did trick us."

"This man's a pro," said Jeff. He was watching the fight with narrow eyes. "He's got experience. He's probably been in the country, working the small tournaments. He might have staged that fight to look slow, so as to get better betting odds."

"That's despicable," said Emily. "How can people be so dishonest?"

"Um, I don't know."

Hal suddenly attacked, leaping forward and swinging his sword in a vertical cut. The blade rang against Bear's steel and for long seconds the two men were all over the ring, weapons glittering in the bright sunlight. There was another round of applause from the crowd, which had grown larger, and Emily saw a few drops of blood on Bear's sleeve.

"Bear's hit."

"Just a scratch," said Jeff.

"Point for Hal, though," said Caroline.

But there was no time for jubilation. Bear feinted, Hal countered, Bear caught Hal's blade with his dagger, and at the same time drove his own sword into Hal's arm.

There were screams from the women in the stands, and some ragged cheers from the men who bet on Bear. The news quickly spread that blood had been drawn, and ticket holders rushed to their seats. Hal staggered back to the edge of the circle. He dropped his dagger.

"Yes!" said Jeff.

"What!" Emily had turned pale. "Jeff, he's hurt!"

"Yes, and it was deliberate. Bear went for his dagger arm! You know what that means? He still hasn't figured out that Hal can parry with the blade."

The tip of Bear's sword had passed clean through Hal's arm, and blood was flowing freely. Caroline felt sick. The spectators were all on their feet now. The Queen was weeping openly, and even the King was out of his seat. Hal's teeth were clenched, and his face showed nothing but pure pain. He put his arm in his pocket to support it. But he still kept his sword up at middle guard. Bear circled him warily.

"Come on, Hal," said Jeff quietly. "Strike now, before you lose too much blood."

Hal apparently had the same thought. He aimed a stab at Bear's chest, but Bear knocked it aside and charged forward. As Hal had no dagger for close-in defense, the big man easily got inside the prince's guard, the points of both his sword and dagger aimed true, victory but an instant away.

Yet even at that last moment Hal twisted his body and Bear's sword passed harmlessly by the young man's head. The miss was by a fraction of an inch, but it was enough. And even as he twisted Hal swept the oriental sword in one of those blindingly fast counterattacks, so familiar in the east, still surprising in the west. Bear felt the point of his dagger penetrate the prince's clothing, but it was too late. The edge of Hal's sword drew a line of blood across the big man's upper arm, sliced through his tunic, and scraped along his breastplate, trailing sparks that were clearly visible to the crowd even in broad daylight. Hal had won.

Applause from the crowd. Hal dropped his sword in the dirt. Bear caught him as he seemed about to topple forward. The next instant Bear was pushed aside as a blond girl in a white dress wrapped her arms around Hal, laughing and crying all at once. The crowd applauded again, more enthusiastically. The blond girl was followed by a raven-haired girl, and finally by Prince Jeffrey. Bear nodded deferentially. Jeff nodded back and put his arm around Hal's shoulders. "Let's go."

"We won," Hal whispered. "Let's collect our bets."

"Let's get your arm taken care of," said Jeff.

Emily had felt like crying all day. She wasn't crying now. And she hadn't actually cried at any time. But she *felt* like crying. And she couldn't explain why.

She made her way through the streets of Melinower, wearing the garb of a sorcerer's apprentice. The city was still unfamiliar to her, but she could find her way to Bungee's tower. He had sent word to her that he had an

ointment to speed the healing of Prince Hal's wound—
Bungee had a firm grip on the business aspects of sorcery and knew the importance of networking. Around
her the streets were filled with nervous, tense people,
with shopkeepers standing outside their doors, looking
up and down the street and chatting with the passersby,
not wanting to go inside for fear of missing something.
It was the kind of shared foreboding that cities get when
word comes that an invading army is just over the horizon, or a severe storm is blowing in from the sea, even
though no overt sign of danger has yet appeared. There
was an awful lot of what looked like soldiers in the streets,
although Emily knew that they were actually the Royal
Guard. Caroline and Jeff and Hal had told her about the
upcoming expulsion. So far the King had made no offi-
cial pronouncement. But he didn't have to, really. Jeff
and Hal said that if you got people stirred up enough,
the thing would take off on its own. The ruler just had to
look the other way.

Happily ever after, Emily thought. Caroline got to
marry a prince. Hal was rescued from being a frog.
Emily got a first-rate apprenticeship. The royal family
would erase its debts. It was amazing how things just
worked out well for everyone. Only the Jews would suffer, and surely they were used to it by now.

So why did she feel like crying?

She reached Bungee's tower, pushed past the impos-
ing iron door, and went up the spiral stairs. And was surprised to find Twigham there. "Twigham?"

The two men were sitting at the long table, smoking
their pipes. From the amount of smoke that still hung

in the air, they had either been there a long time, or had been smoking furiously, or both. There were the remains of tea things on the table and half a plate of lemon cookies.

"Hello, my dear." Twigham rose, and she gave him a hug. "I was just reviewing your apprenticeship with your new master."

"Do you know Bungee?"

"Not until today, no. I hope you don't think I intended to interfere in your schooling. But Ripplebrook has to look after its daughters. Nosiness is one of the prerogatives of being old."

"He wanted to make sure your apprenticeship contract was aboveboard," said Bungee. "Quite right, too. Amanda would have done the same."

"I went over it carefully," said Emily. "What was wrong with it?"

"The contract? Nothing at all."

"Something was wrong." Emily pointed to the empty tobacco pouches and the piles of ash in the tray. "You've gone through about three pipes each. Twigham, you only do that when you've got a particularly knotty problem to work out."

"Ah." Twigham looked at Bungee.

Bungee passed Emily the plate of lemon cookies. "Make yourself a cup of tea, Emily. And then sit down. I've been explaining Amanda's spell to Mr. Twigham."

"The problem," said Bungee, "is that your mother's spell doesn't work."

"Which spell is that?"

"The one by which she turned Prince Hal into a frog."

"Excuse me, Master Bungee. As your apprentice, I don't want to be contradictory. But the fact that the spell *did* work shows that it *does* work."

"And that is the problem. Caroline cannot marry Prince Hal. It lacks magicality."

There was a short silence. Then Emily said, "Was that my cue to ask what magicality is? You've mentioned it before."

"No," said Bungee. "I was just composing my thoughts."

Twigham said, "Master Bungee has been explaining his theory to me. It is quite fascinating."

Bungee put down his pipe, adjusted his hat, and straightened the collar of his robes, all unconsciously, as if he were preparing to make a speech. Since the job of a master sorcerer is to teach apprentices as well as extract work from them, Emily was not surprised to hear him adopt a lecturing tone. She settled back to listen.

"It's one of the eternal questions of sorcery," he said. "Why do some spells work, and others don't? When you're starting out you concentrate on learning how to cast spells and prepare potions and many practical and hardworking sorcerers spend their whole lives perfecting and expanding that field. But some of us seek to go further, to find the underlying principles that govern magic."

"Like the Law of Transformation and the Law of Similarities," said Emily.

"Exactly so. One of the things that has perplexed magicians for years is why a spell will work sometimes and not at other times. Why some things can be magicked and others cannot. Why some people fall under enchantments or curses and others seem immune. I have occupied myself with these questions for many years, and lately I have begun to formulate what I believe is another underlying law of magic. I call it the Law of Magicality, and what it means is that for a spell to work, the spell itself must 'feel' magical."

He paused, waiting for the reaction from Emily, waiting for the inevitable question. Emily frowned. "I know you realize, Master Bungee, that you are not giving me a very helpful definition."

"I do realize that, my dear, and at this point I don't have a very precise definition of magicality, nor have I even come up with a better term. But to give you a working definition, magic works when even an ordinary person, who has no knowledge of magic, recognizes that magic has occurred. If it doesn't seem magical to him or her, it won't be."

Another pause. "I hate to sound obtuse," Emily began.

"Let me see if I understand it," said Twigham. "Emily, if a raven was to fly in through this window, is it possible that it could be enchanted?"

"Certainly it is possible," said Emily, "although it could also be an ordinary raven."

"An owl may or may not be enchanted. Or a hawk. A bluebird."

"Sure."

"What if a squirrel were to run in the window?"

Emily laughed.

"You see," said Bungee. "You laughed at the idea of a magic squirrel. Unicorns are magical, and dragons, and cats, especially black ones, but who ever heard of a magic slug? And in fact, it is nearly impossible to put a spell on a squirrel or a slug, or even a goat, and when it does take it wears off in no time. Fireflies are magical, and so are ladybugs, and you can enchant a spider with ease, but when was the last time you heard of a magic termite?"

"Well, isn't that what you'd expect? You can't create a magic squirrel, so people haven't learned to think of squirrels as being magical?"

"I thought the same way at first," said Bungee. "But now I think differently. Consider the case of a child, switched at birth through some enchantment and raised as a swineherd. Later, through yet more magical means, he finds out that he is really the son of . . . who?"

"A lord," said Emily.

"Perhaps even a king," said Twigham.

"Right," said Bungee. "You never hear of a swineherd inheriting a bricklaying business, even though it would certainly be a step up from herding swine. Wait a minute."

He stepped into a corner of his lab and came back with a chalice. Inside a liquid was bubbling and giving off small clouds of white vapor. He set it in front of Twigham, who put the back of his hand against the cup. It was stone cold.

"One of my most powerful potions," said Bungee. "Notice how it bubbles and steams, even though it is not boiling. Over the years I've noticed that the best potions always bubble and steam. And that they work even better when you drink them out of chalices. People *expect* a magic potion to bubble and steam, and to be drunk from a chalice. Or to be an emerald green liquid, held in a crystal vial. Certainly there are potions that are murky yellow and can be swilled from a wooden mug. But the vast majority of them are ineffective."

"So the potion works because people believe that it works?" said Twigham. "Because it looks magical?"

"No," said Emily. "Real magic works whether you believe it or not. It's one of the ways we tell the real magicians from the charlatans."

"Emily is correct. No, what I call magicality is a property of the spell itself. You can tell if a spell is going to work or not by whether it *seems* magical."

"I get it," said Emily. "Like turning flax into gold. Gold seems magical. No one has a formula that turns, say, mud into cast iron, even though cast iron is more valuable than mud."

"Hmm, yes, you have the idea. Of course, that's alchemy. It's outside my field of study, so I'm not certain that the theory holds up there."

"But isn't this subjective? Wouldn't every person have a different idea of what seems magical and what doesn't?"

"I think not. I have been trying to quantify magicality and have had some little success. I expect the work will take many years. But the results I have obtained so far— well, there is a problem. Emily, we must discuss our Prince Hal."

Emily suddenly found that she was not breathing. She forced herself to start again and hoped the two men hadn't noticed. "What is the problem with Prince Hal?"

"He is not handsome."

Emily looked at Twigham. "Not again. I thought we'd been through all this."

Twigham was scraping out his pipe with a little jack-knife. He tapped the ashes onto his tea saucer. "So did I. Apparently there is more to it."

"Much more," said Bungee. "I don't know exactly how your mother enchanted Prince Hal, and there is no way to find out now. But I have worked through every variation of the frog spell that I can get my hands on, and they are all very clear. The beautiful girl marries a handsome prince. There is no way around it. Anything else lacks magicality."

"We *have* been through this. We all talked it over back in Ripplebrook. To marry any kind of a prince at all is a step up."

"Magic doesn't work that way. You can't negotiate with a spell. A beautiful girl finds the frog and kisses it. There is absolutely no record of a plain girl ever finding the frog. Maybe they never find it. Maybe they find it and kiss it, but they can't break the spell. It's always a beautiful girl, and she always marries a handsome prince."

"But I told you that Hal had been turned into a frog and you know how he looks and you told me to make sure they got married." Emily found herself getting a bit shrill.

"True. Actually I said that Caroline must get married, but that is nit-picking. I had not seen Caroline. I did not realize how attractive she is. Which means she's got to be able to marry a *really* handsome prince."

"But Caroline likes Hal!"

"Marrying a handsome prince is meant to be a reward for her perseverance and self-sacrifice in breaking the spell. She's not supposed to be doing him a favor."

"She's not doing him a favor!" Emily was really

shouting now. "Caroline's lucky to find a boy like Hal. Hal is a very nice person! He's loyal to his family and he's good to people and he's hardworking and smart, and as far as looks go, I happen to think that he's really, really . . . *cute*! Sort of."

She heard a cracking noise. Twigham was trying so hard not to laugh that he bit through the stem of his pipe.

Bungee had also raised his voice. "Emily, look at my bookshelves. You could spend a year combing through the histories, the legends, the tales, and the fables, and you will not find one single story about a beautiful maiden who marries a *sort of cute* prince."

"Fine," snapped Emily. "I'll tell them to break it off right now. You have the ointment or not?"

"By the door."

She scowled at the ointment—it was an emerald green liquid in a crystal vial—and snatched it up as she stalked out. Bungee sat down heavily. "Damn. I should not have raised my voice. I have been too long without a student. I'm out of practice." He looked around for the teapot and tried to pour a cup. It was empty.

Twigham was putting away his pipe things. "Emily will understand. I'll catch up with her. You are quite sure about this spell?"

"You can never be certain of another wizard's spell. Especially Amanda's." Bungee was boiling more water. "But I can tell you there is something wrong with that one. It shouldn't have worked. An unhandsome prince like Hal should never have turned into a frog in the first place. And a beautiful girl like Caroline should not have broken the spell even when it did work, which it shouldn't have."

"So what will happen?"

"She won't marry him."

"Does that mean something bad will happen to Prince Hal?"

"It could."

"I'd better catch up with Emily," Twigham said.

"Here's the problem," Emily told Twigham. "The problem is that a lot of these big-city sorcerers think they're better at magic than Mummy was. Maybe Mummy didn't write learned papers and present them at sorcery conferences, but she knew how to cast a spell. She didn't worry about the 'magicality' of it. If she wanted to turn a prince into a frog, he turned into a frog. End of story."

"Or perhaps the beginning of one," said Twigham. "Your mother was deeper than you give her credit for, Emily. You don't think Bungee is right?"

They were coming up to the gates of Melinower Palace. Emily was now familiar enough to the guards that she could come and go at will, but Twigham was not allowed to pass. "I don't know," she said. "I'm just an apprentice, and I've got two more years to go at that. But it sounds like Master Bungee has come up with a circular argument. He says that certain spells don't work because they're not magical enough, then says that if a spell isn't magical enough, it won't work. Isn't that just saying that a spell doesn't work because it doesn't work?"

"I have to admit it sounded more credible when he described it than when you do," said Twigham.

"Either way, there's nothing I can do about it. Caroline and Hal have made up their minds. And I have to go in now."

"And I must return to Ripplebrook. Give Caroline my best wishes and tell her that we are all happy for you both."

Emily hugged him, then made her way into the palace. It took some time. The hallways were crowded with Royal Guards and their officers, bustling up and down the stairs, shoving through doorways, carrying written orders on folded papers that had been sealed with string and wax. She thought she heard Prince Kenny's voice, confidently shouting commands, but she didn't see him.

The others were in Jeff's suite of rooms—Hal and Caroline and Jeff and Bear McAllistair. Hal was lying on the bed. Jeff was sitting on his desk. Bear was standing at the wall, looking at Jeff's collection of swords. Everyone looked glum. No one was talking.

Caroline took the vial of ointment from Emily and began unwrapping the bandages on Hal's arm. "The Royal Surgeon looked at them while you were gone. He said it's a bad puncture, but clean, and if we keep changing the dressings, it will heal just fine."

Hal gave the slightest wince as she applied the ointment. "Bear, you want some of this also?"

"Guess I wouldn't mind, Your Highness."

Emily asked, "How are your wounds, Bear?"

"Just a couple of scratches, missy." He grinned. "Kind of deep scratches, mind you. I'm still trying to figure out how you won with that lousy sword, Your Highness."

"There's a trick to it," said Hal.

"What about the bets?" Emily said. "Were you able to come up with a way to collect while I was gone?"

Hal looked at Jeff. Jeff shook his head. "Nothing."

"It just seems so unfair. You borrow the money to redeem the chits, collect on the bets, and use the winnings to pay back the loan with interest. You would think that someone would want to make some easy money."

"I've sent couriers to everyone I know," said Jeff. "The problem is that they want to hold the chits as collateral for the loan. And the army officers, of course, don't want to give them up."

"It's not going to happen," said Hal. "If we could borrow money we wouldn't have had to go to the officers' pension fund in the first place. Dad has borrowed too much too often."

"I'll loan you my winnings, Your Highness," said Bear. "I've still got the second-place prize for magic swordfighting. Plus first place for the crossbow contest."

Hal shook his head. "Not enough to make a difference. You keep your money, Bear."

"We still have until tomorrow morning," said Emily. "Something might happen."

Hal said nothing. Jeff said, "All that is going to happen is that the Jews are going to be run out of the country." He heaved himself to his feet, took a sword down from the wall, and strapped it on.

"Where are you going?"

"I'm meeting with some of the officers. We're planning

to go into the city and help stand up against the Royal Guard."

"What?" said Caroline. "The army is going to stop the expulsion?"

"No." Jeff shook his head. "Dad ordered the army not to get involved. This is just some of the officers and myself. Out of uniform and off duty. We can't stop the expulsion but we can prevent some looting, protect people from getting beaten up, that sort of thing."

"You'd be surprised," put in Bear, "how often just a few men with swords have turned a mob away."

"Excuse me," said Hal. "Why wasn't I let in on this? You're going into the city without me? I think not."

"Get real, Hal. You're not going anywhere with that arm."

"Sorry, Your Highness," said Bear.

"You're taking Bear, and I gave him two cuts."

"Yeah, and he's four times your size, so percentage-wise he's half as wounded. Sit down, Hal. You lost too much blood, and if there's trouble, you wouldn't be able to fight."

"I can fight with my left hand."

"You can't fight worth spit with your left hand."

"It's a magic sword. It fights by itself."

"Sit down, Hal. Get some rest. I'll talk to you later."

"It makes sense that the army officers want to get involved," said Caroline. "A lot of the bookmakers are also the moneylenders who are about to get run out of town. I'm sure they don't want them leaving until the pension fund cashes in the bets."

"As a matter of fact, no." Jeff gave her a level, steady

look. "They're doing it because they're decent men who want to do the right thing, and *they're my friends*."

Caroline was embarrassed. "Sorry, Jeff. I guess I'm just feeling overly cynical."

"It's okay. I'll talk to you later. C'mon, Bear."

They left, and Caroline ran to the door to watch them go down the long hallway and down the stairs. She closed the carved oak door and stood with her back against it.

"Sorry about the dowry business," said Hal. "I know you like Jeff a lot."

"Don't worry about it, Hal. I'm engaged to you, and I won't let you down." There was a knock at the door, and she opened it to let Winthrop in.

"Good afternoon, sire." Jeff's valet was pushing a serving cart. "I have extra towels, clean bandages, and hot water for you."

"Put them on the sideboard, Winthrop."

"Also, Mrs. Winthrop has baked a cake for you, sire, and begs you to accept it with her humblest thanks. I took your advice and bet a shilling on the magic sword match. She was very pleased at the result."

"I don't doubt it," said Caroline.

"Great," said the Prince. "At least someone came out ahead on this."

"I wish I had placed a bet myself," said Caroline. "A hundred to one. Imagine."

"Where would you get money to bet with?" asked Emily.

"Can't you guess?"

"Oh, right."

"What?" said Hal. "Where would you get the money?"

"I'd have sold my hair to a wig shop."

"Oh," said Emily. "I thought you meant you were going to spin flax with that dwarf."

"This is one of those cream cakes," said Hal, lifting the cover. "I love these. Give my thanks to your wife, Winthrop."

"Don't be silly, Emily," said Caroline. "The idea is absurd. Besides, you told me that wouldn't work."

"I don't feel like eating anything now, Winthrop. Maybe I'll have some later. What wouldn't work, Caroline?"

"Spinning flax into gold."

"The Law of Similarities," said Emily.

"And the Law of Transformation."

"And what," said Hal, putting the cover back on the cake, "is the Law of Similarities?"

"It just means that if you're going to transmute one substance into another, the two have to look similar to begin with. Golden flax into golden metal, for example."

Hal did a funny thing. He stopped moving with the cover suspended over the cake and held it there for several minutes. He looked at the cake, but it was with that faraway look that meant he wasn't really seeing it. He was so obviously deep in thought that both girls, and Winthrop, stood still and silently watched him.

Finally, he put the cover down, leaned back on the bed, and said, "Okay, so what is the Law of Transformation?"

Caroline, looking at him curiously, picked up the slack on this one. "It means for a transformation to take place, there must be an exchange of magical power. Such as a loss of virginity."

"Right," said Hal instantly. He swung his legs off the bed and rose to his feet. A spell of dizziness overtook him, and he sat back down again, but got up a few moments later. "I'm okay. What was the name of the dwarf again? Was it Gerald?"

"Patrick," said Emily.

"It was Rumpelstiltskin," said Caroline. "How could you forget a name like that?"

"Where is he, do you know? Staying at the Bull and Badger?"

"No, he said he has a room at a goldsmith's shop on the edge of the Jewish quarter."

"I know it."

"He might not still be there."

"We'll find out." Hal was bustling around the room, strapping on his sword, grabbing a fresh shirt, and putting it on with the sleeve pulled down over his bandages. "Never let them see you bleed." He grabbed Emily by the hand. "Emily, do you still have the philosopher's stone?"

"Sure." She showed him the pouch around her neck.

"Then I'll need you to come with me. Caroline, go to the stables and get a coach. Tell them it's for the Prince and get the fastest team of horses they have available. Then you've got to find Jeff and bring him to the dwarf's place. Winthrop, go to Caroline's room, get her cloak, then show her to the stables."

"Right away, sire."

"Wait," said Caroline. "What's going on?" But Hal was already out the door, dragging Emily with him, and was immediately followed by Winthrop, leaving

Caroline alone in room. She picked up the cover herself and looked at the cake. "Either he's come up with
some big idea, or there's something really strange about
this cake." She tasted it. "Not bad." And went off to find
Jeff.

Among those who practice the art of defense, it is ax-
iomatic that a large man is better off with a club, while a
small man is better off with a knife. It is also well-known
that very few men will rush forward into a naked blade.
Something in the human psyche inhibits doing so. So
while a soldier will hold his knife behind him, to lure his
enemy in closer, the man defending his life will hold the
blade out in front of himself, to ward his opponents off.

Rumpelstiltskin was well aware of all of this. In fact he
had two knives, one in each hand, and was brandishing
them at the growing mass of men that faced him. There
were eight of them now, enough for mob psychology to
take effect. It was only a matter of time before the deadly
combination of stupidity, hysteria, and alcohol would
drive the men forward. Rumpelstiltskin knew he was in a
bad position. The location at the edge of the Jewish quarter meant it was among the more vulnerable. And assaults
of this sort, when all is said and done, are as much about
greed as they are about religious bigotry. The chance to
loot a goldsmith's shop was a powerful temptation.

So he paced back and forth just outside the door of

the shop, brandishing the knives and roaring threats like, "Back off, back off!" and "One step closer and I'll gut you like a fish!" and otherwise explaining that anyone who dared attack would be singing hymns with the angels and not as a tenor either.

His enthusiastic band of antagonists had formed themselves into a rough wedge shape, with the biggest of their lot, who was possibly also the meanest, dumbest, drunkest, or all of the above, at the point of the wedge. He was armed with a cudgel and was slowly edging closer, while the others were egging him on with shouts. Rumpelstiltskin had switched from threats to oaths, but these were getting increasingly drowned out by his opponents. The distance between Rumpelstiltskin and the point man was closing. He was swinging his cudgel before him in wide arcs. Finally, he raised it over his head and rushed the dwarf.

And found himself staring right at the point of Hal's sword.

Hal stepped through the doorway he had just opened behind Rumpelstiltskin. He pushed his sword forward, so that the point was just touching the man's chest. "Drop it."

The mob leader dropped the cudgel.

"Now get lost."

The mob retreated. Unfortunately, they did not disperse entirely, as Hal hoped, but merely backed across the street and re-formed. Hal, even with a sword, was not all that intimidating a figure. He realized this and pulled Rumpelstiltskin inside, then put the bar over the door.

"It's a goldsmith's shop," he said. "Barred windows,

heavy barred door. What were you doing outside instead of sheltering inside?"

"Just stalling for time," said Rumpelstiltskin. "It's not my shop. I was doing a favor for the guy who owns it, guarding the front door while he got his stock out the back. Where is Izzy anyway?"

"He's gone. He went out as we came in the back. Emily, you remember Rumpelstiltskin."

"Hello again."

"Charmed," said Rumpelstiltskin. Then recognition flashed on him and he turned to face Hal angrily. "You! Your Highness! Prince Hal! It's all your fault!"

"It is?"

"The match. The swordfight! I lost fifteen crowns because of you and that stupid magic sword. You played us all for suckers, throwing that fight at the tavern."

Hal made a clucking noise with his tongue. "It sounds like you've been gambling, Rumpelstiltskin. I'm shocked, truly shocked. Aren't you shocked, Emily?"

Emily nodded. "I shudder to think what other vices you have developed, Mr. Rumpelstiltskin. You realize, don't you, that impressionable young people like ourselves look to adults like you for role models?"

"Uh, well, it was just a friendly wager," said Rumpelstiltskin. He tossed the knives onto a counter. "Well, I think this part of town is getting too hot for me, especially considering I'm not even Jewish. I'll tell Izzy you came to his shop."

"Wait," said Hal. "Actually, we came to see you. Do you still have that spinning wheel, the one you said was magic?"

"It is magic. You just have to know how to use it."

There was a sudden series of splintering crashes, and the windows disintegrated. An onslaught of rocks came through the iron bars. Rumpelstiltskin ran to the door and flung it open. "Listen, you idiots! There's no gold in here! It's all been taken . . . dammit!" He slammed the door again and dropped the crossbar, just as the door bowed inward under a heavy blow. "These jerks are serious."

"The spinning wheel," said Hal. "Where is it?"

"Upstairs. And you know, right now I can make you a really good deal—" He was interrupted by another heavy crash. The wood around the bolt splintered.

"Guard the door," said Hal. "I'll get the wheel." He started up the narrow wooden ladder to the second floor. "Emily, be prepared to run."

"I'm prepared right now."

"Forget the wheel," said Rumpelstiltskin, as the door splintered further under another heavy blow. "We can come back for it later. They're looking for gold, they won't even notice it." He placed his shoulder against the door and leaned the weight of his small body against it. The next blow knocked him back off his feet. "This is what I get for trying to help people."

"Is this it?" called Hal. He reappeared with a wooden object slung over his shoulder and slid down the ladder, wincing as he hit the ground. "It's some sort of wheel, but it's not a spinning wheel."

Emily looked at it. It was a small, spoked wheel, set in a triangular frame of highly polished, dark wood. "What is it?"

"It's a spinning wheel," said Rumpelstiltskin. The pounding on the door was coming at a steady rate now, and the angry voices outside were growing louder. "Trust me, I've been making wheels since you kids were eating porridge. This kind is called a Castle Wheel. It's for little cottages where they don't have room for a Great Wheel. See, here's your foot pedals, and here's your spindle."

There was a bang. All three looked up. One of the metal bolts had popped from the door. "That's it," said Rumpelstiltskin. "Out the back. You coming, or not?"

"One more question," said Hal. "What was his name?"

Rumpelstiltskin was already sliding between the empty work benches. "Who?"

"The sorcerer. You said a sorcerer commissioned you to build this wheel, but he never showed up to pay for it. What was his name?"

Rumpelstiltskin reached the back door and pushed a chair up against it. He had to stand on the chair to reach the heavy oak bar, which he wrenched up and tossed to the floor. "The sorcerer?" He hopped down, kicked the chair out of the way, and grabbed the door handle. "I think he called himself Torricelli. Why?"

"That's it, then," said Hal. "Let's go." He lifted the wheel with his good arm, grabbed Emily's wrist with the other hand, and in a few steps was right behind Rumpelstiltskin. The three of them burst out the door in one mass, slammed it behind them, and turned into the narrow street.

And came face-to-face with Prince Kenny.

Kenny raised an eyebrow. "Really, Hal. Have you decided to join in the looting? I'd have thought that beneath you."

Kenny was in his Guard uniform, with half a dozen of the Guards with him. They made for a menacing tableau. Unlike Jeff's soldiers, who tended to be well disciplined and professional, the Royal Guards were considered by many to be little more than uniformed thugs. Certainly they were the better class of thug, and corruption in the corps was kept at a minor level, but Kenny's friends did not shy from the use of excessive force. Or miss out on an opportunity to gratuitously break some heads.

Hal looked down the street. He could see Jeff and Caroline, trying to get the carriage through a mass of people. He quickly looked away and shifted the wheel under his arm. "Just picking up some last-minute bargains, Kenny.

Going out of business sales, and all that. Emily saw this spinning wheel in the shop window and had to have it."

"Oh?" Kenny looked at her quizzically. "I didn't know sorceresses spun."

"Oh, I don't," said Emily. "But it was such a good price. Think of all the money I saved."

Rumpelstiltskin said nothing. He knew Prince Kenny was not like Prince Hal, and commoners did not initiate conversations with royalty.

Kenny looked at the shop door. "Goldsmith," he said. "And a moneylender?"

Hal shrugged. "Most goldsmiths are."

"And a bookmaker?"

"Most of the bookmakers are also moneylenders. As our family knows too well."

"Mmm," said Kenny. He turned to his men. "Search the shop."

Jeff and Caroline were just a block away now. Hal stepped aside. The Guards pulled the door open just as a splintering crash came from the front. The shop filled with angry men.

"Looters," said Hal. "We ran into them at the front door."

"Are they?" said Kenny. He smiled thinly.

"Aren't you going to stop them?" said Emily. "They're destroying that man's shop."

"That man is a Jew and won't be returning. But if he left behind any financial records pertaining to Dad's debts, I want to make sure they're destroyed. Get in there," he told the Guards. "And make sure they do a good job."

The carriage was just down the street now. Kenny still hadn't seen it. Hal said, "There's nothing upstairs. I already looked."

"Yeah?" Kenny gave Hal a long stare. "I think I'll check the upstairs myself."

He went inside. Hal grabbed Emily's hand and tore off down the street. He reached the carriage, flung the door open, and tossed in the spinning wheel. He quickly helped Emily inside, just as Caroline and Jeff climbed down from the coachman's seat. Hal pointed to the goldsmith's shop. "Jeff, Kenny's inside there with some Guards. I don't know if he's figured it out, but I don't want to take any chances. Can you make sure he doesn't follow us?"

"No problem. I'll keep him inside until you're away. Where are you going?"

"I'll go with you," said Caroline, climbing inside the coach. Hal was already on top. He snapped the reins, and the coach took off down the street, hell-bent for leather, pedestrians scattering before it, some barely escaping the iron-rimmed wheels.

"Hal!" yelled Jeff. "Take it easy, for God's sake!" and then, "Figured it out! Figured out what?"

The coach took a corner on two wheels, throwing Emily into Caroline's lap. Moments later the two were flung in the other direction, then back again. "Isn't this great?" said Caroline. "I love taking a carriage ride in the country. It's so relaxing."

"I quite agree," said Emily, bouncing nearly to the ceiling. "The gentle swaying—oof—nearly puts me to sleep."

There was a rapping at the coach door, surprising

both girls, since the vehicle was moving at top speed. Caroline pulled back the curtain. A set of fingers was curled over the sill. She leaned out, grabbed a small man by the shoulders, and hauled him in the window. He flattened out on one seat and looked up. "Miss Caroline?"

"Rumpelstiltskin, you have a way of turning up at the oddest places."

"Yes, well I hope you don't mind my inviting myself along for the ride. But it is my spinning wheel, after all."

"The more the merrier. Do you know what Prince Hal intends to do with this wheel?"

"Nope. Do you know where he's going?"

"Nope," said Emily.

"In that case," said Caroline, settling back into a seat cushion, "we'll have to wait and find out. Does anyone have a story to pass the time?"

"Sure," said Rumpelstiltskin. "Whan that Aprille, with hise shoures soote . . ."

"I've heard that one," said Emily.

"Wait!" said Caroline. She yanked back the curtain and looked out the window again. "I remember this. This is the road we came in on. Are we going back to Ripplebrook?"

It appeared so, but there was no discerning Hal's intent. The girls could do nothing but wait, while the horses' rapid pace ate up the miles, covering in an hour a distance that previously had taken them half a day to walk. At this pace the horses didn't last long, but Hal stopped at a military outpost at the base of the foothills and demanded another team. The soldiers were in no position to refuse a prince, particularly one who was wild-eyed and spattered with blood, for the strain of pulling a six-horse hitch had opened up the hole in his arm. Caroline sought to dress his wound, and Emily to question him about their destination, but Hal just shook them off and climbed back up to the driver's seat. There was no choice but to get back in the coach and go along.

But when, an hour later, the coach turned off the road and followed a narrow track into the hills, Caroline was able to say, "I know where we're going. This is the way to that tower."

"Where the girl with the long hair was?"

"Right. Rapunzel. We'll have to get out and walk pretty soon."

She was right. A few minutes later the coach stopped and Hal appeared at the door. It took some work to get it open, for they were hemmed in by saplings, and Rumpel-stiltskin had to help shove from the inside. Hal leaned in and shouldered the spinning wheel. He looked pale and feverish.

"Are you taking that to the tower?" asked Emily.

"Yes."

"Are you all right?"

"No." He disappeared into the undergrowth.

Emily and Caroline exchanged glances. "Go with him," Caroline said finally. "I'll take care of the horses, then I'll follow you."

Emily nodded. The sun was setting, and the forest had already grown dark enough for fireflies to start flashing. With the dim light and the thick woods she couldn't see

Hal, but she could hear him crashing through the brush, and the trail he made was easy to follow. Rumpelstiltskin stayed behind her.

Hal got to the tower well ahead of them. The black column looked strange even during the day, but silhouetted against the setting sun it seemed even more mysterious. Hal kicked aside the blanket over the door, entered, and set the wheel unevenly on the floor. It fell over with a clatter. Rapunzel, sitting on a pile of cushions, looked up. "Prince Hal, what a pleasant surprise! I was just brushing my hair. You know, I really think these silver-chased brushes are—"

"Stow it, Rapunzel." Hal dropped into another chair. "I don't want to hear it." He was very pale now, and his hair was wet with perspiration. He waited while Emily and Rumpelstiltskin entered. "Just tell me where the red mercury is."

Rapunzel opened her mouth, then closed it without saying anything. She stood up and went to a sideboard, her long hair dragging behind her, and poured some water into a basin. Hal watched her. She came back with a sponge and a towel and knelt beside him. "You don't look well at all, Your Highness. You'd better let me tie up that arm."

Hal pointed at the wall with his other arm. "Loose bricks." He kicked at the floor. "Loose tiles. I couldn't figure out why you didn't want to leave after I got you out of the tower."

Rapunzel had rolled up Hal's sleeve and sponged away some of the blood. She carefully avoided meeting his eyes. "I'm afraid you've lost me, Your Highness."

"And all those holes outside. I should have figured it out right away."

"Excuse me, Your Highness," said Rumpelstiltskin. "Of course, it's perfectly obvious to me what you're talking about. Yes sir, just as plain as the nose on your face. But, uh, maybe you want to explain, purely for the benefit of Miss Emily, what this is all about?"

Hal took the towel from Rapunzel and wrapped it around his arm. "Emily explained it all to me," he said.

"I did?"

"The Law of Similarity, she called it. If you want to use magic to change something into gold, it has to resemble gold to start with. Like brass. Not just any brass, but virgin brass. A particular alloy that exactly matches the color of pure gold. Or flax, harvested when just the right shade, unretted to retain its color. Ever looked at gold? Really looked at it?"

"Not nearly often enough," said Rumpelstiltskin.

"Most people think of it as yellow, but it really isn't. It's more like a light brown, with reddish highlights. In fact," and now he slid his hand under Rapunzel's chin and tilted her head so that she was looking directly at him, "it's exactly the color of your hair."

The room was silent. Emily lit a candle. Everyone, including Rapunzel herself, looked at her hair, the unending waves spread over the floor and draped over the furniture, reflecting a soft, golden glow.

"Torricelli was a mysterious man," said the Prince. "It took me a long time to figure out what he was doing.

Why did he kidnap Rapunzel to begin with? Sure, she's very pretty . . ."

"Thank you," said Rapunzel.

". . . so I thought what any man would think."

"No!" said Rapunzel. "Nothing like that happened!"

"No, of course not. He had to keep your virtue intact until the time came to spin the gold. That's one of the requirements for the spell, right? An exchange of magical power."

Rapunzel said nothing. Emily nodded. So did Rumpelstiltskin.

"And in the meantime he wanted you growing as much hair as possible. The more hair, the more gold. He farmed out construction of the spinning wheel to a cabinetmaker."

"That was me," said Rumpelstiltskin.

"And he purchased a philosopher's stone from another magician. Probably he didn't know how to make it himself. But he knew Amanda—he was going to take her daughter as his apprentice. So he placed an order for her to make some stone. I expect she did not know about the kidnapping."

"I'm sure she didn't," said Emily. "Or she'd never have apprenticed me to him."

"Torricelli made the red mercury himself," continued Hal. He looked at Rapunzel. "He told you all about it, I'm sure. Guys just can't resist trying to impress pretty girls with their cleverness. Look at me—I'm doing it right now."

"I'm sure I don't know what you're talking about," Rapunzel said evenly.

"But he didn't tell you everything. He didn't tell you who he bought the spinning wheel from, or the philosopher's stone. So after I killed Torricelli, you decided not to go home right away. Your only chance for getting the gold was to hope that the sellers would deliver the wheel and the stone here. You kept your hair long and waited." Hal shrugged. "And here we all are."

"Wait," said Rumpelstiltskin. "How do you know he made his own red mercury? Maybe he ordered out for that also."

"He made it," said Hal firmly. "He told her. And he hid it in this tower." He kicked at the floor again. "Loose tiles. Loose bricks." He pointed to Rapunzel. "You tore this place up, looking for it. You took up the floors, knocked holes in the walls. You even dug around outside. The holes are still there. So, did you find it or didn't you?"

Rapunzel remained silent. Emily looked from one person to the other and, after a long wait, finally broke the silence. "Hal," she said gently, "you're hurt, and you're bleeding, and you look feverish, and I don't doubt that you're light-headed also. You need to rest. There's no red mercury here. If you were thinking clearly, you'd see that your theory is just based on coincidence and imagination. I don't think you realize just how absurd it all sounds . . ."

"How do I know you have the philosopher's stone?" interrupted Rapunzel.

"Emily has it. She can show it to you right now."

Rapunzel held out her hand. "Let's see it."

Emily hesitated, then dug the leather pouch out of her handbag. The milky white stone dropped into Rapunzel's palm. The girl looked at it carefully, then closed her fingers around it. "How do I know this is really a philosopher's stone?"

"Oh, for goodness sake." Emily was exasperated now. "Why would we lie about it now? What does it look like?"

"I've never seen a philosopher's stone, so I wouldn't know," said Rapunzel stiffly. "Although this is what Torricelli said it would look like," she admitted. "However, all knowledge is subjective, and even though this looks like a philosopher's stone, can I really trust the evidence of my senses? When it comes right down to it, there's no proof that an objective reality actually exists at all . . ."

"You're talking epistemology," said Hal. "How much more proof do you need?"

"Ah." Rapunzel opened her hand and glared at the stone. "So I am. Very well." She gave the stone back to Emily, then rose and went to a cupboard. The top shelf appeared to be filled with bottles of shampoo and conditioner. From it she took a small glass cylinder, which she brought back and set on the table by the candle. Emily picked it up and tilted it. The liquid inside flowed like quicksilver, but had a distinct reddish tinge.

"Where was it?" asked Hal.

"In the teapot. I knew it was magic because it was in a crystal vial."

"All right." Hal looked at Emily. "Does this need any incantations or hand-waving done over it?"

"No, not to my knowledge. All the magic is in the spinning wheel."

"Good. Rumpelstiltskin, you say this thing works at night?"

"Midnight to dawn is what Torricelli mentioned to me."

"That will be magic time, not clock time," said Emily. "Midnight is halfway between dusk and dawn."

"Okay then. That gives us a couple of hours to, um," Hal looked at Rapunzel and cleared his throat. "To take care of this, ah, loss-of-virginity thing."

This came out somewhat flatter than he intended. There was an uneasy silence and an exchange of glances from everyone in the room. Rapunzel was still kneeling near the table. "Excuse me, Your Highness, was that last bit directed at me?"

"Yes," said Hal.

"I see. And who are you proposing that I should give myself up to?"

Hal cleared his throat and jerked a thumb at his chest.

"I see. Well, I'm sorry, Your Highness. No offense is intended, but you are simply not my type."

"Say what?" said Hal.

"I'm not ready for this. I suggest you leave the stone and wheel with me, and when the circumstances are appropriate I will send you your share of the gold."

"If you're joking," said Hal, "we don't have time for it."

"I'm not joking. Now go away. I have my standards."

"Lower them. Think of the gold."

"Ooh Hal," murmured Emily. "Bad move."

Rapunzel stood up, her fists clenched. "How dare you! I don't know what kind of *shiksas* you've been dating, your Highness, but don't expect the same behavior from me! I am not going to give myself up for a little gold . . ."

"Shiksas?" said Rumpelstiltskin.

"Or a lot of gold, or any amount of gold and I will decide when I am ready to do it and who I will do it with. Now get out!"

She reached down to pick up the vial of red mercury. There was a quiet hiss and a thunk and the point of Hal's sword entered the wood just next to her fingers. She looked up into Hal's eyes. There was no anger in them, no flare of danger. They were just very, very tired. Rapunzel felt a sudden icy needle of fear penetrate her heart. She looked back down at the table and slowly drew her hand away from the vial.

"Rapunzel, listen," said Hal, and his voice was absolutely calm, perfectly pleasant, but somehow that seemed to make it threatening. "I know you're a nice girl. I don't know who came up with this nice girls don't, bad-girls-do idea, or why there's never a bad girl around when you need one. I'm sorry this has to be you. But it has to be done."

"Hal!" said Emily.

"There is more at stake here than you realize. We need that gold, and we need it tonight."

"Hal, stop talking like this," said Emily. "Can't you see she's afraid of you? You can't pressure a girl like this. It's like rape."

"When a commoner does it, it's rape. When royalty does it, it's seduction."

"Damn you, Hal!"

Rapunzel stood up slowly. Her eyes were level with Hal's. The Prince was leaning forward on his sword. Emily suddenly realized that he hadn't drawn the sword to be threatening. He was using it to support his weight. She crossed the room and stood beside Rapunzel. "Hal, you can't do this. This isn't right. And aren't you forgetting that you're engaged to Caroline? You can do it with her."

Hal shook his head. "Too much of an unknown. You don't know what kind of spell Torricelli put on that wheel. He set it up intending to use Rapunzel. It *might* work with Caroline. Hell, it will *probably* work with Caroline. But it will *definitely* work with Rapunzel. Isn't that right?"

Emily gritted her teeth, but nodded. She felt a shiver of fear herself, brought on by a sudden flash of insight. She understood now why Hal's father sent him on the tough missions. It wasn't just a matter of image. Beneath Hal's dweebish surface was a core of iron, hard and cold.

"Then we go with Rapunzel." His voice became even quieter, almost a whisper. "We have one shot at this, and we can't afford to take a chance. I really am sorry, Rapunzel. I wish there was time to ride back to Melinower and find a handsome guy for you. But there isn't. You'll just have to grit your teeth and bear it."

Rapunzel was shaking, but whether from fear or anger, or more likely a combination of both, it was impossible to tell. "It's not a question of looks," she began. But then Rumpelstiltskin broke in.

"Do you keep kosher?"

"What?" said Hal.

All heads turned to the dwarf. "I was talking to Rapunzel." He hopped up on a sofa and repeated the question in a cheery, conversational manner. "I said, 'Do you keep kosher?' "

It took Rapunzel a moment to collect her thoughts. "Ah, well, not exactly. I have the separate dishes and all, but generally we only bring them out for the high holidays."

"Yeah, I'm the same way. I'm not really into all the kashrut stuff, but you know, you got to have some respect for tradition."

"I thought you said you weren't Jewish," said Hal.

"Shut up," explained Rumpelstiltskin. He grabbed Hal's arm and began guiding him toward the door. "Rapunzel and I, we need to talk. If you'll just step outside for a few minutes, Your Highness—you too, Miss Emily—I think we can get all this settled."

"But . . ." said Emily.

"Just a few details to work out," said Rumpelstiltskin, shoving them both outside. "Be with you in a minute."

The door slammed. Hal leaned up against the outside wall, then slid down to a sitting position. "Now that was a bit of a surprise."

Emily pointedly ignored him. In fact, she turned her back on him and walked around the tower until she was out of his sight. "Well, fine," he said. He was feeling very tired. He closed his eyes and thought he must have slept for a while, because when he opened them it was quite dark, and the stars had come out. Caroline was shaking him.

"Hal, are you all right?"

"Fine." Hal tried to stand up and found that he couldn't.

"It's getting cool. Maybe you better get inside."

"No, I'm fine. I'll just rest here a bit more."

Rumpelstiltskin came back out. He was carrying a sheet of foolscap with some notes written on it. "That Rapunzel." He shook his head admiringly. "She's one smart cookie."

"You short guys always get the girls," Hal told him. "What did she say?"

"Well, we got a problem, Your Highness. She says nothing doing, not even kissy-face, until she sees at least an engagement ring."

"No problem." Hal reached inside his tunic and brought out a small gold ring with a large diamond. Rumpelstiltskin whistled when he saw it. "Take it with the compliments of the royal family," Hal told him. "And congratulations to you both."

"Thanks, Your Highness. I'll return it as soon as we have a chance to buy another one."

"No, keep it. What's next?"

"I can take care of most of it." He looked at the list in his hand. "As soon as we cash in the gold, she wants me to visit her parents."

"I've met them. They're good people."

"I'm gonna need a new suit. Let's see, she wants a house in Shaker Heights, two weeks each year at the seashore—and I need to see her uncle."

"Her uncle?"

"She's got plans. With our share of the money, we're going into business. I'll make the furniture and her uncle Morty will sell it, she says."

"Sure," said Caroline.

"Her whole family is very big into retail."

"Of course."

"Is there anything else?" said Hal.

"Well, yeah, Your Highness." Rumpelstiltskin looked embarrassed. "Uh, she wants a knighthood."

"Rapunzel wants to be a knight?"

"No, for me."

"A Jewish knight? Impossible."

"Well, it would be good for the furniture business. But see, it's about this expulsion. We kind of think that giving a knighthood to a Jew would help show that the royal court won't support discrimination. It would discourage people from getting behind another expulsion."

"I guess. But Dad would never go for it."

"It's a deal," said Caroline definitely. "Jeff will do it, and he's going to be king. It's a good idea."

Hal rubbed his eyes tiredly, leaving a smear of blood on his cheek. " 'Why is this knight different from all other knights,' " he quoted. "Okay, you've got it."

"That's all," said Rumpelstiltskin. He looked at the ring again. "Guess I better give this to her. Miss Emily's about to cut her hair."

He went back inside. Caroline said, "Do you always carry around diamond engagement rings?"

"I got it for you."

"Oh. Right. Well, thanks. That was a pretty nice stone."

"It's glass. We're broke, remember? You'll have to get Jeff to buy you another one."

Caroline hesitated. "Hal—um—I gave you my promise—if you still want to . . ."

"Forget it." The Prince made a theatrical gesture with his right hand. "I release you from your vow, oh fair one. Go forth and marry whom you please."

"Thank you, Hal."

Emily stalked past, tight-lipped. She went inside without looking at Hal.

"I suppose she's really mad."

"She told me what you said in there. She's jealous. She just doesn't know it. But Hal," Caroline continued reprovingly, "you should have told me first."

"I guess. I couldn't force myself on an unwilling girl anyway. I can hardly stand up."

"It's a good thing we had Rumpelstiltskin along."

"Mmmm." Hal was quiet for a few minutes. Caroline thought he had fallen asleep again, when he whispered, "If I'd asked you, would you have done it with me?"

"Of course, Hal. We're together in this, remember?"

The Prince let his shoulders slump. His head fell forward onto his chest. Caroline had to lean forward to hear him. "You could have closed your eyes and pretended it was Jeff."

She gave him a sad smile. "I wouldn't do that, Hal."

The Prince made no reply. "Hal? Are you awake?" She took his chin and tilted his head up. Hal's eyelids were open, and the eyeballs rolled up in his head. "Hal!"

Hal refocused his eyes. "S'okay."

"You're not okay! What's wrong?"

Hal didn't move. Caroline was wondering if he passed out again, when he pulled up his tunic. Just above the belt line was a small hole, oozing blood. "I took a stab. In the tournament. Right in the stomach."

"Oh my God! Is it bad?"

"Not really. It isn't bleeding much."

"Yes it is! It's bleeding inside, isn't it?"

"At least I didn't put my eye out." Hal managed a weak laugh. "Mom would never let me hear the end of it."

"Hal! Why didn't you say something? We've got to get you back to the city."

"Can't. I really lost that match, don't you see? No one knows. It happened so fast—Bear was so surprised that I dodged his thrust—he didn't know his dagger went in—under my breastplate—then I cut his arm—so he couldn't feel—and the judge didn't see—I didn't flinch, and you couldn't see the blood—I kept quiet—I cheated."

"You're royalty! You can cheat if you want!"

"You're really getting the hang of this, I see." Hal laughed again, then took a shuddering, raspy breath. "Good. You're going to make a great princess."

"I'll get Emily. She knows first aid and might have some ointment or something."

"No!" Hal grabbed Caroline's arm. He struggled to sit up. "No, you can't tell them. Not Emily, not anyone. We can't take the chance."

"Hal, this is not a time to—"

"Caroline, I *lost the match*. That means I lost the bets. If word gets out, the bookmakers won't pay up, and all this will have been for nothing. Kenny will be king, the expulsion will go on, and we're finished."

"Hal, you could die!"

"I won't die. I'm sure I won't die. People live for hours after being stabbed in the gut. Sometimes for days. So don't say a word until we cash in the bets. Just make sure." Exhausted, he slumped back against the wall again. "Just make sure we get the gold."

Caroline ran into the tower. "Okay everyone, let's move it. We've got a busy night ahead of us. Lots to do, let's snap to it."

Rapunzel was sitting in a chair, Rumpelstiltskin was standing on a chair watching her, and Emily was standing behind her with a pair of scissors. Rapunzel was saying, "Rumpy, honey, you've got to leave me *some* hair. I can't go around looking like a monk. A little gold more or less won't matter."

"If it won't matter, then I favor more rather than less. Your hair will grow back, sugar."

"I can do a short flip cut," said Emily. "Off the shoulder."

"Excuse me," Caroline said. "May I see those?" She took the shears out of Emily's hand. "Thank you." Then she grabbed a fistful of Rapunzel's hair, made two quick cuts near the scalp, and let the long tresses fall to the floor. "All done."

"What? What did you do?" Rapunzel looked frantically around the room for her mirror. "Did you just hack my hair off?"

"It's the newest style. You've been out here all summer, so I guess you didn't realize it. All the girls in Melinower are getting their hair done this way."

"Really?"

"Sure. Okay, you two, where's the bed? Upstairs? Then off you go. Time for you to get down and do the wild thing."

"Hey!" said Emily. "Who put you in charge?"

"No one. I'm just helping out."

"Yes, well I don't see why you think you can boss us around. We don't need you here, thank you very much."

"You don't, eh?"

"No, we don't. We're all set. Rumpelstiltskin brought the spinning wheel, I brought the philosopher's stone, Rapunzel has the red mercury and the hair. We have everything we need without you . . ."

"Except someone who can spin."

Emily stopped in midsentence.

"Unless you yourself can spin."

"Um, no."

"Rumpelstiltskin?"

"No. I can darn my own socks."

"Rapunzel?"

"No," said Rapunzel. "I never asked Torricelli about that part. I assumed he'd have someone else come in to do it."

"Then go upstairs and leave it to me." She nudged Rapunzel toward the winding stone staircase, then began piling stuff in Rumpelstiltskin's arms. "Here you go. Candles, flowers, chocolate, a bottle of wine, and a book of slushy poetry. In case you need to get her in the mood."

Emily was looking at the hair. "Can you really spin all this in one night?"

"Oh sure. It will spin up nicely. Look how smooth and strong it is."

Rapunzel called down, "It's because I've been conditioning it with collagen and silk protein."

"Yes, yes. Go on now. Rumpelstiltskin, be gentle with her."

"What are you giving advice for? What do you know about sex, anyway?" said Emily.

"Nothing. What would you say? Slap her around, she likes the rough stuff? Excuse me a moment."

She went out the door and over to Hal. He was still where she had left him, slumped against the castle wall. She felt his wrist. His pulse was unsteady, and his breathing was shallow and ragged. She ran back inside and looked up. "Dammit. What's taking them so long?"

"They've hardly just started. Here, help me set up this wheel." Emily cleared a space in the mass of hair and moved the wheel into the center. She put a stool in front of it. "I've figured it out. The philosopher's stone goes here." She placed it in a cagelike holder that was on the end of the spindle. "Now spin the wheel."

Caroline sat on the stool and worked the foot pedals. The wheel spun, quietly and smoothly, into motion. Carefully, Emily poured the red mercury into a groove on the frame. Slowly it trickled onto the spinning wheel, until the whole circumference of the rim was tinted silver. Caroline stopped the wheel and touched it. It was dry. The red mercury had absorbed into the wood and hardened like paint.

"There!" Emily pointed to the spindle. "That didn't take long. They've done it." At the tip of the spindle, the philosopher's stone was giving off a faint, white glow, like moonlight. "Try it."

Caroline took some hair and wound it over the wheel and around the spindle. She pumped the pedals and got the wheel going again, feeding the hair quickly and expertly through her fingers. After a minute, she stopped. "Something's wrong."

"Nothing's wrong. Why did you stop?"

"It's not working. It looks the same."

"It's supposed to look the same, remember?" Emily unrolled a length off the spindle and bent it between her fingers. It stayed bent. "It's become stiff and heavy. It's metal."

Caroline nodded and got back to work. The wheel spun, the spindle rotated, and the hair flowed through her hands. "Stay with me, Hal," she whispered, and she worked steadily through the night, spinning strands of purest gold.

There comes a time, said Caroline to herself, when you have to face up to unpleasant reality. To admit the harsh truth. To acknowledge that despite all your planning, despite all your efforts, despite all your careful attention to detail, that some things just weren't going to work out the way you wanted.

To be exact, there was no way her bridesmaids were ever going to wear those dresses again.

Still, it had been an exciting two weeks, a time that someday she would tell her children and grandchildren about, with lots of hand-waving and excited gestures. There was the mad ride back from the tower, a frantic

attempt to get Hal to a surgeon, with the carriage careen-
ing all over the road, the horses whipped into a froth, and
a determined dwarf at the reins. And then they had to
change the gold for the betting slips, and that was followed
by an equally furious race through the city. Each of them
took a handful of slips and pushed and shoved their way
through panicked crowds and jammed streets, evading
Kenny's Guards and hunting down the bookmakers, de-
manding payment before they left the country.

And still to come was the great climactic confronta-
tion in the Council of Lords. Caroline had been there,
too, right behind Prince Jeffrey, when he kicked open the
door and strode in, with a sack of gold in each hand, tall
and broad-shouldered and angry. He flung the bags
across the table, and as the coins scattered and rolled, he
demanded authorization to take an army unit and restore
order to the city. Caroline thought that no man had ever
looked so handsome, and she had never been so proud.

Overwhelmed by greed, and fearful of riots outside
their windows, the Council had acquiesced. By nightfall
it was all over—the riots broken up, the looters routed,
the Royal Guards sent back to their barracks, and the
Jews returning to their homes. Everywhere Prince Jeffrey was cheered as a hero, and Kenny was in disgrace.
The next day the King quietly told the Council he was
abdicating and named Jeff as heir to the throne.

Even now, Caroline felt a warm glow of pride when
she looked upon her husband. But still, one had to have
a sense of perspective. "Put down the ledgers," she told
Jeff. She crossed the office floor, took the quill out of his

hand, and kissed him on the cheek. "It's our wedding day. Business can wait until tomorrow."

"So much to do," said Jeff. "And the coronation is only two weeks away."

"I know, I know. And you," she told the circle of financial advisors, "out. There's a wedding reception going on, if you haven't noticed. Get out there. Have fun. Dance, eat, get drunk. Off you go. Shoo."

With backward smiles, they left the room. Jeff started to say something, but Caroline silenced him by hopping into his lap and kissing him all over his face. Then she stood up and dragged him out of his chair. "You, too. You can't miss your own reception. People will think I give dull parties."

He put up his hands "Okay, okay. I'm going." He put on his jacket, but when he turned back around, Caroline had dipped the quill in the inkwell and was making a list on a sheet of foolscap.

"Coronation gown," she wrote. "Portrait sitting. Gifts for ladies-in-waiting. Order tea!" She underlined this last one twice and was about to add a third line when Jeff took the quill out of her hand.

"I can't appear without my wife," he said. "People will think we had a fight."

"I'm coming, I'm coming." She took his hand, and they walked together through the hallways and into the Grand Hall, where the orchestra was playing, the tables were groaning with meats and roasted birds, and the reception dance was going full swing. A multitiered wedding cake, dripping with icing, rose a dozen feet in the air. Two carved ice swans floated in a fountain of wine. Jeff spotted his advisors standing beside it, hooked a glass of champagne from a passing waiter, and went to join them. They immediately began talking finances.

Caroline shook her head, smiled, and began to circulate. She spotted two girls waving to get her attention. They were her friends Ashley and Brenna, who had changed out of their bridesmaid dresses and rejoined the party. "Look," said Ashley. "There's Prince Kenneth. Ooh, I didn't know he was so handsome. Do you think we'll get to dance with him?"

"No! I mean, um, I'll get back to you in a little bit."

Kenny had gotten a consolation prize. He had been named the Crown Prince of Losshire, a protectorate of Melinower, and was wearing the Cross of Losshire as a badge of rank. He was surrounded by his own knot of hangers-on. When Caroline got up close she found, to her surprise, that the oldest prince was talking to Rumpelstiltskin. "There was nothing personal in it," he was saying. "The expulsion was based strictly on financial considerations. Hell, some of my best friends are Jews."

Rumpelstiltskin looked sour, but was diplomatic enough to let it pass. Caroline came up behind him. "That just made it worse," she said. "Persecuting people for money."

"Ah, Princess," said Kenny, with just the slightest sarcastic inflection. "And your own rise to the ranks of royalty was purely the result of unselfish altruism, as I understand it."

"Different context," said Caroline, shortly. She noted with satisfaction that a handful of Jeff's officers kept

Kenny under constant watch. He was going to leave Melinower and he wasn't going to cause any trouble before he left. She switched her attention to the dwarf. "Congratulations on being voted leader of the Cabinet-makers' Guild."

"Thank you, Your Highness."

"Sir Rumpelstiltskin, are you wearing a—is that a yarmulke?"

"Keeping the head covered is a tradition among my people, Princess."

"Right." Caroline moved on. She found Rapunzel chatting with Queen Helen. The girl's hair floated about her head in a cloud of golden ringlets.

". . . so I just trim the ends to keep it short but symmetrical. Then a hot curling iron produces the curls and also adds depth."

"Lovely, lovely," murmured the Queen, looking around a bit desperately. "Oh, Caroline. You know Lady Rapunzel, don't you? So nice to meet you. Excuse me, I must attend to my husband."

Caroline let her escape. "I love your ring," she told Rapunzel.

"Oh, thank you. You don't mind if I keep the glass one, do you? It makes such a wonderful memento, being a gift from Prince Hal and all."

"Be my guest. Have you seen Emily?"

"Why, yes." Rapunzel looked around. "I just saw her a few minutes ago. Over there, by the door."

Caroline made her way through the crowd, smiling and greeting everyone she passed, but getting to Emily eventually. The younger girl was dressed in full formal sorceress attire, including—yes—the midnight blue pointed hat with the star and crescent moon. Caroline hadn't seen her in several weeks. She did not look happy.

"How is the sorcery business?"

"Just fine. I'm learning a lot."

"Getting along with Bungee all right?"

"Oh yes. He's around here now. He has a knack for working a crowd."

"Hal is out of bed, you know."

"I know. I saw him stand up for Jeff at the ceremony."

"I think you should go to him."

Emily looked stricken. "Caroline, how can I see him again? After I was so mean to him that night at the tower? I don't know what got into me. He almost died right outside the door, and I just ignored him."

"He wanted you to."

"He must hate me for thinking so little of him."

"Don't be silly. Hal doesn't hate anyone."

"I should have trusted him more. I know I hurt his feelings."

"Nonsense. Boys don't have feelings. Go and see him."

"I can't."

"You have to. He has something important to tell you." Caroline took her arm and guided her toward the stairs.

"What?"

"He'll tell you. Now go."

Emily made her way up the stairs and through the hallways, which now had a familiar, nostalgic feel to them. Although it was only a fortnight since she had left the palace, it was like returning to her old school. She found Hal's suite and knocked on the door, but there was no answer. Feeling certain she knew where he was, she went through the door at the end of the hall, out onto the terrace, and around the corner. The prince was there, leaning on the terrace wall, looking out across the harbor.

He was wearing the uniform of a naval lieutenant. He looked thinner than before, and the new clothes hung on him even more loosely than his old ones, but there was color to his skin again. His hair was longer and came over his ears, so they didn't seem to stick out quite so much. His face had cleared up somewhat, and he had the beginnings of a beard, which would soon cover his receding chin.

She approached him hesitantly. He wasn't looking in her direction, but he apparently knew she was there, for he suddenly turned and smiled. "Hi."

"Hi," said Emily, and then, "Your beard looks nice."

"Thanks. It was Caroline's idea, actually."

"Your hair looks nice, too."

"Thanks. Rapunzel gave me some stuff to wash it with. She said it would give it more body."

"Yes. Well, it looks nice." Emily found herself at a loss for words. Hal seemed to be waiting for her to say more, and she furiously wracked her brain for conversation, but nothing came forth. She looked away.

When she looked back Hal was holding his arm out. Automatically she linked her arm in his, so that he could pull her close to him. "I missed you," he said.

"I've . . . I've been busy. I had to move, and send for my books, and . . . oh Hal, I'm so sorry."

"For what?"

"For the way I treated you at the tower. For thinking that you were really going to rape that girl."

"Forget it. It was a bluff. You were supposed to think that."

"Caroline didn't think so. She stood up for you, and I should have, too. And she helped you when you were hurt, and I didn't realize—"

"You weren't supposed to realize it. Caroline just has a way about her, I guess. Anyway, it all worked out for the best."

"Your family is out of debt?"

"Not quite. But we're in better shape now. And with Jeff holding the purse strings, we're not heading for bankruptcy. And there won't be any expulsions, at least not while Jeff is king. Kenny is banished to Losshire right after the coronation, and stays there. Of course, he is still planning on collecting a hefty dowry. But now he gets to keep it for himself, instead of turning it over to Dad."

"Good for him, I guess. I have to say I won't miss him."

"He doesn't have much choice. Melinower tradition. Other contenders for the throne have to leave Melinower while the new king consolidates his power. Kenny won't be allowed back. At least now he gets his own tax base."

"It seems so unfair, Hal. Everybody who was involved with the spinning wheel came out ahead except you. I got a really good apprenticeship, Caroline became a princess, Jeff will get the crown, Rapunzel and Rumpelstiltskin got a hefty split of the gold—what did you get out of this?"

"I got to avoid being turned back into a frog."

"Oh. Well, there's that, of course. At least you're not being exiled along with Kenny."

Hal hesitated. He hesitated just a little too long.

"Hal! You're not being exiled also?"

Hal reached into his jacket and pulled out a folded sheet of paper. He spread it open and showed it to Emily. "It's from the Royal Navy. I've been promoted and recalled to active duty. It's a voyage to explore and map the south end of our possessions."

"Hal, that's awful. How could Jeff do this to you? You put him on the throne, you wouldn't try to usurp it. This is so unfair."

"Hmm." Hal pulled another letter from his pocket. "By the most amazing coincidence, this arrived with the orders." He gave it to her.

Emily unfolded it. "It's part of my apprenticeship contract. But who would send you this? And why?"

Hal seemed to be phrasing his words very carefully. "You signed your contract on September 4. Here's the date. And you have two years to run on your apprenticeship. And if you look at my transfer papers, the ship is scheduled to return to Melinower—"

"On the exact same day." A brilliant light dawned on Emily. "Caroline! This was all her idea! She knows I can't do anything with a boy until my apprenticeship is over. Now she's trying to keep you away from girls for the same time."

"It does seem to work out that way." Hal turned his head back toward the harbor, but he was watching Emily from the corners of his eyes. "Um, is that a problem for you?"

"It makes me so mad. That Caroline! She's always been like that, bossing people around, making sure she gets her own way. Where does she get off, thinking she can run my life? Well, princess or not, I'm going to give her a piece of my mind!"

And as if on cue, a window popped open above them. A familiar blond head popped out and yelled, "Emily!"

"What?" Emily snapped back.

"Just kiss him already."

"Go away!"

The blond head withdrew, and the window slammed shut. Emily whirled away. She found herself pressed up against Hal. His arms folded around her, and she turned her face up to his, only inches away. "Actually," he said, "I think that's a pretty good idea."

"I . . . I have to be careful. There's magic in a kiss, you know."

"I know," said Hal, and kissed her anyway.

Definitely magical, Emily decided.